PRAISE FOR *SOMEONE IS WATCHING YOU*

'I held my breath from the first ...
A tense and immersive ad...

...
auth...

'An edg...
keeps ...
PAT...
author o... *...eces of Silva*

'A genuinely chilling horror and a brilliantly
layered tale of toxic friendship ...'
AMY BEASHEL,
author of *We Are All Constellations*

'Tess storms on to the YA scene with a relentless thriller
full of genuine jump-scares and spine-tingling chills ...'
KESIA LUPO,
author of *We Are Blood and Thunder*

'Fast-paced and fabulously creepy ...
The pacy plot kept me turning pages until the early hours,
racing towards a brilliant twist I did not see coming'
SUE CUNNINGHAM,
an early reader

'A tense and twisty tale that won't let you go,
even after the final page'
JENNY PEARSON,
author of *The Super Miraculous Journey of Freddie Yates*

'I flew through this in one sitting – pacey and gripping ...
Don't plan for a good night's sleep after this'
RAVENA GURON,
author of *This Book Kills*

SOMEONE IS WATCHING YOU

TESS JAMES-MACKEY

HODDER CHILDREN'S BOOKS
First published in Great Britain in 2023 by Hodder & Stoughton

1 3 5 7 9 10 8 6 4 2

Text copyright © Tess James-Mackey, 2023
Illustrations copyright © Paul Blow, 2023

The moral right of the author has been asserted.

*All characters and events in this publication, other than those clearly
in the public domain, are fictitious and any resemblance to
real persons, living or dead, is purely coincidental.*

All rights reserved.
No part of this publication may be reproduced, stored in
a retrieval system, or transmitted, in any form or by any means, without
the prior permission in writing of the publisher, nor be otherwise circulated
in any form of binding or cover other than that in which it is published
and without a similar condition including this condition being
imposed on the subsequent purchaser.

A CIP catalogue record for this book
is available from the British Library.

ISBN: 978 1 444 96790 6

Typeset in Adobe Caslon by Avon DataSet Ltd, Alcester, Warwickshire

Printed and bound in Great Britain by Clays Ltd, Elcograf S.p.A.

The paper and board used in this book
are made from wood from responsible sources.

Hodder Children's Books
An imprint of
Hachette Children's Group
Part of Hodder & Stoughton Limited
Carmelite House
50 Victoria Embankment
London EC4Y 0DZ

An Hachette UK Company
www.hachette.co.uk

www.hachettechildrens.co.uk

*For Robyn. May you one day be brave enough
to read my books.*

CONTENT WARNING:

This book contains mentions of emotional abuse, sexual coercion and physical violence.

PROLOGUE

He shrank away from the prowling forms circling him.

'Please,' he begged. 'Please just leave me alone.'

But they wouldn't listen, and his sanctuary – his *home* – suddenly felt like the prison it really was.

Their laughter echoed through the cavernous room. And then the blows landed, one after another. He whimpered as his skin bruised and split beneath their frenzied attack. He reached out, imploring the only one who could help him. But they stumbled backwards, shaking their head in horror as his screams grew louder before they stopped altogether.

His glassy eyes stared up at the bars on the window above him.

And the laughter continued.

CHAPTER 1

An amateurish sign reading Prison Funhouse was Blu-Tacked to the crumbling brick wall. The paper had got wet at some point, the ink dribbling down like mascara tears.

'As *if*,' Nia groaned. Of all the places to spend her Saturday.

Mum was digging around at the bottom of the nappy bag for change as the girl behind the counter grinned manically. Nia turned away in disgust. How could anyone be that chirpy working in a place like this?

Nia couldn't get her head around it. They were at a prison. A literal *prison*. And even though it technically wasn't a prison any longer, it had been packed full of criminals only a year ago. And not just any old criminals, but the worst ones – the ones who killed people and chopped them up and stuffed their remains in the walls. And now . . . ball pits and babies?

'Wild,' she muttered, gazing up at the gatehouse. The wind hurtled through the archway and whistled as it passed through the iron bars of the gate. Nia folded her arms tighter across her chest. The overly cheerful girl in the kiosk didn't seem bothered by her working conditions, even though her nose was bright red from the cold.

'Sorry, how much did you say it was?' asked Mum, as she readjusted baby Deon on her hip.

'Well, adults go free, so you just need to pay for the three children,' Little Miss Pretend-to-be-Perky replied.

Nia tore her gaze away from the entrance gates to glare. 'I'm fifteen. I'm obviously not here to go on the bouncy castle.'

Perky's smile faltered and Nia felt a twist of satisfaction. 'Oh, um, I'm afraid a child counts as anyone under sixteen, I think. I don't actually know.'

Nia groaned. She was probably the only teenager who had ever been dragged here.

'Mum,' she whispered urgently. 'Just let me go home. You don't want to have to pay for me too. It's a waste of money.' She crossed her fingers, hoping that the temptation to save money would be enough to convince Mum to let her leave.

But Mum didn't even look at her as she hissed out of the side of her mouth, 'No, Nia. You're staying here with me, where I can keep an eye on you.'

Nia stepped back, defeated. What was it going to take for Mum to forgive her? She glared at Kayla, who stood quietly next to Mum, her nose practically touching the pages of some boring book she'd been taking everywhere lately. This was all her fault.

Perfect little Kayla. Way-ahead-of-her-seven-years Kayla. Special Kayla, gifted Kayla. Kayla, Kayla, *Kayla*.

Well, perfect little Kayla might be a child genius but she couldn't follow simple instructions. Nia had told her to stay put, not to leave her room, not to breathe a word to Mum and Mark. And she had done the complete opposite.

Nia felt her anger building as she studied her little sister. Her *half*-sister. How was it Nia's fault that Kayla had disobeyed her? Nia hadn't done anything wrong, not really. It wasn't her fault the party had got out of hand. No one had actually specified that she shouldn't have a party while babysitting. She didn't even get paid for babysitting anyway. It wasn't fair.

It wasn't Nia's fault that Kayla got lost.

But Mum and Mark disagreed, and Nia had been paying for it ever since. Surely it was illegal to ground someone for six weeks?

Kayla caught her eye and gave her a shy smile, but Nia tutted in disgust. *Suck-up*.

She stared down at her phone, picking at the Swarovski crystals with a manicured nail. The hot pink looked bright and bold against her skin. Not that she had anyone to show it off to.

No messages.

Come on, Scott, reply already.

'OK!' Mum said, once she'd finally managed to fit her purse back into her bag. 'Who's ready for soft-play!' Her forced cheeriness clashed with the dark shadows beneath her eyes.

She really hadn't picked the right audience. Nia scowled, six-month-old Deon dribbled, and Kayla smiled encouragingly, but it was obvious that all she wanted was to get stuck back into her book.

Mum sighed, and for a moment Nia almost felt sorry for her. But that feeling was quickly replaced with contempt. She shouldn't be here. She should be with Scott.

They trudged towards a second gate, a huge, heavy iron structure that had been decorated with paper chains to make it look more inviting and less prison-like. The unsmiling security guard who let them through made Nia wonder if they'd be allowed back out again.

Why does this place still have guards?

Even Mum couldn't hide her discomfort as they stepped into the courtyard and the prison came into view, and a worried wrinkle pinched Kayla's eyebrows together.

'Creepy, huh?' Mum said as she stared up at the huge building in front of them.

Nia noticed a small brick structure standing separately from the menacing four-storey prison. **INMATE REGISTRATION**. The outside of the door was covered in warnings: **HIDDEN CONTRABAND WILL BE FOUND, SPITTING WILL ADD 30 DAYS TO YOUR SENTENCE**.

Underneath the old warnings was a scrap of paper with an arrow pointing away from the entrance. Written in childish scrawl with brightly coloured crayons: This Way For Play!

This is so messed up.

Nia jumped as the guard swung the gate shut behind them with a loud metallic clang.

'Just head that way,' he grunted, motioning with his head. But Nia didn't want to go any further. Now they were past the gatehouse there were no clues that part of the prison had been converted into a soft-play centre. Why was it so quiet inside these walls – surely they should be able to hear the rumbling background noise from town? Nia's instincts screamed at her to run back to the gatehouse and demand the guard let her out.

'It's been empty for a year. It's just an old building now, nothing to be scared of,' Mum said, as though she were trying to convince herself. 'I must admit, though, it is a strange place to take children.'

Mum's rambling wasn't helping. Why couldn't she have picked somewhere else to come? *Anywhere* else.

'And if you lot start playing up, I can lock you in one of the cells!' Her laugh was unnaturally high, and Nia scowled at her back as they walked away. If she wanted to go to places like this, then whatever. But to force Nia to come too? Unforgivable. 'Look, we need to follow this yellow line.'

Someone had drawn tiny footprints next to the line, no doubt in an attempt to add a bit of cheer to the place. But it made Nia think of tiny ghost children fleeing the monsters locked within the prison walls.

Even though they were still technically outside, the towering wall on the right and the prison on the left made Nia feel claustrophobic. She craned her neck to look up at the bleak sky as they walked, but even that felt smaller somehow. There were no birds.

'I don't like it,' Kayla whispered.

Nia's fingers twitched instinctively to lay a comforting hand on her little sister's plaits, but she pushed it deeper into her pocket.

The prison was so huge that Nia felt like it was wrapping itself around her, swallowing her alive. Four storeys of ancient red brick loomed over them, and the giant chimneys on the roof added to its height. It looked solid, not like a crumbling old ruin but like a fortress that would be impossible to escape from.

The yellow line followed the perimeter of the prison, which was so large that it took them five minutes to get round to the other side, especially with Kayla walking at her usual snail's pace and Mum huffing beneath baby Deon's weight, as well as a nappy bag that seemed to contain half the contents of their house. Eventually they made it to what was once a sports hall for the worst kind of people Nia could imagine, and was now a kids' play centre.

The hall looked as though it had been stolen from a school and flung into the prison grounds. Its white and green walls clashed with the old red brick of the main building. A doorbell was taped to the frame. Nia snorted – no expense spared.

She stared morosely at her phone, the group chat showing that all four of her friends had seen her latest message, but none of them were replying. This had been happening more and more lately, and it left Nia with a cold feeling of terror in her stomach.

She tapped out another message, wishing she could just speak to Scott privately, but knowing he'd be even less likely to reply. What else could she do to keep him? She'd tried *everything*. She'd even kept up with Olivia's stupid dares, which had been getting crazier by the day.

She closed her eyes and stretched her neck from one side to the other. Nia wished Scott would just tell her what was wrong. No, on second thoughts, she didn't. She didn't think she could bear it if he broke up with her. If only she was allowed out of Mum's sight for half a second, then she could be with Scott, trying to make things better. She wouldn't be stuck in this hellhole. She opened her eyes to peer back over her shoulder at the prison.

A pale figure stared back at her through the bars of an upstairs window.

CHAPTER 2

'Hello, sorry about the wait. It's chaos in here!'

Nia's gaze was torn away from the prison window and towards the frantic-looking woman in the doorway. She had a rubber chicken draped over her head.

Nia spun to look behind her again, but there was no figure in the window.

'Mum,' Nia said, but her voice was swallowed by children's screams echoing off the high ceiling and the roaring of the air being pumped into the bouncy castle. 'Mum!'

'Not now, Nia. Come on.'

Mum bustled her way through the scattered tables and chairs with Kayla and Deon. Nia hesitated, squinting back at the window, but the soft-play employee was watching her expectantly as she held the door open.

She reluctantly stepped into the sports hall, widening her eyes in alarm when the smiling woman locked the heavy door behind them. Catching Nia looking, she winked and whispered, 'Can't have the kiddies doing a runner, can we?'

Nia clenched her teeth together, wishing her mind would stop telling her that she should be panicking. She was locked in a prison.

The heat inside the sports hall was intense, and Nia's clothes were already sticking to her skin. A toddler sprinted straight into her legs as they made their way over to a table, and she resisted the urge to push them over.

'Mum, I saw . . .'

But Mum was fishing around in her bag for a muslin to mop up the drool running down Deon's chin. Nia sighed and slumped into a chair – there was no point trying to talk to her when she was flustered.

'Coffee. I need coffee,' Mum said, and she thrust Deon into Nia's arms without looking at her. 'Watch the baby for me, Nia. Kayla, milkshake?'

Kayla shook her head and Nia rolled her eyes. Kayla must be the only seven-year-old in the world who wasn't mad for sugary treats. Nia waited for Mum to ask her the same question but wasn't surprised when she walked away without a word. Girls who threw parties didn't get bought snacks, apparently.

Nia wrinkled her nose as a blob of Deon's baby dribble landed on her hand. *Yuck.* The plastic chair seemed to have been designed to be as uncomfortable as possible, and she wriggled, wishing Deon was old enough to fend for himself so she could dump him on the floor.

Nia shuddered as she looked around. She didn't believe in ghosts. That's not why this place gave her the creeps anyway – it was that she couldn't help thinking about the horrible things that the people who had been locked up here had done. She watched a baby giggling in the ball pit and wondered what was there before all these toys. Had there been gym equipment, or had the prisoners just walked around in endless circles to get their exercise? Nia's phone vibrated and she hurried to get it out of her pocket, nearly dropping the baby in the process. Her heart sank when she saw it wasn't Scott who had finally replied, but Olivia.

Olivia

> Can't believe you're at soft-play. Cringe.

Nia's heart shuddered as three little dots told her that Scott was typing something. But no reply came, and the dots disappeared, along with Nia's hope.

Max

> You on the bouncy castle yet, Nia?

Nia desperately tried to think of a witty reply, something to show them that she wasn't some loser, some stupid kid. That she was one of them.

But Scott was typing again, and Nia was mesmerised by the tiny picture of his face.

Scott

> lol

That was it? Nia blinked at the message, feeling a sudden urge to burst into tears like the toddler sitting at the table next to them. She was clinging on to this relationship with the tips of her fingers, she knew it. *Everyone* knew it.

Scott Pearson was the most popular guy in school, *and* he was in the year above. When he had made their relationship official, people laughed and asked when he would get bored of babysitting. But she had worked hard, so hard, to prove that she was as cool as the Year Elevens. The party she threw six weeks ago was a big part of that.

But now Mum was ruining everything. Why would Scott want to be with a girl who had to be home by seven p.m. every night, and who wasn't even allowed to be alone in her own house?

The sound of Kayla turning a page in her book made Nia look up from her phone. If her sister could have just done as she was told and stayed in her stupid room, then Nia's life wouldn't be ruined right now.

Mum returned, a giant mug of coffee sloshing on to the tray as she swerved out of the way of an oblivious child. She plucked baby Deon out of Nia's arms the second her hands were free, as though she didn't want her precious son being held by Nia any longer than absolutely necessary.

Nia hid how hurt she felt by focusing on her phone. Everything that was important to her was connected to it.

Nia

Are you in town? Xxx

Scott

Yeah

Nia

All of you? Xxx

Scott had seen the message but didn't reply.

Nia put her phone on the table and stared at it, willing it to buzz. All four of them would be together, of course they would. It would be just like it was before Nia appeared on the scene. They were probably overjoyed to be rid of her – Olivia especially had been desperate to get Nia out of the picture ever since she and Scott had started dating.

She'd tried everything she could think of, but she'd never been able to get Olivia to like her. She'd been sweet and complimentary, and Olivia had called her a suck-up. She'd been aloof and indifferent, and Olivia said she was cold. She'd joined in with slating other kids at school, and Olivia had called her out for being spiteful. It could have been because Nia was in the year below them at school, a fact Olivia loved to remind everyone of.

Desperate, Nia had asked Scott what she should do differently, but he'd sighed and told her to stop being so obsessive, that she was trying too hard, that it was embarrassing.

A scream made Nia start in her seat, but it was just some stupid kids chasing each other, eyes wide like sugar-crazed cartoon characters. Kayla didn't look up as they ran past the table. She didn't really have any friends. Not any outside of her books, anyway. Nia studied her, wondering whether she'd prefer to have a screaming, laughing little sister who annoyed the hell out of her, or the quiet, serious girl sitting beside her. Sure, Kayla was kind of peculiar, but at least she wasn't flicking jelly across the room like the brat at the next table.

Mum was as glued to her phone as Nia was. 'Just awful,' she sighed, shaking her head as she jiggled Deon on her knee.

'What?' Nia asked, forgetting that she'd promised herself she would speak to Mum as little as possible.

'That poor girl from your school. Daisy.'

'Oh.'

Why was Mum getting all emotional about Daisy Evans? She'd been missing for weeks now, but everyone at school knew she was just doing it for attention. She was that kind of girl.

'She went missing before,' Nia offered. 'She does it all the time.'

Another message had appeared on the group chat.

Olivia

> I think it's time for another dare.

Nia closed her eyes. Every single time those words were uttered, her life got a little bit worse.

Chloe

> Oooh, whose turn is it?

Nia sighed. Like anyone had actually been keeping track of whose turn it was. If they had, Nia's tally would far outweigh the others'. She waited for Olivia to give her instructions, and glanced up to find Mum looking at her as though she were something horrible she had found stuck to the underside of the sticky table.

'What?' Nia asked, before remembering what they'd been talking about. 'She does. It's not like she's dead or something.'

'*Nia!*' Mum hissed, glancing around as though checking if anyone else had heard.

'*What?*' Nia shrugged. God, she'd only been trying to make conversation, to *engage*, just as Mum was always nagging her to do.

'Honestly,' Mum whisper-shouted as she shook her head in disgust. 'Your behaviour lately, Nia – the parties, the sneaking around at night, and now your complete indifference to whether someone you know is in real trouble.'

Nia flinched at the look in Mum's eyes.

'I suggest you have a good think about what kind of person you want to be, Nia,' Mum snapped as she stood up. She hesitated for a moment, and Nia silently willed her to sit back down. But she only paused long enough to say, 'Kayla, we'll be in the ball pit if you want to join us.'

She pressed baby Deon into her chest and marched away from the table without a backward glance.

Nia stared after her, her throat so tight she could barely swallow. She could go after Mum. She could climb into the ball pit and chat and coo at the baby and make everything better again, couldn't she?

But a cruel voice told her that it was too late, that her relationship with Mum was broken beyond repair.

She stood abruptly, terrified the tears would fall before she could stop them. 'I'm going to the loo,' she grunted at Kayla.

She dug her nails into her palms as she scurried away from the table, following the signs that pointed away from the entrance door, deeper into the prison.

CHAPTER 3

Nia gripped the sides of the sink and glared at her reflection in the mirror. She recoiled from the girl staring back at her. She realised with a sinking feeling that she couldn't remember the last time Mum had looked at her as though she actually liked her.

She closed her eyes and took a breath, her knuckles whitening around the cold ceramic. The toilets were modern, just like the sports hall. This whole section of the prison must have been built not long before the entire thing was shut down. The smell of dirty nappies and baby wipes filled her nostrils. She wished she'd chosen somewhere less disgusting to escape.

Maybe, if Mum could hurry up and forgive her for the party, they could all move on and be a happy family again. *Maybe*, if Mum cared about her as much as she cared about Kayla and Deon, then Nia wouldn't act up. *Maybe*, if Mark was her real dad and not just her stepdad, then she wouldn't get into trouble all the time. Maybe, maybe, maybe.

Her eyes grew hot, and she scowled at her reflection until

the temptation to cry disappeared.

Maybe she should just hide in the visitors' toilets until it was time to go home.

But she couldn't hide from her phone, and the vibrations in her pocket told her that Olivia had set the dare.

Olivia

Niaaaa, it's your turn!

Chloe

Eek, what does she have to do?

Max

It totally has to be something in the prison.

Olivia

Well, duh.

Olivia seemed to be taking her time to decide Nia's fate, which was bad news for Nia. The longer the dares took to set, the more extreme they were.

But what choice did Nia have? Without her friends, she'd only have her family, who could barely even look at her nowadays. She *needed* the four of them, but, god, she wished things could be easier. Would she ever feel like she was one of them, like she belonged? Or was she destined to be a loner, just like—

Daisy Evans . . .

Nia frowned at the mirror. As if summoned by her thoughts, Daisy's image stared back at her in the reflection of the cubicles. It was a Missing Child poster, lopsidedly taped to a toilet door. Nia turned to read the details of Daisy's last known whereabouts and a number to call with information. Daisy wasn't smiling, but she wasn't frowning either. Her face said nothing. It never had. It was one of the reasons she had no friends.

No one at school seemed worried about Daisy's disappearance. She was the kind of girl who bunked off all the time. Olivia had ranted about how Daisy was wasting everyone's time, running away and pretending she was in trouble. This Missing poster was the first time Nia had seen anyone actually taking it seriously.

An idea hit Nia and she ripped the poster off the cubicle wall, dumped it into the sink and turned the tap on before her conscience had time to stop her. She sent the photo to the group message with a speech bubble coming out of Daisy's mouth saying, 'Help!'

Nia added a caption to the picture: **OMG, guys, I found Daisy!**

Trying to ignore the nibble of guilt that suggested Daisy really might be in trouble, she waited, running the hard tip of a nail over her teeth. The water continued to gush over the poster, turning it into a soggy pulp.

The seconds passed as she waited for her friends to respond, and shame pulled her hand down to the sink to fish the poster out. What was she doing? She wasn't this girl, this *mean* girl. Though, if she were being honest, she wasn't sure who she was any more.

As her fingers touched the cold water her phone vibrated, and she hurried to read the replies.

Max

Hahahahaha, that's genius.

Chloe

Ahhhh, I'm dying!

Hope filled Nia's chest. Max was the joker of the group – a lumbering clown of a boy who would do anything in the name of banter. He and Chloe had been a couple since primary school and were so attached to each other it was kind of gross – they even had shared social-media accounts. Nia wasn't sure if Chloe had ever had an independent thought – everything she said or did seemed to be an echo of one of the others, usually Olivia. But this was a start. All she needed now was . . .

Scott

You're hilarious, babe x

Nia beamed at the minuscule photo of Scott next to his

message, pride and relief flooding her body. This was it, they were finally letting her back in.

He'd called her *babe*.

Scott

> What's it like in there?

Nia's fingers trembled in their eagerness as she tapped her reply.

Nia

> It's empty now, but still so weird. Why would someone see this place and decide to turn the sports hall into a soft-play centre for little kids?!

Chloe

> Ughhhh, it's sooo creepy. They should have bulldozed that place.

Max

> Yeah, preferably with the prisoners still inside, haha.

Nia grimaced at the idea, but couldn't stop her smile, the bubble of happiness at being part of the group making her giddy.

Olivia

> I've thought of your dare.

Nia's good mood evaporated. Why couldn't Olivia just drop it? They were all chatting again, as though Nia was one of the group.

But once Olivia had an idea there was no stopping her. And Nia knew her dare would be something to do with this huge, horrible place. They'd been exploring before, but this was different. In those other places she'd been with Scott. And they'd been empty houses, old ruins in the woods, restaurants that had closed only a few months previously. Not ancient buildings full of memories and secrets and . . .

What if a prisoner had been left behind?

Nia blinked. She suddenly didn't feel alone in the toilets.

There was no noise from the corridor, not even the echoing soft-play screams. Daisy's face had blurred into something horrible in the sink.

Could there be prisoners left in here? It had been home to hundreds, maybe even thousands of men, *bad* men, only a year ago. And it was so huge, was it really so crazy to think there might have been someone left behind?

That figure in the window . . .

Nia shivered, and she noticed that one of the cubicle doors was shut. She clenched her teeth in frustration – she was being an irrational idiot. But she couldn't resist stretching her leg out to give the door a shove, just in case.

As it began to swing open, she felt a cold touch on her hand.

Nia shrieked and wrenched her arm away, staggering into the sinks as she spun round. But it was just Kayla, standing solemnly behind her.

'Kayla, you freak! What are you doing creeping up on me?'

Kayla's eyes filled with tears. She was so small for a seven-year-old. So serious and sensitive – everything Nia wasn't.

'Don't cry,' Nia sighed. 'I'm the one who should be crying – I nearly had a heart attack.'

'I'm sorry,' Kayla whispered. She didn't blink often enough, and it gave Nia the creeps. 'I just wanted to check if you were OK.'

I would be, if you disappeared.

A pang of guilt hit Nia as her heart rate returned to normal – she knew she shouldn't think things like that, not after what had happened. But she just couldn't stop seeing Kayla as the reason for her troubles. Even so, every time she snapped at her little sister she felt awful. Then the more she hated herself, the snappier she became. Yet another relationship she seemed to be destroying.

She looked back at her phone, hoping that even if things were getting worse by the minute with her family, at least the situation with her friends was improving.

Olivia

It's a good one.

Oh, for god's sake, just say it already. Nia pushed her thoughts away, as though Olivia would somehow be able to read them through her phone. God knew how she'd react if Nia ever dared to speak back to her like that.

She tried to guess what her dare might be, but she'd never been able to think like Olivia. It was sure to be something messed up, that much was certain. But *what*? She wouldn't make her do anything illegal, would she? The group had done some pretty wild stuff before, but not alone, not anywhere like this.

Nia's fingers tightened over the phone and she looked at the door. There was no way she was about to go poking round an abandoned prison. She wasn't an idiot.

Kayla was watching Nia as though her inner struggle was a TV programme.

Nia stared at the toilet door, its flaky paint giving no clues that only last year this was where women would have cried over their husbands, their sons, their brothers, before visiting them in the vast prison that Nia was already keen to leave. What was in the main building, away from the bright lights and disinfectant smell of the soft-play centre?

Her phone buzzed, and for once she didn't hurry to read the message. She frowned down at the words, wondering what they could mean.

Olivia

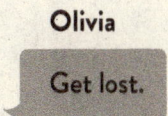

Get lost.

CHAPTER 4

Get lost? That was the dare?

Nia waited for Olivia to elaborate, but no further instructions came.

She nibbled the edge of her nail and tried to decide whether she should say something. *No*, Nia decided, a dare that vague was open to interpretation, and she'd need all the leeway she could get.

Get lost . . . Surely that just meant she should go and explore, right? That wasn't so bad – she was sure to encounter a locked door that would stop her from having to delve too deep into the huge building. How creepy could any of the rooms be anyway? One of them had been turned into a soft-play centre, after all.

She stared at her reflection and nodded. She could do this. She fixed her hair and applied another layer of lip gloss. It was the same shade Olivia and Chloe wore. Nia pouted and tried to embody the natural confidence that came so easily to them.

'Nia, it's this way,' Kayla said, as Nia marched past her to leave the toilets, turning left instead of right.

But Nia was practised at ignoring Kayla and kept walking in the opposite direction from the soft-play area. There were four more rooms on the wide, brightly lit corridor. Two had paper signs Blu-Tacked to the doors, words drawn in black marker declaring their purpose: Craft Room! Birthday Party Room!

Nia curled her lip. This place really was the pits. It could have been all right if a bit of effort had been put in, but the giant soft-play frame in the sports hall looked like it had been rescued from a skip, and the bouncy castle was one good jump away from coming down altogether.

She picked at the corner of the Birthday Party Room sign, revealing its previous use: **THERAPY ROOM A**.

Nia shuddered. The prison reminded her of the black mould she'd tried to paint over on her bedroom wall. No matter how many layers she'd coated on, the grime remained, somehow looking even more disgusting behind the pastel-pink paint.

She carefully pushed the door open. The room was bare, with the exception of a long table in the middle, covered in a plastic, patterned tablecloth. There were paper party hats and plates set out, ready for whichever lucky child got to celebrate their birthday in what was once a prison therapy room. Nia winced as she thought of the secrets and stories that had been shared in here before the prison was closed.

The craft room was similar – colouring books scattered over tables, pots of snapped crayons dotted about, and a Pritt Stick that Nia could tell from a distance was dried-up and useless.

She pulled the door shut and bypassed the other rooms, starting up the stairs. Rubbish playrooms weren't going to cut it – she needed something from the actual prison, something that would make her friends sit up and pay attention. Something impressive that would get Olivia off her back, for now at least.

'I'm just going to have a look around,' Nia said over her shoulder as she climbed.

Panting, she reached the top, wondering which door to take. The corridor was unremarkable, not dissimilar to those at school, which was saying something about her school.

'I don't think you're supposed to,' Kayla said, her small voice echoing up the stairwell. Nia didn't need to turn round to picture her worried face, the little nibbles she would be making at the inside of her lip. Kayla hated breaking rules. That was why Nia had been so sure she would do as she was told the night of the party.

Nia read the signs as she walked past: **STORAGE A, STORAGE B, FACILITIES.**

She sighed impatiently. This place was turning out to be embarrassingly boring. She needed something good to show the others, something juicy.

VISITATION WING.

That was more like it. But the word 'wing' made her pause. She had just wanted to peep into some of the rooms and take a picture of something weird – she hadn't planned on going to an entirely new *wing*. Would it lead to the old, haunted-looking section of the prison that they'd had to walk past to get to the newer sports hall?

The door would probably be locked anyway, though it looked like it only needed a normal key. Surely a prison would have a more high-tech system, like key cards or fingerprint scanners or something? No wonder this place had been shut down.

Nia reached out, annoyed with her trembling hand. What was she getting so nervous about? There weren't even any signs telling soft-play visitors not to trespass, so technically she wasn't breaking the rules. But the feeling that she was doing something very wrong wouldn't leave her; nor would the image of Mum and Mark's disappointed faces.

'Are we going back now?'

Nia gasped. She didn't realise Kayla had followed her up the stairs. 'Not yet,' she replied firmly, Kayla's presence hardening her resolve. She wasn't in any hurry to return to Mum's cold eyes and thin smiles.

Her hand steadied as it closed around the cool metal handle. With a click, the door opened smoothly.

Nia swallowed hard. She wished she was more curious and that every fibre of her being wasn't screaming at her to go back. She peered into the room, waiting for a sharp voice to shout at her for being there, but none came. It was empty.

Though, Nia realised with a shiver, not entirely.

The large room looked like it was ready to receive visitors. Posters giving instructions were stuck to the walls, there were leaflets about mental health on a stand next to the door, and tables that looked like metal picnic benches were spaced across the rough blue carpet. Nia noticed that they were bolted to the floor and wondered why, before picturing furniture being hurled across the room by enraged prisoners in orange jumpsuits.

What conversations had taken place in this room? She could almost hear the echoed memories, the murmur of jumbled voices bouncing between the walls.

'Look,' Kayla said, peering past Nia's waist into the room. 'Books.'

Nia rolled her eyes – trust Kayla to focus on the reading material. A corner of the room had been set up for kids. A garish mural grinned down from the wall behind battered-looking toys, the kind you found in doctors' waiting rooms. The painting was supposed to be Pinocchio, but the artist hadn't got the likeness quite right and his face looked warped and sinister.

Nia looked down at her little sister, who clutched her own book to her chest as she stared at the other titles from afar. She clung on to books in the same way other kids would hold a treasured teddy or blanket. Nia would never understand her.

Nia's life had been altered drastically when Kayla was born, and she wasn't sure she'd ever be able to forgive her for it. For being wanted, when Nia had been an accident.

Mum had never admitted it, but it was pretty obvious Nia hadn't exactly been planned. Mum had only been nineteen, and Nia had never met her dad. She didn't even know his name. All she knew about him was that he wasn't 'part of the picture' any more and Mum refused to share anything else. Then, when Nia was seven, Mark had come along.

He was great. He was friendly and funny and had all the time in the world for Nia. He was everything Nia had dreamed of when she thought about what her dad might be like. But then Mum had got pregnant within weeks of him moving in, and everything had changed.

It took a while. At first Nia was excited to meet her baby

sister – she'd always wanted her family to be bigger. She'd helped change tiny baby Kayla, chosen clothes for her, spent hours playing with her and teasing the tangles out of her hair. But as she got older, they all realised there was something different about her, good-different – she was special.

Words like 'genius' and 'gifted' were thrown around, and Nia watched Mum and Mark as they watched Kayla, their eyes wide with wonder.

All their lives started to revolve around her. Nia's dance classes had to be stopped because they clashed with Kayla's maths tutor, weekends were spent at museums instead of the swimming baths.

Mark was still great. He still took the time to talk to her and play the games she liked and kick a football around at the park. But Nia knew that his eyes didn't sparkle when he looked at her the same way they did when he looked at Kayla. Kayla was his flesh and blood. Nia was just something left over from Mum's old life.

Then Mum got pregnant again. Nia had tried to smile when they told her and Kayla the news, but all she could think about was how the new baby would take even more of Mum and Mark away from her, when she felt like she didn't have enough of them as it was.

Nia tore her eyes away from her little sister. The desire to get out of there was suddenly overwhelming. She took a picture on her phone, but it just looked like a drab room – the creepiness was completely lost.

She needed to go further.

She didn't want to walk across the visitation room – delving any further than this corridor felt like a commitment she wasn't ready to make. But there was a door on the opposite wall of the room, and its contents promised something worth exploring. **PRISONER WING ACCESS. NO VISITORS.**

CHAPTER 5

It would be locked; it *had* to be. But at least Nia could get a picture of the sign, to show the others that she had tried.

She crossed the room swiftly, dodging the chairs and tables and trying not to think about what had caused the stains on the carpet. She snapped a photo.

Nia

> Sorry, guys, tried to take you on a tour, but all locked up.

Nia turned away from the door. It was time to go back. Would Mum be drinking coffee and having a nice time without her there? Kayla was still standing next to the visitation room entrance, gazing at the books in the opposite corner as though hypnotised.

Max

> Aw, man, I wanted to see some freaky stuff!

Olivia

> I bet she's not even tried to open it lol

Irritation made Nia's face twitch. This was a speciality of Olivia's – talking on the group message as though Nia wasn't a part of it. As though pretending she didn't exist would somehow make it so.

She'd just have to prove it then. Nia started to share a live video of herself and gave a little pout to the camera, for Scott. She flashed the lens towards Kayla lurking in the background with her precious book clutched to her chest, then mouthed, 'I have a stalker,' before filming her hand on the door handle. Prepared to rattle the locked door theatrically, she gasped as the handle moved downwards, the door opening with a clunk.

Remembering she was still on film, she recovered quickly and let her friends see a glimpse of her shocked face, before stopping the recording.

Great.

Why wasn't any door in this dump locked? It was practically asking for people to trespass. Nia glanced over her shoulder, wondering if it might be linked to an alarm of some sort. But no one came to stop her.

A rush of cold, stale air seeped through the crack in the door, and Nia took a step backwards. Whatever lay beyond was pitch black. Compared to the bright strip lights in the visitation room, the door felt like it was leading into another world. A world that Nia really, *really* didn't want to enter.

But it was too late now, everyone had seen that the door was unlocked. She didn't have a choice.

The door seemed out of place, older than the rest of the room. She gave it a push with her foot, not wanting to get too close, knowing that if she were in a film there would be something horrible waiting for her on the other side. It swung slowly and silently away from her, revealing a dark, windowless passageway. The light from the visitation room didn't reach the end, so it looked like the walls disappeared into nothingness.

Where was that breeze coming from? The passage smelled like damp stone and mould. It had to be the link between the new part of the prison and the ancient, foreboding section that had loomed over them as they walked through the courtyard.

Nia squinted, willing her eyes to adjust to the light so that she could make out anything other than red bricks and blackness. There was *something* . . . but it was impossible to see properly because it was swallowed by the dark, and when Nia tried to focus on it her eyes struggled and shifted.

'Nia, I don't think we should go down there,' Kayla said, so softly it felt as though she'd whispered into Nia's ear.

Nia pulled her eyes away from the passageway, blinking at the bright lights of the visitation room.

'What do you mean, *we*?' she said. 'There is no *we*. You're going back to Mum.'

But Nia wanted to go back too. She wanted a slice of rocky road and a milkshake. She wanted Mum to smile at her again.

Her phone demanded her attention.

Olivia

> Nia, babes, I think you should go back. I know how scared you must be x

Nia closed her eyes. Was Olivia *really* being nice? *Could* she go back to Mum and still be accepted by her friends, invited to things again like she had been before her disastrous house party? She sighed. No, this was a make-or-break moment for her, she knew it. She could either confirm what her friends already thought of her – that she was a baby and not worth their time – or she could show them that she was fearless and therefore worthy of their acceptance.

There really wasn't any choice.

She turned back to the passageway, but whatever her eyes had tried to focus on earlier had gone. It must have been nothing, just a warped shadow or a pattern on the wall. She took a picture and sent it to the group, though all you could see was a frame of red bricks that gradually disappeared into a black hole.

Nia

> Wish me luck.

She took a step.

'Nia! We shouldn't go in there!' Kayla's urgency made Nia

hesitate – she'd never heard her sound so scared.

She tried to remind herself that Kayla was just a kid. No, not just a kid, her little sister. Big sisters were supposed to take care of little sisters. She was finding it harder to remember that lately.

'Kayla,' Nia said, squatting down to her level. 'Don't worry, you're not going through this door. You're going to go back to Mum and have a nice time and read your book. I'm just going to have a quick look around, then I'll come back too, OK?'

But Kayla was shaking her head, her lip wobbling as tears threatened to spill over. 'I want you to come with me.'

Nia closed her eyes. She couldn't exactly take Kayla back to the table then disappear again. Mum was sure to ask where she was going and insist she stay with them. In fact, she realised glumly, Mum might already be getting frantic if she'd noticed both girls hadn't returned from the toilets yet.

She had an idea.

Nia

> Hey, Mum. Just doing some colouring and stuff in the craft room. Back soon. X

Perfect. Mum would be pleased that she was spending time with Kayla and glad for the chance to drink coffee in peace. And Nia would be able to explore undisturbed. It was a win-win situation.

Now, what to do with Kayla?

'Kayla, why don't you go back to the craft room. You can

wait for me there. Then you'll know I'm not far away.'

Kayla was still shaking her head, and Nia was starting to get annoyed.

'If I leave,' Kayla whispered, 'I'll get lost again.'

Nia narrowed her eyes. That was a low blow. No wonder Mum couldn't forgive her if Kayla kept bringing it up.

'Fine,' Nia snapped. 'If you're so keen to stick with me then you can't be a baby about exploring, OK?'

Kayla wiped her nose and nodded. Though as Nia went to step into the tunnel, she didn't feel so brave herself. She paused, bouncing the door against her palm. Would it slam shut behind them? No, it was heavy and stiff – it should stay open.

If it didn't . . .

She curled her fingers into fists. *Don't think about getting trapped in here.*

Nia stepped through the door.

CHAPTER 6

Nia felt Kayla's icy fingers curl around hers but shook them off. She tried to convince herself that it was because she was irritated with her, but really she didn't want Kayla to feel her own hand trembling.

She held her breath as she groped in the dark for the light switch but recoiled in disgust as her hand touched something cold and slimy. The walls were so damp they seemed to be creating some kind of revolting, moist life of their own. She dry-heaved and tried again, finding the switch and flicking it down.

Nothing happened.

Typical. They'd left all kinds of stuff when they'd abandoned this place but taken the one thing that would be useful to her right now – the light bulbs.

It was a shame they hadn't bothered locking the door, then Nia wouldn't have to be here at all.

Why was the ceiling so low? And why weren't there any windows? Nia longed to retreat to the bright, roomy, newer section of the prison, but her phone vibrated and reminded her why she was there.

Olivia

> Are you dead yet?

Nia resisted the urge to hurl her phone against the wall.

Max

> Bet hers isn't the only body down there...

What? Max had always had a sick sense of humour but, jeez, that was a visual Nia really didn't need right now.

Scott

> You can do it, babe.

A ripple of excitement coursed through her. Scott was on *her* side. That was all that mattered.

A dripping sound from deeper within the tunnel pulled her attention back to the task ahead.

She took a step.

'Come on, Nia,' she muttered to herself. Her voice sounded too loud.

Another step. The ground felt rough beneath her feet, as though there wasn't a proper floor. The light from the visitation room quickly faded, and Nia could barely see a metre in front of her face.

If only her stupid, ancient phone wasn't broken – the section on the back containing her main camera and torch was shattered. She could only use her selfie-camera, which hadn't been a problem before now. But right now she really wished the torch worked.

She held her phone above her head, using the glow from the screen to light the way, though it only illuminated a few centimetres in front of her feet.

She took another cautious step.

What was that noise? It didn't sound like dripping.

Step.

Kayla's fingers plucked at the hem of her top.

Step.

There was something there in the endless dark, the same something she had struggled to make out when she had first opened the door.

Step.

What *was* it?

Step.

The murky shades of light shifted, and the shape disappeared so quickly that Nia gasped. Whatever it had been, it wasn't there any more. There was nothing to focus on, just a gaping black mouth ready to swallow her. She furrowed her brow, trying to force her eyes to make sense of the shadows hiding in the dark. She could have sworn she'd heard something, but her heart was thumping so hard that all she could make out was her own blood rushing through her body.

She turned back to look at the door, the square of light further away than she would have liked. Kayla stared up at her, her pupils huge.

'Did you see—'

'Shh,' Nia hissed. She didn't want to know what Kayla had seen. She wouldn't be able to convince herself it was all in her head if Kayla had seen it too.

This is a terrible idea.

Nia's phone buzzed in her hand, and she only just managed to stop herself from screaming.

It's just an empty old building. Keep it together.

Nia was distracted from her phone by a particularly disgusting section of the wall. She tried not to study the green-and-black slime too closely but couldn't help noticing protruding clumps of fuzzy white mould. Goose bumps crept over her entire body and she tried to fold in on herself, away from the rankness surrounding her.

She turned her phone light upwards. The corridor was wired with long strip lights that were identical to those in the newer section of the prison building.

If only the stupid things worked.

Nia could just make out another heavy metal door at the end of the corridor. It was open, but only revealed more darkness beyond.

Nia swore under her breath. What if none of the doors were locked, and she had to keep going deeper and deeper into this hellhole?

'How much further are we going to go?' Kayla whispered, reading Nia's mind.

'Just through this door,' Nia promised herself as much as Kayla. 'I'm going to lean through and take some pictures, then we can get out of here.'

'OK.'

Nia turned and gave Kayla a little smile. She was being pretty brave, despite the evident fear in her eyes. She clutched her book like a life buoy and took a deep breath that, even in the dark, Nia could see made her small frame tremble.

Even as they crept closer, the weak light coming from her phone screen wasn't enough to illuminate what lay beyond the doorway – the darkness swallowed up the light completely. Their cautious footsteps echoed through the corridor and Nia found herself running through a plan of action in case anything leapt out at them. She would turn, grab Kayla under one arm and run. Her phone buzzed again and she swore, unable to resist the need to check it.

Olivia

It's been ages, why isn't she sending any pictures?

Olivia

She's definitely dead.

Olivia

Bye, Nia.

Nia clenched her teeth. It was impossible to complain, to tell Olivia she'd gone too far, when she could respond with, 'God, I was only *joking*!'

But instead of scaring her, as she was sure was Olivia's intention, the messages spurred Nia on. She pictured the smug smile being wiped off Olivia's face when she proved her wrong, and stepped forward with a renewed sense of determination, not stopping until she had reached the doorway.

She hadn't yet entered the room, but she could feel the gust of cold air coming out from it, brushing against her face. Even though she couldn't see a thing, Nia could *feel* the empty space in front of her. She wasn't sure which was worse – the cramped corridor or the vast nothingness. A shiver raced up her arm to her neck.

'Nia?'

Kayla's voice bounced around the dark room, confirming Nia's suspicions – this place was big enough to create its own echo.

'Don't worry,' Nia whispered, not wanting her own voice to echo. 'I'm just going to have a quick look and then we can go.'

But as she went to take a step forward on to what looked like a metal grate, tiny hands plucked at her jumper, not strong enough to stop her, but enough to make her hesitate.

'No, wait!' Kayla insisted. Nia was used to brushing her little sister off, ignoring her questions and requests, but she sounded different this time. 'Feel for a light switch first.'

Nia rolled her eyes. The corridor lights didn't work so why would this room have functioning electricity? She ignored her and inched forward.

'Please!' Kayla's voice was loud, and her plea was repeated over and over again around the room, sounding more urgent each time. 'Please . . . please . . . please . . .'

Nia sighed and turned back to her little sister. 'Kayla, just relax, will you? You don't have to come in. Just stay here and wait for me. I only need to get close enough to something so that I can take a picture. Then we can go back, OK?'

But Kayla was shaking her head, her eyes huge, her fingers tight around the spine of her book.

'Please, please, *please*, just check for a light. I've got a really bad feeling.' Nia opened her mouth to snap, but Kayla interrupted, her voice barely a whisper now. 'You don't know what's in there.'

Nia tried to swallow the pang of fear Kayla's words brought, but it stuck in her throat, making her feel like she might choke.

Kayla was right. She had no idea what she was leading them into.

Could she turn back now? Could she fake a picture to send to the group, something that would make it look like she had explored further?

She looked around desperately, but there was nothing apart from bricks and mould. She needed more.

'OK,' she said, forcing her voice to be steady. 'I'll check.'

'Don't reach too far!' Kayla reminded as Nia stretched her arm around the door. Why was Kayla so worried about her stepping into the room? Nia's imagination answered, and she pictured gnarled fingers seizing her the second she breached the doorway. Her hand withdrew involuntarily and Nia clutched it to her chest.

Come on. It's just an empty room. There's nothing there.

Giving it a comforting squeeze, she sent her hand back into the gloom. She patted the wall, grimacing as she felt something damp and cold, picturing the moist white mould in the corridor. But revulsion was better than terror, so Nia focused on that as she searched blindly.

Nothing.

She shook her head impatiently. She shouldn't have listened to Kayla, then she wouldn't have a hand covered in some disgusting unknown substance. She stretched higher, twisting her arm around, careful not to step through the doorway . . . just in case.

There was something there.

It didn't feel like a light switch, not the regular kind, anyway. It was a box, about the size of Nia's hand. It was smooth with sharp corners and wasn't as cold as the metal door – it felt like plastic. Frustrated that she couldn't see what it was, Nia tried to shine her phone on it, but she couldn't reach, not with her feet still in the corridor.

It was no good. She couldn't get a proper feel of it with her arm twisted round at an uncomfortable angle like this. She changed positions, turning to hug the corridor wall and reaching her left hand round the corner. She closed her eyes and concentrated, trying not to think about the filth on the wall she had her body pressed up against.

Please don't let there be spiders.

This angle worked much better. She could get her fingers round the entire box now and could feel something – a cable – feeding into it from above. Her nails found a seam and she picked at it.

The lid flipped up, and she felt a light switch nestled beneath the plastic casing.

Bingo. She half expected all this effort to be for nothing. After all, what was the chance the light would even work? She flicked the switch, and the room lit up.

CHAPTER 7

Nia winced and shielded her eyes from the blinding strip lights as they clunked and buzzed, struggling to come to life. One of them flickered, sounding like a giant moth flapping frantically against the bulb.

As her eyes adjusted, the sight in front of Nia sent her staggering backwards. She clutched on to the frame of the doorway and instinctively threw an arm out to hold Kayla back, even though she hadn't made any move to come closer. Nia couldn't make sense of what she was looking at.

An old, crumbling walkway circled the perimeter of the room. Nia took a shaky step forward and peeked over the edge. Below them was what appeared to be another level with a similar doughnut arrangement of cells, and what must've once been a communal area in the centre. Remnants of an old pool table lay scattered below. She looked up and saw the underside of a similar walkway and a glimpse of more metal bars – yet another level of cells.

Much of the walkway had fallen away, twisted metal angling

downwards and piercing the huge net that hung below each level. The metal grate Nia had been about to step on to was attached to the floor by a single rusted bolt. If she hadn't listened to Kayla – if she'd taken another step forward in the darkness – she would have fallen at least ten metres on to the solid concrete below. Her heart lurched and she took another step backwards, her knees trembling as she imagined her body plummeting.

Nia braced herself on the wall, past caring about the mould. That had been too close. She frowned, remembering again Kayla's insistence that she didn't step through the doorway.

'How did you know?' she asked as her heart began to calm a little.

'I don't know,' Kayla whispered.

Nia watched her, but Kayla didn't speak again. She just stared. There had always been something strange about her – Nia had felt it from the start. She was so serious and quiet. She listened so much more than she spoke, and she was so smart that Nia often felt like a fool in comparison.

'You're so creepy,' Nia whispered.

'I know,' Kayla said sombrely.

It could have been the near-death experience, or it could have been Kayla's solemn little face, but Nia started laughing.

The sound was alien in the murkiness of the corridor, and it ricocheted around the cell block. It sounded like there were a hundred girls, all laughing hysterically, which made Nia laugh even harder. Kayla looked uncertain, but then a smile flickered at the corner of her mouth and her high-pitched giggle soon joined Nia's.

The thought brought reality back to her, and her sniggers tapered off. She smiled uncertainly at Kayla. It was the first time in a long while they'd laughed together like this. She wished Mum were here to see it.

'Thank you,' Nia said.

Kayla smiled back at her and Nia almost reached out to stroke her hair. But a buzzing in her pocket forced her attention away from her little sister.

Scott

> Babe, you OK?

Nia's focus was fully back on the boy at the end of the phone.

Nia

> You won't believe this.

She turned back to the door, but it was impossible to get a picture of the entire cell block with her tiny selfie-camera, due to the sheer size of it. She sighed angrily as she looked at the photo she had captured. It wasn't nearly as impressive as the reality.

She gingerly sat down and took a picture of her feet dangling over the edge, but even that didn't look scary because the perspective was off – it didn't look like a drop you could twist your ankle from, let alone die.

Olivia

> Believe what?

Olivia

> Helloooo, anyone home?

'All right, Olivia, just wait,' Nia muttered.

'Who's Olivia?'

'No one, don't be so nosy,' Nia snapped. She instantly regretted reverting back to her usual irritated tone with Kayla, but she had more pressing concerns.

She sent the picture of the drop. Olivia's reply was brutally quick.

Olivia

> Why are you sending us a photo of your knock-off Nikes?

Nia studied her shoes. Was it that obvious they were knock-offs? She had begged for the real deal, but Mum had laughed as though Nia had suggested they buy her a Porsche or something. Mark had found these for her and she'd tried to look pleased. She *was* pleased. Sure, they were fake, but they were a symbol of Mark caring about her.

That had been before the party.

Nia sent the picture of the room, not that it was any better.

She couldn't get a proper shot because of the broken platform obstructing her view.

Olivia

> What even is that? You're just taking random pictures to make it look like you went exploring, aren't you?

A shout of frustration left Nia's mouth and the cell block shouted back. What was she going to have to do to convince them that she really was in the prison?

Nia

> I can't get a proper picture, but I'm in a cell block! It's massive, but the walkway is all collapsed so I can't go any further.

Scott

> LOL. Yeah, sure, babe. You've been busted.

No, no, no! Not Scott too. He was supposed to believe her. He was supposed to be on her side.

Nia's eyes began to itch, and she squeezed them shut, refusing to let the tears escape. This moment was important, she could feel it. This was her chance to finally show everyone that she deserved to be part of the group.

They'd tested her since day one, ever since Scott spotted her walking home from school six months ago and wrapped his arm around her shoulders. He'd introduced her to Chloe, Max and Olivia, who'd laughed at her spluttering after taking her first drag of a cigarette. It was gross but she felt like she couldn't refuse – not with Scott's piercing eyes watching her every movement.

Scott had asked for her number and promised to message her. She stayed by her phone the entire weekend, chewing her fingernails until the flesh around them was raw and painful. By Sunday afternoon she was a complete mess. Her mind had been consumed with him since the moment he'd smiled at her, but he'd probably forgotten her the second he'd walked away.

Then on Monday morning he'd grabbed her hand as she stood waiting to go into her classroom, pulling her out of the line. He apologised for not getting in touch, but his words washed over her as she stumbled against his chest. The feel of his muscles beneath his school shirt and the fresh smell of his skin made her feel delirious. And then he'd kissed her. Right there, in front of everyone. She'd stood in the corridor long after he'd left, feeling exposed but excited, like she knew her life was going to change.

But some people were scared of change. Nia had been friends with Lucy and Anna since primary school, but their routine was becoming tedious, even before Scott noticed Nia's existence. They were friends out of habit, rather than choice. Or at least that's how it felt to Nia. While other people in their year group posted pictures online of parties that people talked about in the school corridors for weeks, Lucy and Anna filled their weekends with family camping trips. When Nia had half joked about sneaking some of Anna's mum's white wine from the fridge after a long day of studying in her kitchen, both girls had reacted like she was trying to pressure them into a life of hard drugs and crime. Besides, Lucy and Anna had always been a lot closer to each other than they had ever been with Nia.

So it was hardly a surprise when instead of being thrilled for her when she told them about Scott, they'd tried to ruin it for her.

'He's a bad influence!' Anna had insisted, sounding more like her mum every day.

'I've got a really bad feeling about this,' Lucy had whispered, her round eyes bulging in warning.

When were they going to realise that there was more to life than plaiting each other's hair at sleepovers?

Nia was ready to experience the exciting and dangerous world that Scott and his friends were rulers of. And once school broke up for summer, it was easy enough to stop replying to Lucy and Anna's messages, though it took them a while to get the hint.

She did wish she had someone to confide in, though. Someone to speak to about Scott and ask advice about how to get him to like her as much as she adored him. She'd thought Chloe might be that person at first – she seemed sweet despite, Nia suspected, not having much between the ears.

They'd spoken a few times in a chat separate from the rest of the group. Nia had messaged first after seeing the devastation on Chloe's face when Olivia had laughed at her new jacket.

Nia

> I liked the jacket, by the way. It wasn't nice of Olivia to laugh at it like that x

Chloe's response had taken a long time to arrive, as though she were carefully deliberating her words before pressing send.

Chloe

> That's just the way she is.

Nia waited an age as Chloe continued writing.

Chloe

> But you're right – it's cute, isn't it?!?

Nia grinned at the phone. She wondered how long Chloe had been at the receiving end of Olivia's scorn, which must have been ten times worse without Nia around to soak some of it up. Maybe it was something they could bond over. She pictured them teaming up to tell Olivia that enough was enough – she couldn't treat people like they were toys to be picked up and discarded at will.

But the messages stopped abruptly one day, and Nia was sure Olivia's hatred of her had ramped up a notch at the same time. She suspected their conversations had been discovered, and that Olivia had quickly put a stop to them.

But it didn't matter, not really, not as long as she had Scott.

Until she'd ruined everything by acting like the baby everyone kept calling her. Scott had told everyone when she didn't want to do anything more than kiss. She had thought that sort of thing was supposed to be exciting, not scary, which is why she had stopped him. He hadn't been happy about it.

She knew she wouldn't have many more chances with him, not unless she could prove that she was the fun, daring girl he wanted to be with.

He had to believe her.

Nia

I'm not lying.

Olivia

We'll believe you when we see a photo of you inside a cell.

Nia glared at Olivia's request. No, not request. Olivia didn't make requests. She commanded.

She should have known something like this was coming – the dare couldn't stay as vague as 'Get lost'. What choice did Nia have? She had to prove herself to her friends. She'd already lost Lucy and Anna, and it felt like she was losing her family too. She wasn't sure she could lose anyone else.

Nia looked warily over the edge and withdrew her feet when she imagined someone shoving her from behind. This passage couldn't be the only route into the cell blocks, surely? There had to be other wings, and they couldn't all come through this one to get to the visitation room. She racked her brain, trying to remember the route they had taken to get to the sports hall. Were there any more open doors, other ways she could get inside to take this picture?

Nia stood and tapped her fingertips on her temple. Had she noticed another way out of the soft-play area? No, the sports hall was strangely separate from the rest of the prison, as though it had been dropped there from a height and had been wondering why it was there ever since. And going back outside to check for open doors on the perimeter of the prison wasn't an option – she'd have to walk past Mum, and there was no way she'd let Nia go sneaking around.

It had to be here, in this cell block. Just the small issue of a sheer drop to contend with, that would surely kill her if she fell.

What about the level she was on now – could she get to any of the cells up here? The walkway on the right had completely fallen away and a large section of it had broken off and crashed to the floor below. Nia tried not to think about the way she had dangled her body over the drop as she reached for the light switch. She marvelled again at Kayla's instincts. As much as she didn't want to think about it, the kid had really, truly saved her life.

To the left, remnants of the walkway clung to the wall, a small section still attached to the corridor, which was what she'd seen with her phone light. The metal grate dangled over the massive room, creating a steep slide to the floor below, where it had pierced the netting and continued down to the ground.

Nia groaned – there was no way she'd be able to climb across to a cell on the floor she and Kayla were on. But . . . the top of the makeshift slide was only a metre or so away from the doorway. If she could get to the dangling walkway, she might be able to get all the way down to the ground floor.

If.

Was it really worth the risk? Nia thought of the expressions on Mum's and Mark's faces when they looked at her, ever since that night of the party. It didn't feel like things could get much worse at home.

Yes, it was worth it. She *needed* her friends. They were all she had.

Kayla hadn't made a sound for a while, but she was standing in exactly the same spot when Nia turned to her.

'I've got to go a bit further,' she explained, trying to keep her voice steady, hoping her confidence would put Kayla at ease. 'You wait here.'

In case I fall and need you to run for help.

Nia readied herself for Kayla's protests, but she just said, 'I wish you wouldn't go. I wish you'd come back to Mum.'

Nia wasn't convinced Mum would be bothered if she didn't come back – Kayla was the precious one. At least she'd be safe up here, so Nia wouldn't get into trouble for losing her. Again.

'Just wait here,' Nia instructed, already turning away from Kayla. 'And this time, do not wander off!'

CHAPTER 8

She couldn't jump, not at this angle. She'd need a decent run-up, which would mean sprinting along the corridor, leaping out of the doorway and then somehow turning ninety degrees in mid-air.

Not happening.

She'd have to climb over. The walls were made of the same old brick as the passageway, though thankfully there wasn't the same build-up of slippery mould out here. She picked at the cement between the bricks closest to her and it flaked away easily. Still, she didn't fancy clinging on to the shallow holes with her fingertips and leaving her feet dangling.

Nia frowned, spotting a small object on the wall at the same height as her feet. She lowered herself to all fours and craned as far out of the doorway as she dared to get a better look.

It was a piece of metal sticking out of the bricks, like a bracket of some sort. She looked further along the wall and saw more of them, at the same level as the first. They must be where the walkway had been connected to the wall before it collapsed.

She stood and checked the state of the wall at head height. The cement between the bricks seemed more crumbled here. Maybe, just maybe, crumbled enough to make decent handholds.

Clutching on to the corner of the door, Nia reached out with her foot and tapped it firmly on the first metal bar. It held.

Knowing what she was about to do was insane, she got her phone out, unable to prevent the thought that it might be the last message she ever sent.

Nia

I'm going to climb down.

Nia

If I die, it's Olivia's fault.

Nia shook her head and deleted the last part. It would just annoy Olivia, and though it was hard to imagine her being even more unbearable than she already was, Nia didn't want to take the risk.

She wedged her phone in her back pocket next to her lip gloss, wishing she had somewhere safer to put it. If it fell out and smashed, all this would have been for nothing. Turning so that her stomach was pressed up against the wall, she took a last look at Kayla, who still hadn't moved an inch, then stepped out of the door.

What the hell am I doing?

Nia balanced with her right foot on the metal bracket and her left still in the corridor. She could feel the deadly open space behind her and pressed her body against the wall, her fingers wedged as deep as possible into the bricks. How was she going to get to the next piece of metal without taking her foot off the first one?

Her fingers started trembling, the effort of clinging on making them cramp. The brick was rough against her palms and the pressure on her false nails stung like hell. She only had two options: dangle from her fingertips and swing to the next metal support, or somehow swap feet so she could step over.

Option one wasn't actually an option, she quickly realised. Her acrylics were too long – the nails would be ripped off her fingers. They still felt awkward on her hands, no matter how much she tried to copy Olivia's elegant gestures. The occasional wrenched finger and jabbed eyeball had been worth it, though – the nails had brought her a step closer to being one of the girls. But right now she wished she had her natural short, stumpy nails that didn't feel like they were being prised from her nailbeds.

She considered option two. She'd have to rotate outwards so that she was facing the drop, instead of the wall. The bile rising from her stomach told her that she would surely fall if she tried that.

She needed her left foot to replace her right foot on the first metal bracket. If only there was room for both feet at the same time, but the support wasn't even as long as her foot.

It was *wider* than it, though.

She twisted so that her right foot was as far away from the wall as possible, her heel pointed back towards the doorway and her body angled towards the next support. That left about eight centimetres for her left foot. She squeezed it on, pressing it as close to her right foot as possible. Then, a millimetre at a time, she shuffled her right foot off the support.

She'd done it – her right foot was now free to stretch to the next bracket.

She lunged slowly over and found handholds above the second support. Only one more to go until she reached the platform.

But there was something strange about the third support. It didn't look like the others, it looked like . . .

A screwdriver.

Nia tried to understand what it could mean, but she didn't have time to waste, not when the skin surrounding her nails had started to bleed from the strain of gripping the wall. A squeak of pain escaped her lips as she repeated the stepping process. The screwdriver wasn't as secure as the brackets, and for a sickening moment Nia thought she was about to fall. But it was wedged in just far enough to hold, and she made it to the platform.

The walkway rattled and groaned beneath her weight as she landed, lurching sickeningly above the huge drop. She crouched and laced her fingers through the metal grate floor, wincing as the sharp edges hurt her hands. The slide looked a lot steeper this close.

No turning back now.

Trying not to think about how difficult it was going to be to get back up to the doorway, she started to inch down backwards.

Just like climbing down a ladder.

Nia tried to remember if she'd ever climbed down a ladder before. It was something everyone should be able to do, though, surely? Then why were her knees shaking so hard that it made the walkway bounce and sway beneath her?

The metal scraped her hands, and the holes in the grate weren't big enough for her feet, so she could only get the tips of her shoes in. She whispered thanks to her trainers, knowing the rubber grip was one of the only reasons she wasn't sliding down towards the concrete two floors below. These 'knock-off Nikes' were keeping her alive right now.

The platform groaned as it swayed beneath her weight. She passed the netting, wondering why it was there. In case people dropped things off the top floor maybe?

Yeah, like bodies.

She tried not to think about falling, looking anywhere but down. She spotted a dead pigeon tangled in the net next to her face and a shiver ran down her spine. Its neck was bent so dramatically that it touched the back of its body, as though it had broken itself in half in its desperation to escape. Bile scorched her throat again.

Almost there, Nia. You're almost there.

Her phone vibrated in her back pocket and, in a moment of stupidity, she reached to get it out, her hand responding automatically to its call. Her balance was thrown and she felt the world shift beneath her before she quickly pressed herself back on to the grate, gripping tight with both hands again. She closed her eyes, breathing deeply to calm her racing heart.

When she opened them again she was face to face with the glassy stare of the pigeon. A thin trickle of blood stained its crusty beak.

Nia fought the urge to flinch away, clenched her jaw and reminded herself why she was doing this.

Keep going.

Then, just when the pain of the metal on her palms started burning more than she could bear, her feet reached the end of the walkway.

She grinned victoriously, but her elation evaporated when she realised she wasn't yet on the ground.

CHAPTER 9

Nia stretched a leg down and tapped the air in search of the floor, but found nothing. She craned her neck, trying to see how far away from the ground she was. She guessed there was about a two-metre drop between the end of the platform and the cell-block floor.

Looking down, the drop seemed huge, but was it big enough to seriously injure her? Her fingers were so sore from clinging on to the grate that she worried she might lose her grip. She needed to do something, fast.

She'd have to lower herself down using just her hands. Already knowing how much it was going to hurt, she took a breath before letting her feet dangle off the end.

She couldn't help the shout of pain that escaped her lips as she shuffled downwards. She'd never been athletic. She couldn't even do the monkey bars at the park, which was the closest thing she could compare to this. Now, as well as her hands screaming in pain, it felt as though the muscles leading from her armpits to her elbows were tearing.

She couldn't hold on any more. She took a peek, and the ground looked so far away. She'd made a terrible, terrible mistake.

Nia shrieked as she landed heavily on her ankle. There was a loud crunch and the pain that shot up her leg was worse than anything she'd ever felt. She rolled on to her side, hugging her knee to her chest with a soft whimper. Fearing the worst, she peered at her foot, sure she was horribly injured and mentally preparing to see bone jutting out of flesh.

But her ankle looked fine. There was no sign whatsoever of the agony within, and Nia didn't understand how something so painful could be invisible. Surely it had to be broken?

She cautiously tried moving it, and shockwaves of pain made her yelp. Broken or not, she sure as hell wasn't going to be able to walk on it.

She rolled on to her back and gingerly climbed to her feet, taking care not to put any weight on her bad leg.

Kayla must have been terrified to see her fall. Nia looked up, amazed at how far she had come. The doorway looked like a small dark hole in the distance.

Kayla wasn't standing in it.

Nia closed her eyes, trying not to be angry with Kayla for, yet again, disobeying her and refusing to stay put. She was scared, and who could blame her? Nia was scared too. Her hands were raw and covered in cuts; there was no way they'd support her weight if she tried to jump up to the platform and climb back out.

She was stuck down here. The realisation sent a rush of panic into her chest that clamped her lungs in a vice-like grip.

A tiny, terrified noise escaped her lips.

Nia clenched her mouth shut and forced the tears away, even though there was no one there to see her cry. She couldn't bear the thought of Mum's face when she saw the trouble Nia was in, the disappointment. How serious was this? Would the police be involved?

Nia sniffed. If Kayla had just done what she was told, then everything would've been fine. But she had to go running off to tell Mum, of course she did. Now it would feel even more like she was the outsider of the family, the one nobody wanted around.

'Well,' she said to the empty room. 'I may as well get what I came for.'

Olivia

> Are you dead yet then?

There was a good chance she *would* be dead, after Mum found out what she'd done. But, for now Nia had survived the drop and was going to make sure she reaped her rewards.

Mum couldn't actually physically stop her from going out to see her friends, could she? Nia had gone along with the punishment for losing Kayla, but there was nothing to stop her ignoring whatever over-the-top penalty she'd get for exploring the prison. It's not like Mum could hate her any more than she already did, so why bother doing as she was told?

Feeling more determined, she balanced on one foot and took a picture of the row of cells. She sent it to the group without a caption – there was no need for one; the proof was enough.

Olivia

> That could be any random picture off the internet.

Nia shouted into the room, clenching her fists in frustration. Would anything she did ever be good enough?

She closed her eyes and wondered whether, if she wished hard enough, she would open them and be back home. Actually, if she was wishing for things, she may as well go back in time as well, to the night of the party.

But the pain in her ankle wouldn't let her escape for long, and it yanked her back to reality.

She wondered if anyone had ever fallen down on one of the walkways. If there had ever been a fight up there, a face crushed against the sharp metal, beneath another prisoner's boot.

She shuddered, hating her mind for always imagining the worst possible thing.

How was she going to get out of here? She pictured a fireman throwing her over his shoulder and carrying her up a ladder, television reporters keeping their cameras focused on her bum and screaming questions at her: 'Nia, what made you come down here?' 'Nia, how can you be so stupid?' 'Nia, why did you put your sister in danger *again*?'

Well, if the whole town was going to turn up to rescue and ridicule her, then she may as well get this stupid picture Olivia was so desperate for.

She looked around the cell block. Bathed in fluorescent light, there was nothing she couldn't see, no hidden corners, no mystery tunnels.

But it was still the creepiest place she had ever been.

Maybe it was because she knew it would have once been full of bodies and sound, a hundred men jostling for space while guards patrolled, keeping an eye out for trouble. Now it felt like the emptiest place in the world.

Nia hopped awkwardly to the wall, glad no one could see how stupid she must look. Using it for support, she shuffled forward as quietly as possible, hating the way every sound she made echoed back at her, bouncing off the walls and ceiling of the giant room. Reminding her how alone she was. It was cold outside, but somehow she was sure it was colder in here. She could see her breath steaming in the air.

The pool table in the middle of the room was the only thing that was a colour other than the cold metal grey of the walkways or the sickening cream that had been painted over the brick walls. The tattered green cloth looked like it had been savaged by a wild animal. One of the cues had been snapped in half.

A couple of months ago, not long before the party, one of Olivia's dares had taken Nia and the others into an abandoned restaurant. The place had been a mess – graffiti covered the walls, all the furniture had been smashed up, and there was evidence of a pretty wild party from whoever had broken in before them. They themselves had left their own stamp on the building, of course. Nia managed a faint smile as she thought about the heart Scott had drawn on the wall with their names entwined inside. Her smile faltered when she remembered that was the same night Scott had called her a baby for not wanting to take things any further with him. She shuddered at the thought of the disgusting old mattress in the corner of the room.

Inside the cell block there was no mess. It was as though no one had set foot in here since its doors had closed a year ago. Like a giant concrete tomb that had been sealed and forgotten about.

Nia wondered if a prisoner had smashed the pool cue as one last act of defiance before being transferred to another prison. Or a guard, maybe.

But how had the walkway collapsed? Nia knew this place was falling apart — that was why it had been abandoned. But surely a solid metal platform hadn't ripped itself out of the wall all by itself? And it hadn't been *that* long since the prison was closed down.

Nia glared up at the ceiling high above — one of the lights was still groaning and flickering, making her head ache. She brought her attention back down to the ground, warped shapes dancing in her eyes from the imprint of the harsh light. Apart from the pool table, there was only one other thing on the ground floor of the cell block. She approached it warily. It was a tiny room, more of a box, really.

It looked different to the rest of the block — newer, flimsier. The bottom half was made of plastic and the top was see-through, but again looked like plastic rather than glass. Nia's reflection stared back at her. She flattened a wayward patch of frizz and laughed weakly. If Mark could see her now he'd be sure to make a joke about her worrying about her hair despite being trapped inside an abandoned prison. Well, he would have before, anyway.

She opened the door. The box was only big enough for a desk and a chair. It must have been some kind of prison guard office. What a job, sitting in a plastic box watching criminals play pool all day.

Nia was tired. Tired of this place, tired of always messing up but most of all, tired of never being good enough.

A surge of pain shot through her ankle and she lowered herself to the floor of the guard box, resting her head on her knee and closing her eyes. When she opened them, she noticed something underneath the desk . . . a notebook.

She sighed. She didn't want to stick her hand under the desk, sure the notebook was guarded by some horrific spider that would run up her arm the second her fingers went exploring. But what if there was something scandalous written inside? Something secret that would make the others gasp.

She had to know.

Nia glanced around the room, checking each corner for spiders, but there wasn't even a cobweb. She tentatively reached for the book and dragged it out, sliding it away from her body in case any creatures clung to it. There was no label on the front, no clue as to what lay inside.

She picked it up by a corner, not really wanting to touch it, but not knowing why. The book was immaculate. There wasn't even any dust on it, as though it had been used just yesterday. Nia flicked it open, revealing the cover page beneath.

INMATE DISCIPLINARIES.

CHAPTER 10

Nia shivered. Did she really want to read more? Curiosity tugged at her, and her hand turned the page before she'd had a chance to think it through.

The logbook started immediately, obviously carrying on from an earlier version. There was no introduction, no explanation or warning of what was contained within the pages, it simply started with:

02.05.21 – Warren, A. (8763). Spat at officer. 5 days' isolation.

Nia pulled a face and removed her finger from the page.

07.05.21 – Warren, A. (8763). Trashed room. Claimed to be hearing voices. 5 days' isolation.

Nia's eyebrows shot up. She didn't know much about hearing voices, but surely this person needed help, not locking in a cell on their own?

12.05.21 – Warren, A. (8763). Flipped pool table. 5 days' isolation.

She glanced over at the pool table. It looked like someone had decided to nail it to the floor after this incident. Had the Wolverine-style slashes across the green felt been made then too, or was that kind of thing just an everyday occurrence in prison?

10.05.21 – Murrell, F. (7892). Possession of contraband. Stripped of privileges.

Nia had been beginning to wonder if anyone other than A. Warren would feature in the incident book.

17.05.21 – Warren, A. (8763). Punched another inmate. 5 days' isolation.

Nia flicked on through the pages. A. Warren's name appeared over and over again. It seemed that as soon as he was let out of isolation, he did something to get himself back in there.

She pictured a giant of a man with tattoos on his split knuckles and scars on his face. She shuddered at the idea of being locked up with a brute like A. Warren. All the other inmates must have been terrified of him, dreading the days he was released from isolation, knowing that he was sure to kick off again.

Some people deserved to be locked up.

If this logbook didn't count as something juicy, she didn't know what would. She took a picture of a page that featured no other names other than his and sent it to the group.

Nia

A. Warren is baaaad.

Max

> Whoa, that's crazy.

Chloe

> He sounds horrible.

Nia waited for three little dots to appear, announcing Olivia's typing of some witty comment, but nothing came. She smiled. If Olivia couldn't think of anything to say, then Nia was winning.

A noise made her whip her head round. A metallic groaning, like the sound the walkway had made as she'd climbed down. The sound stopped, but Nia could see the walkway slowly bouncing and swaying. She froze, unable to take her eyes off the platform or think of a plausible explanation for it moving by itself.

The dead pigeon was no longer in the netting. Nia could see its tiny body on the floor of the cell block, one wing bent over its broken neck.

It must've come loose and hit the walkway on the way down, that was all. She turned back to the logbook, trying to convince herself that the pigeon falling had been enough to make the walkway move like that, but unable to rid herself of the feeling that there was something, or someone, else to blame.

She used the tip of her nail to flick through the logbook – the words within made the paper feel dirty. A. Warren's offences seem to be getting worse, but his punishment remained the same every time: five days in isolation. Although it sounded like A. Warren needed to be kept away from other people, she was beginning to question whether the punishment should have been reviewed – it wasn't exactly keeping him out of trouble.

She kept reading, unable to tear her eyes away. His crimes were becoming more erratic. There was something almost . . . desperate about them.

12.08.21 – Warren, A. (8763). Threatening behaviour towards self, other inmates and officers. 5 days in isolation.

17.08.21 – Warren, A. (8763). Attacked officer. 5 days in isolation.

22.08.21 – Warren, A. (8763). Attempted to jump off upper walkway. 5 days in isolation.

Nia looked out of the guard-box window, back towards the destroyed netting she had climbed past. Images of falling bodies flashed through her mind and she shook her head, blinking them away. Did A. Warren have something to do with the broken platform?

She curled her hot-pink nail around another page and turned it over. There was only one entry.

27.08.21 – Warren, A. (8763). Brawl instigator. Fatal stab wound. Deceased.

Nia gasped.

A. Warren was dead.

She didn't know why, but the discovery made her feel . . . something. She shouldn't care – A. Warren was some violent nobody and the world was probably a better place without him. But knowing that didn't stop the feeling of cold shock.

She flicked the book closed and the hardback cover landed with a snap that felt too loud. She looked over her shoulder, her eyes drawn to the dead pigeon, half expecting it to have moved.

Why weren't there any more entries in the logbook? Had the prison closing been something to do with A. Warren's death? Everyone said it was closed because it was falling apart, which Nia didn't doubt, given the state of the walkway dangling above her. But what if there was something more, something to do with the man in the logbook?

She squeezed her eyes shut. She was being ridiculous. The weirdness of this place was turning her into a conspiracy theorist. The logbook ending where it did was just a coincidence, and chances were that the cell block had become a much more peaceful place – as peaceful as a cell block full of prisoners could be – once A. Warren had gone.

A puff of cold air on her neck made her snap her eyes open and spin on one leg. But, of course, there was no one behind her. The walls of the cell block towered above her, making her feel tiny, vulnerable. The logbook was messing with her head and she wished she'd never found it. She tapped out a message, trying to ignore the growing feeling of panic inside her chest. This place was becoming too real now that she could picture the kind of people who had called it home.

Nia

Bad news, guys. A. Warren was murdered.

Chloe

> No waaaaay. OK, that place is 100% haunted.

Nia looked around the cell block, wondering where he had been killed. Her eyes were drawn back to the pool table. Was that a stain on the floor beneath it? She sighed, angry with herself for letting her imagination run wild yet again. Possible bloodstains were not something she needed on her mind while she was down here, on her own, with absolutely no way out.

She was sharply reminded of the seriousness of her predicament. Where was Mum? Surely she would have come running the second Kayla returned without her?

She looked up to the doorway, wishing more than anything to see Mum standing there, promising that she wasn't angry, that she just wanted Nia to be safe. That everything would be OK.

Nia reluctantly opened Mum's contact details, her thumb hovering over the call button.

Things had been bad enough before. Now Mum was never going to let her leave the house again. But at least she had shut Olivia up; that was something.

The buzzing of her phone told her she had celebrated her victory prematurely, and Nia closed the phonebook app, opening the group message instead.

Olivia

> I said we needed a picture of you in a cell.

Great.

Olivia

Preferably locked in, haha!

Fantastic.

She'd come too far to give up now. With the biting pain in her hands and ankle, and the world of trouble she would be in when she finally made it out of here, she needed this to be worth it.

Mum would have to wait.

CHAPTER 11

The cell doors were all shut. Nia gritted her teeth and limped over to the nearest one, hissing with pain every time she was forced to put weight on her bad ankle. She gave the metal door a gentle push with her fingertips but it didn't move – a door that size was going to take more than a little nudge, even if it happened to be unlocked. She tried again, using the heel of her hand to shove a bit harder. The door groaned on its hinges as though it hadn't been opened in . . . well, it had been a year now.

It opened just a few centimetres, revealing a sliver of darkness, and Nia stopped pushing. A series of horrible images flashed through her mind: a hand creeping round the frame; a red-rimmed eye staring back at her from the dark; a dead body slumped in the corner of the room.

What if A. Warren had been killed in there? What if he was *still* in there?

Get a grip, Nia.

She tried to convince herself that there was nothing to be

scared of, that she'd been in the cell block for at least twenty minutes now and nothing bad had happened. But the cells felt different to the communal area. They were closed off, and they were where the inmates had *lived*. What's more, the idea of the door slamming shut behind her was making her shudder so violently she had to scratch her arms to get rid of the feeling.

It's just an empty room, Nia.

But no matter how hard her mind insisted, her hand just wouldn't respond and push the door open. She couldn't stop thinking about A. Warren and how he might have died.

'Come on, Nia!' she hissed, frustrated that she was standing in front of her chance to finally prove Olivia wrong, and she was dithering instead of going for it.

Then she realised what the raised section of metal on the outside of the door was: a hatch.

'Of course,' she sighed, relief flooding her body. The guards would have needed a way to look into the cells to check on the inmates without having to open the door. She pulled the catch, but stood back before sliding the cover aside, just in case.

She couldn't see anything.

Nia groaned. She was going to have to get closer.

Reluctantly, she pressed her face up to the Perspex screen that covered the small hatch, squinting into the dark room.

Someone stared back out at her.

Nia screamed so sharply that it hurt her chest. She flung herself backwards away from the door, scrambling across the floor as quickly as she could. She didn't stop until her back hit the leg of the pool table.

She couldn't take her eyes off the door. She couldn't blink. She was frozen, her ankle throbbing, her mouth hanging open.

There's someone in there, there's someone in there, there's someone in there.

She just *knew* some nightmarish creature was going to emerge from the cell. She pictured rotting flesh covered by tattered prison overalls. A gaping hole where a mouth used to be. A finger outstretched, pointing at her.

But nothing came.

Who or *what* was in there? Was it even alive? The speed with which her imagination whirred through the possibilities made Nia feel dizzy, despite being on the floor. Whatever it was, it was nothing good – harmless things didn't hang out inside abandoned prison cells.

But the seconds passed and the door stayed closed. Was it possible that she was so tense she had simply . . . seen something that wasn't there? Eventually her breathing calmed and her heart stopped trying to explode out from behind her ribs. She slowly gained control over her body and rose cautiously to her feet.

Had it been in her head?

No. She was certain she had seen something. The image of the bloodshot eyes would be forever etched into her memory. So why wasn't whatever it was coming out of the cell?

She waited another few minutes, her eyes trained on the door, before calling, 'I know you're in there!' Her voice was squeaky and made it painfully obvious that she was just a scared teenage girl.

No reply.

'I'm not scared,' she shouted, sounding terrified. What were they *doing* in there?

Whoever, or *whatever*, was lurking inside the cell obviously wasn't coming out. Nia considered getting as far away as possible from the door and just waiting – Mum was sure to appear soon.

But she knew she couldn't bear the suspense. Her heart was still throbbing, and she couldn't cope with it any longer, jumping at every sound, convinced that something was going to burst out of the cell and attack her.

She took a step forward. Her pulse started racing again and she wondered if she was going to throw up. She needed to get it over with, find out who was in there before her heart gave up on her completely and she dropped down dead.

Nia hobbled towards the door, adrenaline dulling the pain in her ankle, and flung the hatch open.

They were still there, staring, unblinking, furious.

Her panic threatened to go into overdrive again, but something stopped her from letting go of the hatch and backing away. Something wasn't right. The eyes looked different.

She forced herself to take a breath and look properly.

Her terror was replaced by relief, then anger. There was no one in there. Someone, some *idiot*, had drawn a pair of eyes on the back wall of the cell. They were convincing, especially in the dark, but Nia couldn't help but feel embarrassed that she had been so scared she thought she would have a heart attack.

It felt good to be angry, better than feeling scared, anyway. Nia used the emotion to wrench the heavy door open, exposing the cell fully.

The cell was so tiny that for a moment Nia wondered if she'd opened a storage cupboard by mistake. A rush of stale air greeted her and she wrinkled her nose at the smell of cold damp.

The walls were the same sickly-cream-painted brick as the rest of the cell block, but black mould crept from the corners and made the paint peel. The floor was the same cold concrete. A single strip light was in the middle of the ceiling but there was no light switch – it must have been controlled by a central switch somewhere. Nia thought of Mum's obsession with 'mood lighting' that she created with a variety of lamps in their living room, barely ever using the main light. She would hate prison.

A metal toilet with no seat or lid perched in one corner of the room beneath a window that was too high to see out of. The small square of sky it framed was bleak and grey. A narrow bunkbed frame took up half of the floor space. Nia could see that there was no water in the bottom of the toilet, but there was a dripping noise coming from somewhere within the cell.

And drawn on the back wall, staring directly towards the hatch, a pair of eyes that looked so realistic Nia couldn't help still being frightened by them.

There was nothing else in the cell. Nia hadn't seen anything so depressing in her life. She couldn't believe that *two* people would have lived in here. She wasn't claustrophobic – at least, she had never been before today – but she still didn't want to step inside. The ceiling was too low, the walls too close.

She often heard people grumbling about how prisoners had

it easy nowadays. She'd seen memes online suggesting that war veterans and inmates should swap places, because inmates were treated better – they had a roof over their head, three meals a day and their own televisions and games consoles.

Nia took another look at the cell. There was no way a television would fit anywhere in here, even a tiny one. And the toilet was about a metre away from the bed. Imagine if your cell mate needed to go while you were trying to sleep. She shuddered and promised herself that she would never break the law – she wouldn't survive a day here.

Unless breaking into an abandoned prison was enough to get her locked up in one? If she hadn't felt so wretched she would have laughed at the irony. She couldn't get into trouble with the police for this, could she? The door to the cell block had been open. It didn't count as trespassing if no one had bothered locking the doors, did it?

Well, if she was going to be sent to some kind of young offender institution, she may as well make the most of the risk she'd taken.

She sent a selfie to the group message, the cell behind her. She couldn't resist adding a snarky caption:

Nia

Happy now?

She triumphantly waited for a response, a sense of peace coming over her now that she knew this part of her struggle would be over at least. She frowned at the screen as the messaging app told her that all four of her friends had seen the picture – why weren't they saying anything?

Finally, three dots told her that someone was writing a reply.

Olivia

Wow

Nia sighed. It was impossible to tell, but, knowing Olivia, 'Wow' didn't mean she was actually impressed.

Olivia

It's like, bigger than your bedroom, Nia. Are you going to stay?

A lump formed in Nia's throat and she watched as more dots appeared on the screen. She prayed it was the others writing to defend her, to tell Olivia she was out of line.

Chloe

Ouch, burn!

Max

Hahahha, shots fired

Someone was still writing. *Please, Scott, please*.

Olivia

> And you're still not inside the cell. God, Nia, it's not difficult!

Nia closed her eyes and breathed heavily through her nose. She shouldn't be surprised by their reactions. They had been like this since the day she'd started hanging around with them. But that didn't make it hurt any less.

She wished, not for the first time, that the door to the cell block *had* been locked. Maybe the pictures of the visitation room would have impressed Scott enough to give her another chance, even if Olivia had demanded more.

But Nia just *had* to push further, didn't she? She had to make everyone like her, no matter the cost. And now she was trapped inside a prison, her ankle aching, her hands bloody and sore, and she seriously doubted it would even change anything with her friends. She'd still be the baby of the group, the boring one, the loser.

She wanted to tell Mum how she was feeling, to lay her head on her lap and feel the weight of her hand combing through her hair, reassuring her. But Nia wasn't sure she'd ever be able to do that again.

Where *was* Mum?

Her breath paused as she realised things could actually be worse than she thought. What if Kayla hadn't made it back? What if she hadn't told Mum where Nia was? What if she *had* told Mum, but Mum didn't care?

What if this was her punishment for losing Kayla on the night of the party?

CHAPTER 12

The adrenaline pumping through Nia's veins melted away and she staggered out of the cell, slumping heavily to the floor outside. She could feel the coldness of the cream brick wall through her jacket but didn't have the energy to shiver.

The idea of Mum leaving her down here was ridiculous. It was too crazy to even think about. But Mum's expression that night was vivid in her memory. Maybe, just maybe, it wasn't such a crazy thought after all.

It had just been a party. It should have been harmless. It *was* harmless, but Mum and Mark had acted like Nia had killed someone. They were *still* acting like that.

They'd gone out for dinner for the first time since Deon had been born. It was their anniversary or something. Nia had stopped paying attention after she'd heard, 'We're going out for the evening and we're leaving you in charge.'

They'd taken Deon with them, thank god. He was only four months old and glued to Mum's boobs most of the day. Kayla was easier to deal with – the only difficulty they had with her at bedtime was convincing her to put her book down and turn the light off.

Nia hadn't hesitated before sending a message to her friends. It had only been a week since they had broken into the abandoned restaurant. A week in which Scott had barely said two words to her, but people pointed at her in the school corridors, and someone stuck a sign on her back that said *'Frigid'*.

She was being given a chance to redeem herself. A chance to prove she wasn't just some stupid kid. A chance to show Scott that she really loved him.

'Nia, can I stay up late so we can watch a film tonight?' Kayla had been as excited about the evening without Mum and Mark as Nia was, but for entirely different reasons.

'No, Kayla. I'm going to be busy.'

'Oh.' Kayla hadn't pouted. She wasn't the kind of kid to make a fuss. But she chewed her lip and said, 'Please?'

Nia was too busy forcing her curls through the straighteners to bother looking at Kayla, but the whininess in her voice irritated her. 'Why would I choose watching some stupid baby film with you over seeing my friends?' she snapped.

She swore as Kayla's questions distracted her and she burned her finger. Her hair wasn't behaving — it never did. It would never be straight and silky like Olivia's.

Kayla had disappeared from Nia's room, and Nia didn't give her a second thought until someone knocked on the front door.

They were here.

'Kayla,' Nia shouted through her little sister's open bedroom door. 'You need to stay in your room this evening, OK?'

'But I haven't had any dinner,' Kayla squeaked.

The door again. Nia sighed. She didn't have time for this.

She shouted, 'Coming!' and ran down the stairs.

The letterbox was pushed open as she approached, and Olivia's mouth appeared. 'Oh my GOD, Nia. Hurry up, it's freezing out here!'

Nia apologised and fumbled with the door, letting them inside.

'Finally,' Olivia huffed as she strode past Nia, leading the group as always. 'What took you so long? It's not like you live in a mansion.' Her eyes scanned the interior of Nia's house as she said this, her expression making it clear what she thought of the three-bed semi.

Olivia looked gorgeous. Her perfectly flat stomach was exposed and Nia eyed her belly-button ring enviously. Mum would never allow her to have one. Olivia's hair was long and glossy, the complete opposite to Nia's tight curls that still rebelled despite the constant straightening. And her make-up was flawless, perfectly contoured and blended, as though it had been done by a professional.

Although, Nia had recently overheard a conversation between Olivia and Chloe that made her wonder if perfection came at a price higher than it was worth.

It was that night at the abandoned restaurant. As Nia was dashing out of the building, away from Scott and his impatient hands, soft voices had piqued her interest.

'It's only a pound,' Chloe said soothingly from behind a crumbling wall in the courtyard. 'You can get rid of it again, babe, I know you can.'

'It's not that easy,' Olivia hissed, and Nia could picture her slapping Chloe's comforting hand away from her. 'When you're as slim as me, every ounce matters. I've got a casting call next week and all they're going to be able to see is this fat bulge on my stomach.'

'You're not fa—'

'Tell that to my mother!' Olivia shrieked. 'If I don't get it under control by my next weigh-in she said she'll confiscate my Prada handbag!'

Nia frowned. Olivia's mother *weighed* her? And punished her if she gained weight? Even if she found it difficult to sympathise with a punishment of confiscating a designer handbag, Nia couldn't deny the tug of sympathy she felt towards Olivia.

Maybe this could be the moment they became friends. Nia could reveal herself, tell Olivia that she was beautiful just the way she was. She could be a shoulder to cry on, just like Chloe was.

But the idea of Olivia's reaction after discovering she'd been overheard during her moment of vulnerability sent a wave of fear pulsing through Nia's chest. So she'd kept quiet and scurried home.

And now Olivia was in her front hall, looking past Nia as though she were a piece of furniture. 'Who else is here?' she asked.

'Errr . . .' Nia replied. What was Olivia talking about? She *knew* they were her only friends; who else could possibly be here?

'Don't tell me it's just us five?' Olivia laughed. 'Some party!'

Chloe and Max dumped their coats in Nia's arms and followed Olivia into the house. Max ruffled Nia's hair on his way past her as though she was ten years younger than him, instead of one. Chloe smiled, but Nia could see something else in her eyes, the same hint of cold fury that appeared whenever Max paid Nia any attention. Nia wished she could tell Chloe that she had no interest whatsoever in her boyfriend, that she only had eyes for . . .

Scott finally shuffled into view as the others squeezed further into the narrow hallway.

'Hey,' Nia smiled, a little bubble of warmth spreading through her whole body. She stepped closer for a kiss, wishing she wasn't weighed down by Max and Chloe's winter coats.

But Scott didn't even look at her as he walked past. 'Got any booze?'

'Um,' Nia stuttered, following the crowd into the kitchen and putting their coats down. Of course she didn't have any alcohol. She was fifteen; how did they expect her to get served? She seriously doubted any of them could either. Well, except for Olivia. Nia suspected she could get anything she wanted.

'Eugh,' Olivia said as she pulled a bottle of wine out of the rack. 'Your parents have got cheap taste in wine.'

Nia's cheeks burned. Why couldn't Mum and Mark be cool parents? If they were, they'd have thrown a party for her and even let them have a few drinks.

Olivia opened the fridge. 'Ew, it smells like something died in here. Doesn't your mum ever clean?'

Nia knew Olivia wasn't her friend, not really. She suspected

Olivia wanted Scott for herself, and this weird pretence that they were friends was part of Olivia's plan to show Scott what he was missing, being with a loser like Nia. But that didn't stop her words from stinging.

'This will do, I suppose,' Olivia said, and pulled a bottle out of the fridge. 'Not the best vintage but I suppose beggars can't be choosers.'

She held a bottle of champagne in her dainty hand. Mum and Mark had bought it to celebrate – they must have been saving it for when they got home from the restaurant.

'Scott, sweetie, will you do the honours?' Olivia passed the bottle to Scott, somehow getting close enough to him in the process to brush her chest up against his arm.

Scott smiled down at her and Nia clenched her jaw. She would do whatever it took to get Scott to look at *her* like that again. She'd do it tonight.

'Nia?' a voice called softly down the stairs. She'd completely forgotten about Kayla.

'I'll be right back,' Nia said, grabbing some ham out of the fridge that Olivia hadn't bothered closing. She took a loaf of bread with her too, and heard a *pop* as she ran up the stairs. Mum was going to be furious.

'Here,' she snapped, thrusting the food into Kayla's arms and dismissing her plea to stay and read with her. 'Just be quiet and stay put.' Nia paused, knowing she needed to make it clear how important it was that Kayla didn't leave her room. Nia did not want to be disturbed tonight. She turned, bending over so she was barely an inch from Kayla's face. 'Do not set foot out of this door, do you understand? If you do,

I'll be so angry with you I'll never speak to you again.'

Kayla's eyes filled with tears, but she nodded.

Why hadn't she stayed in her room?

CHAPTER 13

If it had just been the stolen champagne, then Mum would probably be here right now, rescuing Nia. But that wasn't the only thing that had happened that night, and Nia wasn't sure she'd ever be forgiven.

The cold of the prison made her shiver as she sniffed and squeezed her eyes shut, refusing to cry. She *never* cried. It was something she was strangely proud of.

Her phone vibrated and she fished it out of her pocket, preparing herself for yet another bitchy comment from Olivia. But this time it was a picture posted online, and it was so much worse.

Olivia was holding the camera, angling it down at the four friends. Chloe and Max were in the background, kissing as always. But in the foreground, so close to the camera that Nia could see every sickening detail, was Olivia. She had her lips pressed up against Scott's cheek.

Olivia

> How weekends are supposed to be spent.

If it had been anyone else, Nia could have passed it off as an innocent comment about hanging with your friends at the weekend. But she knew Olivia. She knew she'd tagged Nia in it, then removed the tag, just so she would get a notification. She knew how much Olivia resented Nia coming into their lives, turning their four into a five and making her the odd one out. She knew just how much meaning there was behind everything that Olivia did.

Nia tried to figure out where they were from the photo, but their faces filled the entire screen. Had they been together the whole time she had been messaging them? It wasn't unusual for them to all be on their phones at the same time, but the idea that they had been discussing Nia's predicament in person stung.

Nia had to *do* something. But what could she possibly do, stuck in here? She needed to remind Scott that she was his, that she was better than Olivia – not that she believed she really was. The least she could do was show that she was true to her word and finally get this stupid picture of her in a cell.

She didn't want to go back into the creepy-eyes cell, so she scanned the row of identical doors. One of them caught her attention and she stood, wincing as she took the weight back on her sore ankle. The cell was set away from the rest of them, with a bigger gap between it and its neighbour. There were bars in front and a see-through sheet of thick plastic instead of a door. It looked like a cage.

There was a sign on the wall next to it, and her eyes widened as she read: **ISOLATION CELL**.

Now not only did she have a cell, but she also had a backstory to link it to, something that the others wouldn't be able to resist feeling curious about. She decided not to give Olivia the satisfaction of knowing that she had seen the photo of them all and sent a picture of the sign to the group.

Nia

> Found A. Warren's crib.

She had pictured the isolation cell being a little more... isolated. But the only thing that made it seem any different to the rest was that it was slightly further away in the corner of the cell block. And the weird door. Maybe it was more of a confinement cell, and A. Warren would be kept in there for five days straight every time he did something violent, not even being allowed out for meals or exercise.

Nia tried to imagine it. She didn't think she'd be particularly calm and ready to integrate with the other prisoners if she kept getting locked up in a minuscule room.

Grimacing at the thought, she decided to go straight into the cell without giving herself the chance to overthink it. The longer she dithered outside the door obsessing about A. Warren, the more opportunity her mind had to play tricks and convince her there was someone in there.

This door didn't groan on its hinges; it swung open smoothly, as if it had been used more than the other one. The cell was just as tiny, but there was a single bed instead of bunkbeds. Everything else was the same; the metal toilet, the cream brick walls, the too-high window. The only difference was that the isolation cell wasn't empty.

Nia tried to make sense of what she saw. On top of the threadbare mattress, a pile of what looked like clothes and blankets had been neatly folded. On the floor between the toilet and the wall there was a messy bundle of material, reminding Nia of her dirty-clothes pile in her bedroom. A plastic bag full of empty crisp packets and drinks bottles hung off the back of the door. But by far the strangest thing in the cell was the walls.

Every square inch was covered. Grey pencil sketches, poems, shiny sweet wrappers, sharpie doodles and even a smudged charcoal landscape decorated the walls, hiding the cream paint beneath. Nia gawped at the artwork, overwhelmed and unsure what to feel. There was something strangely familiar about the pictures. Some of the drawings were terrifying – the stuff of nightmares, screaming figures clutching their faces and clawing at the walls. But between these images, sweet cartoon characters smiled and frolicked, waving down at her.

Was this A. Warren's work? It had to be – according to the incident book, no one else had spent nearly as much time in here.

She took another look at the sweet-wrapper section and realised with astonishment that the scraps of rubbish had been stuck together to create the face of a woman. She was smiling, peaceful, beautiful. How could the same person who drew such awful images create something so stunning?

She got closer, wanting to see the detail. She tried to avoid looking at the nightmare images, sure that she'd never be able to forget them if she did. She squinted at a poem, trying to make out the words, and laughed aloud. It was a haiku, the kind they had to do in school. This one, however, was about a particular guard, and it was filthy.

She found more of the same, each one funnier than the last, and all signed *A. Warren* in childish handwriting. Nia found her opinion of him starting to change. The brute with a shaved head and bloody knuckles that she'd pictured couldn't be the creator of such incredible art and witty poems, could he?

Nia was totally absorbed and, for the first time since she'd entered the prison that morning, she wasn't thinking about Scott, or Olivia, or Mum, or anything other than what she was looking at.

The pictures and poems seemed to tell a story, she realised. It started on the left wall, the cartoon characters interacting and playing, their huge eyes making them look cute and carefree. But things started changing. Their expressions grew darker, their surroundings bleaker, until, finally, all that was left were screaming faces and other things Nia really didn't want to see.

What does it all mean?

Nia knew she should send pictures to her friends, captioned with comments about A. Warren being a psychopath. But it felt wrong. She didn't want him to be ridiculed, for his innermost thoughts to be mocked by a group of teenagers who would never understand him. She swallowed, suddenly feeling sick at the thought that the artist was no longer alive. Standing there, with his creations, in the cell where he had spent so much of his time, she felt close to him.

What had happened to him? And why was he in here in the first place?

She sighed, frustrated at the lack of information. She wanted to know more. She wanted to know everything there was to know about A. Warren. Would a prisoner getting killed in prison make the news, or was that sort of thing happening all the time? Would anyone even care if it was?

Nia pulled her phone out, ignoring the notification from the group message and going straight to the internet. But all she could find was a tiny article in the local paper:

Prisoner Left Dead Following Brawl. On 27th August 2021, Andrew Warren died from a stab wound to the abdomen while incarcerated in HMP Staffbury. The prison governor confirmed that Warren was a known troublemaker and had instigated the fight with other inmates: 'Though this incident was unfortunate, I am confident that correct procedures were followed, and it was the victim's actions that caused his unfortunate demise.' There will be no subsequent inquiry into the death.

Nia frowned as she pocketed her phone. Was that it? A man was killed; surely there had to be an investigation? She looked back at the walls, feeling like Andrew Warren deserved an apology. She squinted – there was something she hadn't noticed before.

She took a step closer to the right-hand wall – the wall with the terrifying images. Right at the end there was a blank space. A space that Andrew Warren might have filled in, if he'd lived long enough to do so.

But there *was* something there, in the space. When Nia realised what it was, she felt the muscle around her heart clench tightly. It was a photo. A photo of Daisy Evans, the missing girl from her school. A photo that had been cut from the poster asking for information about her whereabouts.

There were black holes where her eyes should have been.

Surrounding the photo, letters had been cut from the text on the poster and arranged like a kidnapping ransom note. They read: DEad giRL.

Nia stepped backwards, her thoughts whirring so quickly she was scared she might faint.

This was *new*. Someone had been down here. Someone had been down here very recently. Maybe that someone was *still* down here.

She'd been standing there admiring the artwork on the walls without thinking about what the other things in the cell could mean.

Idiot, Nia.

There was someone living here. Someone who kept their clothes folded and put their rubbish in a bin bag. The same person, she realised with a shudder, who had been staring at her from the window as she'd waited to enter the soft-play centre. She looked again at the plastic bag and saw a second one hanging next to it, full of unopened snacks and drinks.

They could be back at any moment, this nutter who cut up

photos of missing girls and claimed they were dead, and Nia really, *really* did not want to be here when they returned.

It was time to call Mum and get the hell out of here. Forget the trouble she'd be in at home – she could be in even worse trouble stuck down here with some psychopath who lived in a jail cell. She reached her hand down towards her pocket to retrieve her phone, but as her fingers grazed the material of her jeans, a hand seized her wrist.

CHAPTER 14

The confined cell made Nia's scream sound so sharp that her ears rang. She snatched her hand back to her body, tripping backwards over the bedframe as she spun to look at the intruder.

Kayla stood over her, as serious as ever, her precious book tucked under her arm.

Nia spluttered, her mouth flapping open at the same rate as her heart hammering in her chest. She finally recovered enough to whisper, 'What? How did you . . . ?'

But her thoughts re-ordered themselves as her shock diminished, and her terror was replaced with fury. 'Why did you follow me?' Nia screamed. She rose to her feet and towered over Kayla. 'Why don't you *ever* do as you're told?'

Kayla took a step backwards, her bottom lip quivering. But Nia was too angry to care. For a moment, when those cold fingers had clamped around her arm, she'd thought she was about to die.

But it was Kayla. Kayla was to blame for her terror. Kayla was to blame for *everything*.

'Why didn't you say something?' Nia shouted. 'Why didn't you call my name instead of sneaking up on me, you—' Nia snapped her mouth shut, biting back all the words she wanted to call her, a little voice reminding her that once they escaped her lips they couldn't be unsaid.

'I'm sorry!' Kayla said, and her face contorted as the tears arrived. 'I was scared.'

Nia felt her rage trickle away, and not for the first time she wished she hadn't been so harsh on her. Kayla may be gifted, she may be Mum and Mark's favourite, but she was still just a naive seven-year-old kid.

'Forget it,' Nia sighed, wondering whether her heart could take any more shocks today.

She couldn't shake the fear that the cell's current resident would be coming back at any moment. She couldn't stop looking at Daisy's face on the poster. What did that message mean? *Dead Girl*. Had whoever was staying in the cell – the owner of the bundle of clothes and blankets in the corner of the room – done something to Daisy?

Nia shook her head. She wasn't some kind of teenage Sherlock Holmes. She wasn't about to go digging for clues about a missing girl. She needed to get herself and – more importantly now – Kayla out of there.

But a movement caught her eye and she turned slowly to the corner of the room, wishing she hadn't seen anything.

'Kayla, did you see—'

Kayla was nodding, her eyes wide in terror as she looked at the heap of rags between the toilet and the wall, the pile that Nia had assumed was dirty clothes.

It was *moving*.

Nia was sure it would be something repulsive, something she'd have nightmares about for years to come. She didn't want to know what it was. Then why was she being pulled towards it, as though by some force stronger than common sense or fear? Why was she reaching her foot out to flick the top layer off the pulsing mound of material?

Rats.

A whole family of them, squeaking and squirming over each other, naked and wriggling. Their eyes were clamped shut and Nia could see their bones and organs beneath their translucent pink skin. The mother glared furiously up at Nia, her slimy-looking tail coiled around her greasy black fur.

Nia retched and ran out of the cell, hastily ushering Kayla before her. Her entire body rippled with repulsion as she shook her arms, trying to banish the image from her head.

Rats.

Was that who had been living in the cell, Nia wondered, before remembering the plastic bags.

No, rats couldn't unwrap a Mars bar and put the rubbish in the bin. But Nia had noticed bottle lids full of water and broken-up crisps dotted around on the floor next to the nest. Someone had been feeding them. The same someone who made deranged artwork of missing teenage girls.

'We need to leave – now!' Nia gasped.

Kayla's eyes widened and fresh tears threatened to spill. Nia cursed herself for failing to keep the panic out of her voice. The last thing she needed was a hysterical child to look after, not when the crazy rat-keeper could return at any moment.

Nia took a breath and tried to wipe the fear off her face as she smiled at Kayla. 'Sorry, I'm just not keen on rats! Let's get back to the soft-play and have a hot chocolate, yeah?'

Her cheeriness sounded forced, but it seemed to relax Kayla – her tears were under control and she gave a watery smile. Every fibre in Nia's body told her to get away from the isolation cell, the rats and the entire cell block. But she needed to find out how Kayla had got down here. And to do that, she needed to keep them both calm.

She sat down, glad to take the weight off her ankle. She leaned against the guard box and patted the hard floor next to her.

'So,' Nia said, 'you didn't tell Mum what had happened?'

Kayla shook her head as she folded her legs. 'I didn't think you'd want me to.'

Nia couldn't be angry with Kayla for that. She'd only done as she was told. In any other circumstance, she would have been furious with her for telling Mum, especially about something that broke the rules as badly as this.

But something didn't add up. 'Where have you been this whole time? I've been down here for ages.'

Nia saw Kayla's lips move as she sat hunched beside her, but couldn't hear what she said.

'Say again?'

'I don't know,' Kayla whispered.

Nia felt herself becoming annoyed again. She really didn't have time for stupid kids' games. 'What do you mean, you don't know? How can you not know what you've been doing for . . .' she checked the time on her phone, 'the last half hour?'

'I don't know,' she squeaked, her voice even smaller.

Nia exhaled heavily through her nose, knowing that if she lost her temper Kayla would withdraw even further into herself. 'Kayla, it's really simple. Just tell me what you did after I climbed down here.'

Kayla's eyes were glazed, as though she were seeing something that wasn't there. 'I watched you climbing,' she whispered. 'I was so scared that you would fall.'

The sores on Nia's hands reminded her of how long she had spent clinging to the rough bricks, then gripping on to the sharp metal grate. There was no way Kayla could have managed it, so where was the other way down here? She was desperate to ask, but Kayla was speaking again so she closed her mouth. If she interrupted her now, she might get flustered and stop altogether.

'You got to the bottom of the metal thing.' She nodded up at the walkway dangling above the floor. 'And I remember you slipping and falling.' Kayla's eyes darted from side to side. 'And then I was here, standing behind you.'

Nia tried not to let her impatience show and kept her voice calm. 'No, Kayla, that's not what happened. I started climbing at least half an hour ago. And you couldn't have just magically transported from up there,' she nodded at the doorway floating where the upper-level walkway should have been, 'to down here, could you?'

'I don't know,' Kayla whispered, and curled into an even tighter ball.

Resisting the urge to shake her, Nia tried again to prise the details from her. 'How did you get down? Did you come the same way as me?' She tried to imagine a seven-year-old child taking the same route she had. Maybe, Nia mused, it would have been easier for Kayla, seeing as she was so much lighter than her.

But this was *Kayla*, not some sporty, gymnastic kid. Kayla hated pretty much all physical activity. She avoided exercise to the extent that Nia wondered if she had any muscle mass at all.

Kayla's lips were still moving and Nia leaned closer to her.

'I can't. I can't. I can't. I can't,' she muttered on a continuous loop, so quietly that Nia had to press her ear to her lips to hear her.

'Hey,' Nia said. 'Stop that.' She reached her hand out to touch Kayla's arm and snap her out of it, but Kayla snatched it away and scrambled to her feet.

'I can't. I can't. I can't. I *can't*!' she squeaked, her eyes frantic, her hands curled into claws.

Nia stood too, moving slowly as though Kayla were a feral animal. 'Kayla, it's OK.'

What was wrong with her sister? Nia had never seen Kayla like this. She was always so calm and controlled. *Nia* was the dramatic one, the one who misfortune and chaos followed around.

'It's OK,' she repeated, trying not to make any sudden movements. 'I'm going to get us out of here.'

'I can't tell you!'

'I know, Kayla,' she reassured her. 'We'll figure it out, OK?'

She pulled out her phone. She'd brought Kayla into yet another dangerous situation. Mum would have been angry before, but she'd be absolutely livid now that Kayla was stuck down here too. But what choice did Nia have? She needed to get Kayla out of here.

Nia tried to plan what she would say, but flinched as she imagined Mum screaming down the phone, the disappointment in her voice that said what Nia had always known: 'Why do I have to have you as a daughter?'

So she took what she knew was the coward's way out, and texted her.

Nia

> I need to tell you something, but you have to promise not to get mad, OK?

She stared at the screen, waiting for the reply and hoping Mum would be worried instead of angry. Her phone came to life in her hands as it vibrated with Mum's incoming call. Nia cut it off – she really, *really* didn't want to have to speak to her. Mum called three more times before giving up.

Mum

> What's happened, Nia? What have you done?

Why did Mum always have to assume the worst about her? She hadn't *done* anything. OK, maybe she had. But it wasn't her fault she was stuck down here. If the platform hadn't been broken she'd have been in and out before Mum had even realised she'd gone. And Kayla wouldn't have had to be involved at all.

Nia looked over at the end of the platform that was suspended in mid-air. *Could* she still get out by herself? She hadn't even tried.

'Come on,' she whispered to herself as she stood beneath it. She stretched up but couldn't reach the end of the platform. Standing on one leg, she bent her knees and jumped upwards, grunting with the effort. Her fingertips brushed the cold metal.

'Come *on*.'

She could do this; she was *so* close. She jumped over and over, but she never touched the platform again, her jumps becoming lower as she grew tired, her landing leg exhausted from the impact and her bad ankle aching.

If only she could climb on top of something to get higher. Nia looked around, but *everything* – the pool table, the beds, everything – was nailed to the floor. And even if they weren't, she realised, she'd still have the issue of getting Kayla out. She doubted she'd be able to climb all that way back up.

Defeated, she returned to Kayla, and saw that she had four more missed calls from Mum, and two messages.

Mum

> Where are you? I've checked the craft room and it's empty.

Mum

> Nia, tell me what's going on right this second.

Nia closed her eyes. There was no avoiding it, she was going to have to come clean.

Nia

I'm trapped inside the prison.

She realised she hadn't mentioned the thing Mum would be most concerned about, and hastily tapped on the screen.

Nia

Don't worry, Kayla is with me. She's safe.

Mum's reply took an excruciatingly long time to come through, and Nia imagined her head exploding as she tried to control her rage.

Mum

Is this your idea of a joke?

CHAPTER 15

Nia stared around at her grim surroundings. Being stuck inside an abandoned prison was definitely not her idea of a laugh.

She had no idea what to say. Was she going to have to send Mum a picture to prove she wasn't making some seriously unfunny joke? Or a picture of Kayla, who was still standing against the guard box like a tiny statue. That would make her realise she was being serious.

But as she aimed her camera at Kayla, another message from Mum appeared on her screen.

Mum

> You've done some stupid things lately, Nia, but even you aren't idiotic enough to go wandering around an abandoned prison. Tell me where you really are.

Nia blinked at the message, willing it to rewrite itself into something that didn't feel like a knife to the heart. Mum had never spoken to her like that before. It looked like her patience had finally worn thin, and now Nia finally had it – proof that Mum really did hate her.

She turned her back on Kayla and felt the muscles in her face spasm as they furiously fought tears. She clamped her eyelids shut, clenched her fists and forced the crying to stop. Her head hurt with the effort, as though it were going to split open from the building pressure. But she had it under control. No more tears.

What had she done to deserve this? Yes, she had thrown a small party and her friends hadn't exactly been respectful of the house. And yes, Kayla had wandered off when she was supposed to be looking after her. But before that, Nia hadn't been a bad daughter, had she? Why couldn't they forgive her for that one mistake?

Things hadn't been right for a while, though, she knew. She'd been horribly jealous of the attention Kayla got from them for years. She hadn't been the best sister. And when they announced that they were having another baby Nia had withdrawn even further from the family. She stopped going on family outings, stopped watching television with them, stopped doing *anything* with them. She had thought they'd be relieved that she was removing herself. That way they could pretend she didn't exist, and enjoy their perfect family without her.

Tiny cold fingers touched her arm, but Nia didn't scream this time.

'Nia, you're sad,' Kayla said matter-of-factly.

Nia shook her head, knowing the tears were too close to risk speaking. If she opened her mouth, who knew what would come out.

'I'm sorry,' Kayla whispered.

That was the problem with Kayla. No matter how vile Nia was to her, she was always there, always adoring of her big sister, always sorry. But it wasn't Kayla's fault; it never had been. Nia stared at her through foggy eyes. She wanted to crouch down and wrap her arms around her, tell her that *she* was sorry, that she wanted to be a family again like they had been when Kayla was tiny, before they knew how special she was. But Kayla looked so small and frail, like she was barely there. Nia was scared she would break her if she hugged her.

She took a breath and smiled at her instead. 'I'm OK. I'll be OK.'

Her voice wobbled threateningly and she sucked in a breath of cold air. Somehow she felt a bit better. Maybe it was this small moment with Kayla. Nia couldn't remember the last time she'd really smiled at her sister, and the thought filled her with guilt. She was going to be better, she promised herself. Once they got out of this place she was going to be a good sister. Even if Mum never let her leave the house again, she would at least spend time with Kayla, instead of hiding in her room and resenting her.

Her phone vibrated and she hurried to look at the message, hoping it was Mum telling her that she believed her, that she didn't think she was an idiot, that she was on her way. That she loved her.

But it was just a stream of meaningless chat from her friends.

Chloe

What was the cell like, Nia?

Max

Show us some pictures!

Then there was a gap in the timeline, and Nia realised that they must have left wherever they had been together.

Olivia

Today was so fun, guys. We should do it again soon! I miss you three crazies already xxx

Scott

Nearly home now, keep laughing to myself about what Max did haha.

Olivia

Not as funny as what YOU did!

Chloe

Wonder what happened to Nia.

Olivia

Maybe A. Warren has finished her off.

Chloe

OMG

Olivia

Or maybe Nia has decided to live in the prison now . . . upgrade!

Scott

Ouch, bit harsh, Liv.

Olivia

Aw but you love me anyway.

Scott

😉

Nia's fingers tightened around her phone. She looked at Scott's reply again – had he been defending her? His wink after Olivia suggested that he loved her took any hope Nia had been feeling and crushed it.

If she had seen the conversation ten minutes ago, before the message from Mum, she would have been even more devastated than she was now. But she was too tired. She just wanted to go home.

She looked at Mum's message again. It didn't make any sense. Nia had expected Mum to send all the emergency services, then tear the building apart brick by brick with her bare hands to get to Kayla. Did she really trust Nia that little that her first thought was that she was playing some weird prank? Was she really not coming for them?

'Can we go home now?' Kayla asked, reading her thoughts.

'I'm working on it, kid,' Nia said gently.

Nia's thoughts were interrupted by a loud grinding groan, the sound of a heavy door being pushed slowly open. Her wide eyes swivelled to where the sound came from, towards the end of the cell block.

CHAPTER 16

Nia held her breath. Images of the contorted figures with leering mouths and black eyes on the wall of the isolation cell flashed through her brain. She saw the heaving pile of twisting rats, their naked flesh pulsing, beady eyes glaring. She saw Daisy's face, the words *Dead Girl* warning of what was to come, or what had already been done.

The Ratman was back.

She instinctively shielded Kayla from the direction of the noise but had no idea what else she could do, how else she could keep them safe.

Think, Nia.

There was no escape. They were trapped in a prison with someone who slept with rats and cut up pictures of missing girls.

Could she get Kayla out if she lifted her up to the platform? Kayla would have to climb all the way out on her own, though. Nia gasped as she pictured her falling backwards through the air, her arms waving frantically.

'This way!' A tugging at her sleeve – Kayla was pointing to the opposite end of the cell block, away from the sound of approaching footsteps.

Nia hopped behind, not knowing – or caring – where they were going, as long as it was away from the Ratman.

They arrived at an old door with as many bolts and locks as the one they had used to enter the cell block on the upper level. Nia crossed her fingers as she approached it, praying that now wasn't the time one of the doors would actually be locked.

It wasn't, and she almost shouted with relief.

She heaved it towards her, its hinges protesting as it opened. The stupid door was going to tell the Ratman exactly where they were. 'Shh,' Nia whispered, as though that would make any difference.

Behind the door was another dark brick passageway.

She hesitated for only a second before stepping inside, beckoning Kayla to follow her and closing the door behind them. It was pitch black.

Nia pressed her ear to the inside of the door but all she could hear was the whooshing of her blood. Were they safe in here, or did the Ratman know where they were? *Nia* didn't even know where they were.

It was dark, darker than Nia thought it was possible for a place to be. And the passageway was even mustier than the one that had led them to the cell block. She was sure the walls would be coated with cold slime.

Weren't prisons supposed to be clean and clinical, like hospitals? That's what she'd seen on the awful television dramas she used to watch with Mum, anyway. Once Kayla had gone to bed, they'd share a bag of popcorn, a glass of wine for Mum. Mark would pretend to be uninterested, but always ended up as invested in the ridiculous story as they were. The memories felt so distant that Nia couldn't bear to think of them.

So why was this prison so dark and dingy? It was like a medieval dungeon, something that should be a tourist attraction, not a place to keep the county's most dangerous men. No wonder they had closed this place down. The sooner they demolished it, the better.

Her heart gradually slowed, but she still couldn't hear anything through the thick door. Maybe they were safe. Maybe the Ratman hadn't seen them come in here. Maybe he wasn't even dangerous, just some loner who had decided to live in a prison with a family of rats . . . and make collages of a missing girl with her eyes scratched out and a sinister message scrawled over the top.

Yeah, right.

They couldn't go back into the cell block, not with that maniac waiting for them. Nia turned to look down the passageway, not that she could see anything. She held her fingers in front of her face and waggled them, but she couldn't even make out the movement. There could be absolutely anything in front of them.

Wait, where was Kayla? She hadn't made a sound since Nia had closed the door behind them. Nia thrust her hands forward into the air but she couldn't feel her, couldn't sense her. She held her breath and the silence engulfed her. She felt utterly alone.

'Kayla?' she whispered, her voice muted by the thick walls surrounding them.

'I'm here.'

Nia clutched her chest as she sighed in relief.

'So,' Nia breathed, 'you're not going to like this, but we need to go that way.' She nodded away from the door. Kayla wouldn't have been able to see the gesture, but it wasn't like there were many ways to interpret *that way*.

Nia prepared herself to comfort Kayla, to assure her that she'd be safe with Nia looking after her. But Kayla just said, 'OK,' as though Nia had suggested they go for a walk in the park to feed the ducks like they used to when Kayla was a toddler.

Nia blinked in surprise as tears threatened yet again. Why had that memory made her feel so emotional? Their little trips must have meant more to her than she'd realised at the time. They'd go there this afternoon, as soon as they got home, she promised herself. If Mum didn't lock her in her room and throw away the key, that was.

Her hands grappled along the walls. She was past caring about the disgusting texture of the mould, she just wanted to be able to see again. Her fingers gripped the edges of a small box, the same as the one Kayla had told her to search for in the cell block.

'Yes,' Nia breathed as she hurried to open the cover. 'Please, please, please.' She flicked the switch but nothing happened.

'Oh, come on!' she groaned, frantically clicking it up and down. Of all the places she could have really done with the light working, this windowless tunnel was at the top of the list.

Her phone screen cast a pathetic, short beam of light that made the shadows come to life and sent her imagination running wild. She wondered if it would be less scary to just close her eyes and feel her way. Something dripped on to the floor in the distance.

'This has to be a way out,' she told Kayla, wishing she had more confidence in her words. 'They must have a way out of each cell block, right? In case the prison officers need to escape or something.' Nia knew she was clutching at straws, but what else could she do?

A thought struck, and she turned to shine the light on Kayla.

'Kayla, is this the way you came? Is this how you made it down into the cell block?'

But Kayla dropped her gaze, once again muttering, 'I can't say.'

Can't say? The words made Nia pause, but she didn't press any further – she didn't want to send Kayla back into that weird state. Nia couldn't be sure, but she was guessing that the door wasn't soundproof, and a hysterical child would surely alert the Ratman that they were there.

She was right about this passageway, though, she had to be. There was no way Kayla would have been able to make the climb down to the cell-block floor. She must have found some hidden way in and got confused about the route she'd taken. Nia shuddered – it was lucky she'd found her way down here at all. Imagine if she'd taken a wrong turn and had got lost in the depths of this giant, hellish building?

She looked at her phone. It had been an hour since they'd crept into the first tunnel. Mum hadn't said anything else. But even more worrying was the red icon on her screen, warning her that she only had seventeen per cent battery life left.

'Oh god.'

Nia had been due a phone upgrade but Mum refused to let her have one after the party, no matter how much Nia had insisted her phone was ancient and she had to charge it twice a day. She thought of the portable charger nestled in her handbag, back at the table in the soft-play centre. What were they going to do if her battery died?

Keeping her phone unlocked to use the brightness from the screen couldn't be helping – she'd watched the battery drop from seventeen to sixteen just in the time she had been worrying about it. She locked it, plunging them back into darkness.

'Kayla,' she whispered. 'I need to save my battery so we'll have to feel our way along the walls, OK?'

Kayla didn't answer.

Nia realised she couldn't hear her soft breathing or sense her presence behind her again. She waved her arms around in the dark, but found nothing.

'Kayla,' she said, her voice edged with panic. 'Are you still there? I can't feel you.'

'I'm here.'

Nia breathed. She had been so sure she was alone again. She needed to stop doing this – her constant panicking wasn't going to get them out of here.

'Hold on to my jacket and don't let go, OK? It's so dark in here, if we lose each other I might not be able to find you again.' Nia cursed herself for being so dramatic. She was supposed to be keeping calm, so Kayla didn't get scared. But she was the one acting like a terrified child.

She could barely feel Kayla's hand gently plucking the back of her jumper, but it helped her focus.

'Let's go.'

She didn't creep this time. She'd seen the passageway, knew it was empty. The Ratman was behind them. This way led to their escape. There was nothing to be scared of.

There's nothing to be scared of.
There's nothing to be scared of.

The mantra got her all the way to the end of the tunnel, one hand trailing along the damp bricks, the other thrust out in front of her. She kept her eyes tightly closed so that she couldn't convince herself she'd seen something lurking in the dark.

A spider's web wrapped around her face and Nia shrieked, flapping her arms across her head and hair. She was sure she could feel the heavy weight of something huge and hideous on her shoulder and smacked it away as she danced on the spot, swiping her body and praying the creature would get trampled to death under her feet. The reaction felt automatic, an instinct that was completely out of her control.

She backed away and tried to calm down, but a thought repeated itself over and over and filled her with dread.

If this was the way Kayla had come into the cell block, wouldn't she have broken the spider's web?

The urge to let the panic consume her was overwhelming. She wanted to scream, to run, to fling herself on the floor and insist that she couldn't do it any more. She wanted Mum.

But more than anything, she wanted to get out of the tunnel.

'Hold my jacket, Kayla!' she shouted, the adrenaline pushing her forward into a jog, her arm covering her face to fend off anything else that waited for her in the darkness.

Her elbow collided with something solid.

'Yes,' she whispered, using both hands to yank the door open, relieved that the owners of the building hadn't decided to start locking the doors at this point. The same characteristic groan came from the hinges and Nia prayed the Ratman hadn't heard. Hopefully he had gone back to his creepy artwork and had no idea they were even there.

The room they entered had windows, thank god. Nia had to squint to see as the brightness stung her eyes. The first thing she did was check her entire body for spiders, tipping her head upside down and ruffling her hair in case any unwanted guests still clung to her. A shudder ran from her toes to the top of her scalp. She would never put herself in a situation like that again.

Finally, more composed, she looked around the room. There were two doors, both with signs indicating where they led:

F-WING COURTYARD. Nia felt elated. This was the way out, it had to be.

But she read the second sign and the words froze her to the ground.

HANGING ROOM. NO EMPLOYEE ACCESS – FLOOR UNSAFE.

CHAPTER 17

Hanging Room?

People weren't hanged in this country any more. They hadn't been for . . . Nia had no idea how long. She wished she'd paid attention in history lessons.

The building was obviously old, that was clear from the crumbling brick and creepy passageways. But surely this room hadn't actually been used for hundreds of years?

Nia grabbed her phone. This was worth sacrificing some battery life for.

When was the last person hanged in the UK?
13 August 1964.

Nia's mouth dropped open. *That* recently? There must be some mistake, surely?

When was the last person hanged in Staffbury prison?
The last Staffbury prison hanging occurred in 1963.

Nia thought she might throw up. Hangings were things done in the Middle Ages, where peasants watched and threw vegetables at the condemned. How was it possible that something so gruesome had happened so recently, in a time where they had television, feminism and all that hippy stuff that was going on in the sixties?

Her legs twitched as though they wanted to take her through the door despite her brain screaming, 'No, don't do it!'

She looked at Kayla, who stood watching, as always.

Her phone buzzed.

Scott

> Did you bottle it in the end then, Nia?

Nia thought of the passages she'd crept through, the cells she'd explored and the terror she'd felt. It was all going to be for nothing, because she still hadn't got a decent picture, something that would impress her friends. Something that would show Scott she was exciting.

She sent a picture of the sign. No caption was necessary.

The replies came in quick. Nia winced, knowing she was sacrificing precious battery life she might need to get them out of this place. But it was worth it, for the reactions she was getting.

Chloe

> Eeeeeeeeek!!!

Max

> AS IF

Chloe

OMG, Nia, this is soooo freaky. You're going to be a legend at school on Monday!

Scott

Jeeesus. That's mental.

She smiled, relief flooding her body. She'd done it.

Olivia

It's just a photo of a sign. What's the big deal? I might be impressed if you sent a picture of the place they actually hanged people.

Nia's nostrils flared. Olivia always had to take things one step further and Nia was done trying to impress her. She wasn't going to waste another second of her life worrying about—

Scott

Yeah, babe. That would be cool.

Was Scott calling *her* babe, or Olivia? Her anger pulsed in her chest and turned into something else; a deep longing, a *need* for Scott to like her.

'Nia,' Kayla squeaked, as though she could tell what she was about to do.

'I'll be really quick, I promise.'

But Kayla was shaking her head. 'Please don't go. Please, let's get out of here.'

'I just need one photo, then we can go.'

'That's what you said last time.'

Kayla was right. Last time that 'one photo' had led to them both being stuck inside an abandoned prison with an artistic maniac.

But she was *so* close. She'd just have to go through one more door, take a picture, then they really could get out of there. They could even leave before Mum really believed they were missing. Nia could just go along with what Mum already thought – that she was playing some sort of weird joke. Would that get her into less trouble than the truth?

Nia turned to Kayla. 'Wait here,' she instructed, feeling an overwhelming sense of déjà vu. 'Don't leave this room, OK?'

'But—' Kayla squeaked, her eyes widening in alarm.

Nia turned away from her sister before guilt could stop her doing what she'd come here to do.

Just one more picture.

Nia opened the door. Another corridor.

She groaned. She'd just promised herself that she would never creep down another one of these horrible passageways. How far away was the hanging room? She didn't want to leave Kayla here for any longer than necessary. But, she realised, this corridor wasn't that long – she could see a staircase at the end, leading upwards. It wasn't pitch black either, which made it a serious upgrade from the spider's lair in the last one.

She limped down the passageway without another glance at Kayla – she didn't want to see the look in her eyes.

The stairs were steep and crumbling, slick with green slime and water that dripped in from a gaping hole in the roof. There were marks on the wall where a banister had once been, but now all Nia had to hold on to were the walls. She winced as her raw hands rubbed against the rough brick.

'Just one photo,' she muttered as she scurried up the stairs. She'd said that exact phrase too many times to count today, but this time it *had* to be the truth. They were so close to getting out, she could feel it.

How long had it been since anyone had been up here? They seemed to have unlocked every single door in the prison before abandoning it, possibly to stop idiotic teenagers getting stuck inside for ever. She tried not to think about how *she* was one of those idiotic teenagers. But when had the hanging room last been visited before the prison was closed? And why hadn't it been turned into something else?

Nia pulled a face, imagining a hanging room being used for another purpose. Maybe it was for the best that it was closed off and left to rot.

She reached the top of the stairs and was faced with four options: **EXECUTIONER'S OFFICE, HOLDING CELL, VISITOR ROOM** and a fourth, unmarked door.

It felt colder up here.

Nia cautiously pushed open the door to the holding cell, revealing a space no bigger than a cupboard. There was a hard wooden bench along the back wall and an old bucket in the corner. She didn't want to think what the bucket had been used for. She shuddered, imagining sitting on the uncomfortable bench, staring at the door a metre in front of her face. Waiting to die.

The visitor room was larger, but just as bare and hard. A metal table was bolted to the floor, with four chairs attached to the base, just like in the visitation room she'd first come across. There was a small divide in the middle of the table, enforcing a distance between the people who sat around it. Nia wondered how many tears had been cried in this room.

She didn't bother looking in the office. She couldn't help but feel repulsed by the person who would have sat at the desk in there, looking at the list of people he would kill that day. The prisoners who had been put to death had probably done awful, unspeakable things. But Nia couldn't help feeling sorry for them, thinking about how scared they must have been.

The fourth door beckoned.

Nia's senses were on high alert, convincing her that it grew colder with every step, that the air smelled different, that there were whispers behind the door. Even the throbbing in her ankle seemed to dull as her feet carried her closer.

Her fingertips touched the door and she got a sudden overwhelming sense that there was somebody standing right behind her. She spun. The corridor was empty, but the hairs on the back of her neck still stood up.

Just one picture.

But something was screaming inside her, telling her to go back.

CHAPTER 18

'Hello?' she called loudly, surprised that her voice didn't shake.

It felt good to speak, like she was taking charge of the situation.

'I'm coming in.'

She opened the door.

A rope, tied into a noose, dangled from a beam in the centre of the room.

Nia flinched, every fibre of her being telling her to run. But the rope had hypnotised her, and she stared at it without blinking.

Move, Nia.

Get out of here, now.

Her knees trembled, like they wanted to be running, but her feet remained planted to the floor.

She slowly got over the shock of seeing the rope hanging there and took in the rest of the room. The brick walls were painted cream, just as the cell block had been. The two windows had also been painted over, allowing chinks of light to shine through cracks in the sickly paint but obscuring the outside world.

Nia thought she would like to have one last look at the sky, if she were about to die.

A single chair sat in the corner of the room, and Nia wondered who it had been for. A prison guard? A reporter? The criminal's mother? Would she have sat there, insisting that her son was innocent, screaming as the trapdoor beneath his feet opened? Or maybe a relative of the victim, eager for some form of justice?

The rope was attached to a thick beam running the length of the room. Beneath the rope, a section of the wooden floor was squared off with white paint. There was a large black lever next to it.

Goose bumps crept up her arms and into her hairline, then shot down her spine. She wrapped her arms around herself. She didn't think anything could ever convince her to pull that lever, no matter what the person standing on the trapdoor had done.

Why had they just left the hanging room as it was? Surely they could have taken the furniture and used it somewhere else? Nia eyed the rope warily. They could have at least taken that down.

She really didn't want to step any further into the room, but she couldn't get a good photo of the rope from where she was standing. So she took a step.

The floorboards creaked and she remembered the sign: *floor unsafe*.

She scanned the ground. It didn't *look* unsafe. It looked solid and felt sturdy beneath her feet.

Just a little bit closer.

The picture wasn't particularly clear because the window frame in the background stopped the rope from standing out, but it would do. She pressed send and couldn't resist adding a message.

Nia

> Happy yet?

Now, finally, she could get out of there. She was turning to leave when she received a reply.

Olivia

> OMG, Nia, stop sending pictures that could be stolen off the internet. We need to see YOU next to the noose!

Chloe

> Olivia, maybe she shouldn't.

Olivia

> Extra points if you put it round your neck.

Nia gasped. What was *wrong* with Olivia? She knew she had a dark sense of humour, but this was taking it too far.

She remembered the warnings Lucy and Anna had given her. It was this kind of twisted shit they'd been trying to protect her from. Nia was starting to wish she'd listened to them.

She watched her screen, waiting for Scott to step in, to agree with Chloe that it was a bad idea.

But Scott's reply only consisted of a stupid emoji.

'Nothing I do will ever be good enough, will it?' she said to the tiny picture of Scott's smiling face, a face she saw in her dreams. She angrily brushed her tears away before they could fall.

It wasn't right. She knew it wasn't right, the way they treated her. But what other choice did she have? When Scott had chosen her, she had discarded Lucy and Anna like they were nothing. Not that it had stopped them trying. All summer they'd messaged her, asking if she wanted to hang out at their houses, to go to the cinema, to go shopping. They'd even turned up at her house, but Nia had hidden in her room and begged Mum to tell them she was sick. When term had started in September there had been a moment Nia was tempted to catch up with them, link arms and apologise for being such a crappy friend.

But then Scott had called her name, and Lucy and Anna had become invisible to her once more. They finally got the message, and she guessed she became invisible to them too.

And Nia didn't even have a family to rely on, not any more. If Scott and the others ditched her, she'd be alone.

She fished her lip gloss out of her pocket and slid it over her lips. At least she could try to look like she had her shit together for the photo. Nia wished she could check it in a mirror. The bubblegum pink looked great on Olivia and Chloe, but Nia wasn't sure it was her colour. The sneer on Olivia's face when she'd bought it hadn't exactly boosted her confidence.

The floor groaned under her weight as she took another step towards the noose.

Why was the rope moving? It was barely noticeable, but she could swear it was gently swaying back and forth.

Get a grip, Nia.

The floor felt springy beneath her feet. Not as solid as it looked.

Just do it.

She stepped on to the trapdoor and reached forward to touch the noose. Repulsion rippled through her body as she thought of the necks that it had broken.

With a colossal bang, the floor gave way beneath her.

She felt her mouth open in horror as she plummeted downwards, her arms desperately windmilling. She imagined the noose tightening around her neck, but her fingers found the edge of the trapdoor and she dangled, her eyes wide with terror.

She was alive. A strange, guttural noise escaped from within her and she struggled to pull herself up, her arms shaking with the effort, her already-sore hands scraping against the splintered wood of the platform. Her legs scrabbled up the side of the hole and she finally clambered up, rolling away across the dusty floorboards.

She lay on her back, clutching her heart as it threatened to leap out of her mouth. The flaking ceiling warped in her vision and she wondered if she was going to pass out. She had been sure, *so sure*, that she was going to die. In the split second that she was falling, she had thought she had already put the noose round her neck.

Imagine if she had?

She would be dead. And it would be Olivia's fault.

No. It would be her *own* fault.

A sob echoed around the room and she brought her hand to her mouth to catch it. How could she have been so *stupid*? All this, risking her life more times than she could count now, and for what? For a boy, and his spiteful friends.

The tears rolled down her cheeks and into her ears, forcing her to sit up to escape the unbearable tickling sensation. She allowed herself to cry into her sleeve, just for a moment, before taking a shuddering breath and telling herself, *no more*.

She felt different, as though the shock had snapped her out of some kind of fog. As though she were seeing things clearly for the first time in a long while.

She needed to get back to Kayla. She would have heard the deafening noise of the trapdoor swinging open. She could be coming up here right now to check Nia was OK, and she really didn't want her little sister to see this room.

Nia pocketed her phone, which had skittered across the floor when she'd slipped. She peered cautiously over the edge of the trapdoor into the pit below. It looked to be about three metres deep. She would have broken something for sure if she'd fallen, or worse. The pit was painted that same nasty cream colour, but there were darker stains across the walls and floor. Nia didn't want to think about what they could be.

She tore her eyes away, the thought that she could have

died making her feel small and vulnerable. She was done – no more passageways, no more dangerous situations, no more hurting her family. And if that meant no more Scott then – she gulped – so be it.

She hurried down the stairs, nearly slipping, but saving herself by bracing against the walls. She limped along the corridor. The door had swung shut behind her and she pulled it open. This time she wouldn't hesitate before giving Kayla a huge hug.

Kayla was gone.

CHAPTER 19

'Kayla?'

'KAYLA!'

She'll appear any second. Nia chewed her lip until she could taste blood.

'KAYLA!'

She's just hiding behind one of the doors.

'KAYLA!'

She has to be here.

But she wasn't. Kayla was gone.

The room whirled around Nia as an unwanted memory pushed into her head.

The panic in Mum's voice, the confusion in Nia's as she ran up the stairs.

'What do you mean, where's Kayla? She's in her room.'

Reaching the tiny bedroom, tripping on the uneven carpet as she squeezed through the doorframe. Finding Kayla's room empty.

Nia leaned against the wall, sucking in air, willing the

dizziness away. She couldn't freak out right now. She needed to find Kayla.

Think, Nia.

Which way would she have gone? Back down the passageway to the cell block? No, there was no reason to go back there. Kayla knew they couldn't get out that way.

The other door then. The door to the courtyard, the door Kayla had wanted Nia to choose.

How she wished she'd chosen that door now.

She yanked it open, willing Kayla to be standing on the other side, bathed in sunlight, smiling.

The courtyard was empty. Kayla wasn't there, nor was it the route to their freedom, as Nia had been so sure it would be. It was no bigger than the footprint of her house. The walls were sheer and high, framing a square of grey sky above. The rain fell into Nia's eyes as she stared up at the cell-block windows surrounding her. There was no way out, just another door, leading straight back into the prison.

'Kayla!' Her voice was muted, the sound swallowed by the towering walls. Somehow it felt even more claustrophobic out here than it did inside.

She spun around, checking the corners. Kayla was only tiny; maybe she had missed her huddling into the dirt and stone.

Weeds pushed through slivering cracks in the tarmac, snaking their way up the walls and across the ground. But no Kayla.

Keep searching. Must keep searching.

Nia wrenched the other courtyard door open, straining with the effort. Would Kayla even have been able to open it? She must have, there was no other option.

Another corridor. More bricks. More darkness.

No Kayla.

'Kayla!' Her voice ricocheted down the passageway then returned to her, fainter. She stretched her neck forward, frozen, listening for a reply. Nothing.

Pain shot up her leg as she set off at a jog, but she clenched her teeth and forced herself onwards. There was no time for pain, or fear of spiders, or the dark this time. The danger was real now. Kayla was lost, *again*.

She stopped calling Kayla's name as she ran. The sound was distorted, confusing her, warping and sounding like Kayla calling back to her.

Another door. Would there ever be an end to the doors, the corridors and the empty spaces where Kayla should have been?

Nia opened it. Two large barred windows were at either side of the room. Between them were eight identical doors.

'Come *on*!' Nia shouted. This was impossible. Where could Kayla have gone? She could be trapped inside the belly of the prison, wandering for days, scared, alone. And it was all Nia's fault.

A moan of despair left her lips and she considered slumping to the floor, giving up.

No, Kayla needs you. Think, Nia. Where would she have gone?

The doors were unhelpfully signposted – **WING C, CELL BLOCK D, GOVERNOR'S OFFICE**, the list went on. Why couldn't there be one that read **ESCAPE ROUTE**?

What would Kayla have done?

But Nia had no idea. She'd been so desperate to grow up that she had forgotten what it was like to be a child.

She chose a door directly opposite hers: **CELL BLOCK D**. A short passageway revealed another heavy door, which opened into a cell block that looked exactly the same as the one they had climbed down into. Except the upper walkway was still intact and there was a blackened pile of burnt rubbish in the middle of the room.

'Kayla?' Nia called, wincing at the echo of her sister's name.

Daunted, Nia retreated. The cell block was too huge to search, not when she couldn't even be sure that Kayla had gone that way.

She tried the door to the governor's office, but it was so heavy that it was almost impossible to open. 'Not this one,' Nia whispered, thinking of Kayla's tiny arms.

The third door led to a room with even more doors, and Nia was close to despairing. Panicked, she ran crookedly, flinging doors open, running down passages, screaming Kayla's name. Her chest tightened and her breath came in short gasps, even when she stopped running.

'KAYLA!'

What if Nia had got it wrong? What if Kayla *had* returned to the cell block they had started off in after all?

What if the Ratman has her?

Nia felt as though someone had thrown a bucket of iced water over her.

She ran, smashing her elbow into a wall but not stopping, despite the flare of pain that shot through her arm. She needed to get back, needed to save Kayla.

But wait. Which door had she come through? Nia spun, completely disorientated, every door looking the same. This wasn't even the same room she had started in – there was no governor's office.

How far had she gone, how many doors had she run through in her panic? 'No, no, no!' she cried, cursing her stupidity. She opened doors and shut them again, praying for some glimpse of familiarity.

Her dare had been completed. She was lost.

CHAPTER 20

Nia nearly dropped her phone as she pulled it out of her pocket, her trembling fingers struggling to grip it. Through her tears, she ignored the notifications and found Mum's name.

Mum answered the phone before it had even rung once. 'Nia, Nia, where are you? You're worrying me now.'

Nia's face crumpled and she bent at the middle, her mouth open in a silent scream. She couldn't breathe. Her inhale sounded like she was in physical pain. She *was*.

'Mummy,' she wailed, but it barely sounded like a word.

'Nia? Nia, baby? What's wrong? Where are you? Oh god, what's happened?' Nia could hear the tears in her voice too.

She gulped air noisily, knowing she needed to get control of herself. This wasn't about her. It was about Kayla.

'I've lost her!' she sobbed. 'I've lost Kayla again!'

She waited for Mum's panic level to join hers, for the questions, the hysteria, the accusations. But Mum was quiet for so long that Nia said, 'Mum, did you hear me?'

Silence.

'Mum!' Nia screeched. 'Did you hear me? I said Kayla's lost! She followed me into the prison. I was trying to keep her safe.' Nia closed her eyes, hating herself because that wasn't true. 'But I lost her. I've been looking for ages, but now I'm lost too.'

'Nia . . .'

Why wasn't Mum screaming? Why wasn't she running, calling the police, doing *something*?

'Nia . . . hear . . . Nia?'

What?

Nia took the phone away from her ear to look at the screen. The signal bar flickered between one and nothing. Snatches of Mum's voice crackled down the line.

'Mum, the signal's bad in here. The walls must be blocking it out or something.' Nia spun in a circle, feeling even more trapped, even more unreachable. 'I'll try to get back to the courtyard!' she shouted, not knowing if a single word she said was reaching Mum.

She hobbled towards the door that felt the most likely to lead back the way she'd come.

Then her battery died.

She stared at the screen, unable to believe what she was seeing. The reflection of her terrified face stared back at her.

'Please,' she whispered, holding the on button down. 'Please!'

The screen remained black.

Her legs finally gave way and she wilted to the floor, wailing into her arms. Her stomach hurt, like a hand had gripped it and was twisting, twisting.

It felt good to cry, to *properly* cry, without worrying about what her face looked like, or the sounds she was making, or how it made anyone else feel. It felt like something she had needed to do for a long, long time.

But the longer she cried, the more afraid she was of stopping. As soon as the tears dried up, she was going to have to act. But what else could she do? The more she searched for Kayla, the more lost she herself became. She'd probably got further and further away from her as she ran deeper into the depths of the prison while Kayla was out there, with the Ratman.

A fresh bout of tears juddered through Nia's body. This was all her fault, just like the night of the party had been. She'd spent so long feeling sorry for herself, fighting against her parents, insisting that she wasn't to blame for Kayla leaving her room, that she'd never actually said sorry.

She was sorry now.

An hour ago she would have done anything to win favour with Scott and the others. *Anything*. Now she would throw all that away in a heartbeat just to be reunited with Kayla. But had it taken her too long to figure out where her priorities were? She hoped she would have the opportunity to put it right again. Not just with Kayla, but with Mum and Mark, with Lucy and Anna.

She hoped so hard it hurt.

Nia found herself making promises; she wasn't sure who to. Promises that she would be good, she would stay home, she would ground *herself* for eternity if that's what it took to earn her family's love and trust back. No more Friday nights lurking in parks with Scott and the others, sharing a bottle of cider. No more doing whatever it took to impress her friends. No more dares. No more sneaking into abandoned buildings, even if Scott was tugging her hand, insisting it would be *fun*.

She would put her pyjamas on as soon as she got home from school. She would plait Kayla's hair after her bath and read her a bedtime story, no, *two* stories. She curled her fists as she recalled lost memories of snuggling beneath the covers with her little sister and having to untangle their limbs after she'd fallen asleep, so she could sneak to her own bed.

Why had that stopped?

Nia could just about remember the exact moment she had decided to completely pull herself away from her family.

It was the night they had broken into the empty restaurant, another one of Olivia's dares. She had pushed Scott off her as they lay on the filthy mattress. Nia had returned home in tears. She felt dirty, but also ashamed of herself for running, for making a fuss.

She curled up on her bed and apologised to Scott again and again, leaving messages, even voicemails, on his phone. But he ignored her, cut off her calls, and eventually told her to leave him alone. Was he testing her? Nia typed out a promise that she would do what he wanted next time, then deleted it. She wasn't ready. She wanted Mum.

So she crept down the stairs. Her dressing gown hid the clothes she wore beneath, the jeans that were stained with grime.

'Do you think he'll look like Kayla?' she heard Mum saying to Mark, as they snuggled under a blanket in the living room. Nia stood in the hallway, drawing her dressing gown tightly across her stomach as she spied on them through a crack in the door.

'Hopefully,' Mark replied. Nia could hear the love in his voice as he gazed at the sleeping four-month-old on Mum's chest. 'Hopefully he'll get more than Kayla's beauty, he'll get her brains too.'

Nia waited for Mum to suggest what part of Nia she wished the baby would be gifted, but she just sighed and said, 'I love you. Our family is whole now.'

Nia was numb, sure that they despised her, that they wished she'd disappear. Since when had their family been less than whole? Then she realised – when Deon had been born they had a boy and a girl who were both a hundred per cent theirs. Their perfect *whole* family. Nia was just some half-thing – something left over from an accident in Mum's previous life. The truth hit her like a slap.

They didn't want her.

She crept up to her room and pretended to be asleep when Mum came in to check on her. The next day she went grovelling to Scott.

He'd accepted her back, begrudgingly. But things hadn't been the same. He'd been off with her, dropping comments about how she owed him, about how she was immature. She'd planned to change all that at the party.

Things *had* changed at the party, that was for sure.

The memories filled her with regret, and she wished she had set aside her pride and spoken to Mum about what happened, let her know how she was feeling. Then she wouldn't be lost in an abandoned prison, and Kayla wouldn't be in the clutches of a maniac.

She had no more tears left. She was thirsty, and hungry, and so, so tired.

But she had to keep trying. There was at least a chance she would find her way back to Kayla if she kept searching. But if she sat here and did nothing, then she'd be giving up on her little sister.

She took a breath and pushed the air noisily back out. Wiping her sleeve across her cheeks, past caring about the state of her make-up, she stood and stared at the door in front of her. She would open every single door in this place, sprint down every single corridor and check every single cell until she found Kayla.

As she took a step forward, a noise behind her made her spin. One of the doors was opening, and a skeletal white hand snaked through the gap.

CHAPTER 21

Nia didn't stop to think. Trusting her instincts, she stepped behind the opening door. She scanned the area, but there was nothing she could use as a weapon. Her phone would have to do. She wouldn't hurt him too much, just enough to let him know that she wasn't scared of him. Then she'd force him to take her to Kayla.

She tried to convince herself that she wasn't more terrified than she had ever been in her life, but she could barely hear her own thoughts over the thumping of her heart.

The pale fingers were still on the door, and Nia considered wrenching them back. No, that wouldn't be enough. She needed to go for his head. The hand was smaller than she had expected, almost dainty, but filth was packed under the fingernails. She pictured a twitchy little man with a pointy nose, just like one of his beloved rats.

That was good, though; he wouldn't be too much bigger than her.

She was going to have to time this just right. Too soon,

and he could retreat back into the corridor. Too late, and he'd realise she was standing there, then she'd be the one under attack. The only thing she had on her side was the element of surprise.

Nia had never been in a fight before, but somehow she was sure that she knew exactly what she needed to do. She was going to do it for Kayla.

He was taking his time entering the hallway. Could he sense she was there?

Come on, just a little closer.

He took another step and the tip of a scuffed black shoe appeared.

Just one more step.

The second foot joined the first.

Nia pounced.

As she hurled her body around the door, she screeched. She raised her phone high above her head and brought it down as hard as she could. Just at the last second, as she realised what she was seeing, she hesitated long enough for the Ratman to raise his arm in front of his face, blocking her fist with his forearm.

The Ratman was half a foot shorter than Nia. He had long, matted hair that looked like it might have once been blond. He cowered away, his eyes full of fear, instead of the malice Nia had been expecting.

It was Daisy Evans.

'What are you doing, you psycho?!' the smaller girl screamed, once she had recovered from the shock of being attacked.

Nia gaped at her, taking in her bedraggled appearance, her

head bursting with questions. What the hell was Daisy Evans doing down here? But there was only one question she really wanted the answer to.

'Where is she?' she roared, raising her phone again.

Daisy tripped to the floor as she scrambled backwards, shielding her head with her hands.

Nia stood above her, her face contorted with rage. 'Where IS she?'

'Don't!' Daisy whimpered, pushing herself along the floor but never taking her eyes off Nia.

Nia crouched, grabbing the front of the smaller girl's hoodie in one hand and keeping her other hand above her head, ready to bring her phone smashing down into Daisy's face. 'Tell me where she is!'

Daisy's mouth was flapping open and shut but Nia couldn't make out a word she was saying.

'Tell me!' She gave Daisy a shake, her back hitting the hard ground below.

'I don't know what you're talking about!'

'I swear to god, Daisy Evans,' Nia hissed, pushing her face closer. 'If you don't tell me where Kayla is right this second, I will *hurt* you.'

Nia meant it.

The terror in Daisy's eyes flickered for a second, and her eyebrows came together in the middle. 'I-I-I—'

'Come on, spit it out!'

'I don't know what you're talking about!'

Nia roared with frustration. She didn't have time for these games.

'Kayla,' Daisy said. 'Th-That's your sister, right?'

'Yes,' Nia growled, wondering if she *should* hurt Daisy. Every word she said that wasn't Kayla's location was a waste of time.

'She—' Daisy seemed to be struggling to find the words and looked almost close to tears. 'She's not here.'

Fear clutched Nia's heart and she lowered her phone to grab Daisy's hoodie with both hands. 'What have you done to her, you freak!?'

Terror and confusion mixed on Daisy's face. 'I— Nothing! Nia, *nothing.*'

'Then *where is she?*' Frustrated tears gathered in Nia's eyes, threatening to spill over and drip down on to Daisy as she cowered beneath her.

'I – I don't know,' Daisy whispered. 'I promise.'

Nia's energy drained out of her as suddenly as it had come, and she let go of Daisy, leaning back to slump against the wall. She screamed into the air before covering her face with her hands. This was hopeless. If Daisy knew where Kayla was, then she was the most effective liar she had ever met. And if she was lying, threatening her wasn't working.

Nia glared at Daisy, waiting for her to run, ready to tackle her back to the floor. She wasn't going to let her out of her sight. She was her only chance of finding Kayla.

But Daisy wasn't running. She picked herself up, moving slowly as though a sudden movement might set Nia off again. She turned so that her back was against the opposite wall, and they sat face to face.

Daisy looked awful. She'd never looked great at school. She

was always a bit greasy, a bit smelly, a bit weird. No one really paid her any attention – she had a way of disappearing into the background. When she had gone missing, jokes went around school, mainly started by Nia's new friends:

'Disappearing Daisy? She's sitting right there, can't you see her?'

'Who? Oh, she's been missing for four years, hasn't she?'

But here she was, looking as though she'd been living in the prison for weeks.

But Nia didn't care about Daisy Evans. She just wanted her sister back.

'I know you've seen her,' Nia said, her voice cold and hard. 'I know you've been sneaking around after us.'

Daisy shook her head and a thought struck Nia.

'Who then? Who else is down here?'

Daisy was still shaking her head, and Nia resisted the temptation to make her stop.

'N-no one. There's no one else, it's just me . . . and you now.'

'And *Kayla*,' Nia snarled.

Daisy swallowed and eyed Nia as though she might pounce again.

'Nia, I'm sorry ab—'

'Just,' Nia interrupted. 'Just tell me where she is, *please*.' Nia didn't want to start crying again; she wasn't sure she'd be able to stop if she did. She'd cried more in one day than she had in a very long time.

'I don't know,' Daisy repeated, and Nia groaned and threw her head back. 'But . . .'

Nia snapped her head forwards, willing the next words to come out of Daisy's mouth to be something useful.

'I'll help you.'

CHAPTER 22

Could she trust her? Did she have a choice? She may be bigger and stronger than Daisy, and Daisy was obviously scared of her. But in here, she wasn't sure if she had the upper hand at all.

'How? How can you help me if you don't know where she is?'

Daisy pulled her tatty sleeves over her pale hands. 'Um, I know my way around down here. I can help you look?'

Nia narrowed her eyes. 'Yeah, right. You'll just take me even deeper into the prison and leave me there to rot.' She cursed herself for putting the idea into Daisy's head. What the hell was Daisy even *doing* down here?

'I wouldn't do that,' Daisy insisted, widening her eyes earnestly. 'Honestly, I wouldn't hurt you. I'm not like that. I'm not like . . .'

'Like who?'

'Nothing, no one. Never mind.'

But Nia wasn't letting her off the hook that easily. 'Like

who? Like the person who's down here with you? The freak who did all those drawings in the isolation cell?'

The Ratman.

Nia wasn't sure Daisy had enough blood in her body to blush, she was so pale. But she dropped her eye contact and looked embarrassed, as though she had been caught out.

Was the Ratman some kind of child abductor? Had he kidnapped Daisy and been keeping her down here? By the looks of her, she'd been here a while. What horrible things had he done to her? What horrible things was he doing to Kayla?

'Please, Daisy,' Nia tried, softening her voice. 'Tell me who he is. He could have Kayla.'

Daisy looked at her again, her lips parted, her eyes conflicted. But she quickly made her face blank. 'I'm telling you the truth, Nia. There's no one else down here. Just us.'

'Then who—'

'Me! The freaky artwork is all me!'

It had been *Daisy*?

But Nia found she wasn't that surprised. Daisy always had been a bit odd. She could picture her frowning at the walls of the cell, smudges of pencil on her face, lost in her own head.

Which meant... there was no Ratman. No deranged girl-killer stalking them. It meant that maybe Kayla really was just lost.

Nia's reality had been distorted. She had been so sure that the Ratman had been living in that cell. He was a fully formed person in her mind. So to discover that he didn't exist made her feel like there was a hole left where he once stood, filling her thoughts.

But this whole time, it was *Daisy Evans*?

'Are you nuts or something?' Nia snapped.

Daisy flinched and stared at the holes in her jeans. 'Maybe,' she whispered.

Nia suddenly felt a pang of guilt. Daisy seemed so genuine that Nia desperately wanted to trust her. It would be so much easier than being in here alone.

What was the alternative?

She sighed. 'OK, let's go.'

Daisy's body shrank a little, as though she had let go of the tension that was making her sit straight.

'OK.' She rose gingerly to her feet, and Nia felt a rush of shame as she noticed her wince. How hard had she slammed her to the ground?

Her hand twitched as it instinctively went to help Daisy up, but Nia forced it back down by her side. Daisy wasn't normal. The artwork in the isolation cell was proof of that. And even if she was telling the truth about being down here alone, what was she *doing* here?

'So,' Daisy said, drawing out the word as though sudden sounds might make Nia freak out again. 'Where do you want to . . . look?'

'Back the way I came, obviously.'

Daisy nodded but didn't move. They stared at each other, both framed by the brick walls and the low ceiling of the passageway, waiting for something to happen.

'Do you want me to go first, or . . . ?'

Nia nodded slowly. No way was she about to let Daisy creep around behind her.

Another painful silence stretched between them.

'Well?' Nia snapped, done with Daisy's games.

'Oh, um.' Daisy pulled an awkward face. 'I, um, kind of need to get past you then.'

Nia tried to play it cool; the last thing she wanted was Daisy knowing how completely disorientated she was. But the reality was, she could lead her anywhere and Nia wouldn't have a clue whether they were going back to the cell block or deeper into the prison.

She crossed her arms and stepped aside, scowling at Daisy as she passed, hoping her bravado was convincing. Daisy chose the door opposite them, and Nia's suspicions grew.

'Wait a minute,' she said, refusing to step into the next passageway. 'How is it this way, if you were coming from that way?' She nodded over her shoulder, her eyes locked on Daisy.

Daisy couldn't maintain eye contact, but she looked embarrassed rather than deceitful. 'Um, I've been following you.'

Nia narrowed her eyes at the idea of Daisy skulking around in the dark after her. 'Yeah, and I came from Cell Block B, so why wasn't that where you were coming from too?'

More squirming from Daisy, and Nia was tempted to shake her again. 'You, um . . .'

'Um, um, um, what, Daisy?'

Daisy flinched but held her ground. 'You were running around hysterically. You crossed your path so many times that you were basically just running in circles for half an hour. You even ran past me a couple of times.'

Nia gawped at her. *Impossible.* There was no way she could

have missed seeing another person in here. But she scrutinised Daisy, who looked like she probably could fade into a wall and become invisible, which had been her speciality at school too. And Nia hadn't exactly been in a calm state of mind when she'd realised she'd lost Kayla.

She blinked quickly, refusing to let her fear rule her again.

'It's this way,' Daisy said. 'You can trust me.'

That word again. *Trust*. What choice did she have?

'Go on then,' Nia instructed, and Daisy led the way.

Daisy walked slowly but surely, holding a small keyring torch in front of her. She hadn't been lying about knowing her way around this place at least. They moved in silence, but a whirlwind of thoughts and questions flew through Nia's head. She had to know.

'What happened to you?'

She saw Daisy's shoulders tense, and her pace quickened.

'Seriously,' Nia pressed. 'Why are you here?'

A bizarre noise, which Nia realised was Daisy's laugh, echoed down a lighter, airier corridor than the ones Nia had previously come across. She'd never heard anything so forced.

'Why not?' she asked, her voice unnaturally high. 'You can't tell me you don't think it's cool?'

'Er, I can actually,' Nia replied truthfully.

'Well, why are *you* down here then?'

Nia shrugged and stared at Daisy's shoes. There was a gaping hole in the back of one of them.

'Dunno, just am.' The last thing she wanted was to admit that she was here because of a dare. That she had lost her sister because of a *dare*.

'It's because you were curious, right? You can't deny there's something about this place.'

Nia wrinkled her nose at a particularly disgusting patch of mould on the wall next to her face. There was something, all right.

Nia wasn't stupid. It was obvious what Daisy was doing – flipping the question back around to distract Nia from getting a proper answer from her. She clearly didn't want to talk about what she was doing here, so Nia decided to change tactics.

'You like art then?'

Daisy didn't reply for a moment, and Nia studied the back of her head as she walked. Her greasy hair was scraped back into a long, limp ponytail.

'I love it,' she finally answered.

Nia remembered something, a collage hung outside the art studio at school. It was of a girl, hunched over, her face hidden, but her body telling a story of sorrow and loneliness. It was so captivating that the whole school had been talking about it for weeks, especially as it had been signed *Anonymous*.

The whole thing had been made of scraps of rubbish, and Nia realised why the artwork in the isolation cell had felt so familiar.

'It was you, wasn't it? The person who did that rubbish collage at school?' Nia shook her head. 'Not *rubbish*, but you know, *rubbish*.'

Nia could have sworn she saw Daisy's ears twitch. Could she be smiling?

'Yeah, that was mine.'

Nia blew air out of her cheeks. Sure, Daisy was weird, but

she couldn't deny that she was talented too. Nia had even taken a photo of the collage on her phone and would look at it occasionally, especially after a fight with Scott or her parents. She'd wondered about the artist – it was as though they had recreated something Nia kept hidden deep inside. She'd never thought it would be Daisy Evans.

They passed through another door and Nia was amazed at how far she'd travelled in her blind panic. She shivered, wondering how long it would have taken anyone to find her if Daisy hadn't been there. Could Kayla be running through these same passageways, lost and terrified?

Nia's heart threatened to go into overdrive again at the thought of Kayla being in danger. She focused on Daisy's thin shoulders as she walked in front, and tried to convince herself that the girl was telling the truth – there was no Ratman.

'Why didn't you tell anyone it was you?' Nia asked, desperate to distract herself from the certainty that there was someone else down here with them. 'You could have been—'

'Popular?' Daisy laughed – a real laugh this time. 'People like me will never be popular, Nia. Not like you could be.'

'What's that supposed to mean?' Nia snapped, disliking her tone.

Daisy sighed and turned to face her, the light from her torch casting dark shadows under her eyes. 'You're not going to throw me to the floor again if I tell you?'

There was something different about Daisy now. A spark in her eyes that suggested she wasn't really the scared loner Nia had pinned to the floor only minutes ago.

'That depends.' Nia crossed her arms, but Daisy raised her

eyebrows, waiting for assurance that Nia wasn't going to attack again. 'Fine, whatever. Just say it.'

'It's just, we're different.'

'Well, duh.'

Daisy continued, unfazed. 'I'll never be popular. Even if I had a makeover, changed my entire personality and did everything required to be one of the popular kids, it just wouldn't happen.'

Was Nia imagining it, or did Daisy put emphasis on the word, *required*?

'My weirdness – or my uniqueness, as my dad used to call it – would always find its way through the cracks.' She smiled to herself, the idea of never being popular not seeming to bother her at all. '*You*, however . . .'

Nia tensed, ready to tear holes in whatever Daisy had to say about her. There was no way she had come this far to stand here and let Daisy Evans take jabs at her.

'*You* were always popular.'

OK, she hadn't been expecting that.

'Maybe you weren't the most well-known kid in school, but you had good friends, you got on with teachers, you were invited to all the parties. Everyone liked you.'

Daisy's words seemed like they were supposed to be compliments, but Nia wasn't enjoying her use of the past tense. 'What do you mean, "*liked*" me?'

'Well, do you get invited to parties any more?'

Nia laughed. What a stupid question. Did Daisy even know who Nia hung around with nowadays?

'I mean, parties thrown by other kids in our year,' Daisy explained.

Nia snorted. But she realised that she couldn't think of the last time she'd been to a Year Ten party. Maybe there just hadn't been any for a while? No, that couldn't be right. There had to have been something.

Daisy smiled apologetically and turned to go, as though she had made her point.

'Yeah, OK, so what?' Nia said, forcing Daisy to turn back to her. 'I've made new friends, what's the big deal?' The parties she'd gone to with Lucy and Anna had been embarrassingly lame anyway. She was sure she wasn't missing out.

'The big deal,' Daisy said calmly, 'is that your new friends have made you even more unpopular than me.'

Nia's jaw hung loose in amazement at the nerve of Daisy, the most unpopular girl in school, calling *her* a loser.

Daisy turned away from Nia and continued walking. 'Sure, Olivia and her posse may be "popular",' Daisy made little quotation marks in the air with her fingers, 'but no one actually *likes* them.'

Nia rolled her eyes. Daisy was plainly off her rocker.

'Do *you* even like them, Nia?'

Nia glared at the back of Daisy's head as they walked. She knew nothing about her, and here she was reading her as though she were her best friend.

'*Yes*,' she insisted. 'Of course I do.'

She was lying through her teeth.

Daisy stopped and spun to face Nia. Her eyes were bright and bored into Nia's as though searching for the truth behind them. 'And Scott?'

Nia shook her head and widened her eyes, demanding

further explanation from Daisy.

'Do you really like Scott?'

'Yes,' Nia said, not needing to lie this time. She thought of his easy smile and the flecks of orange in his eyes that made her stomach flutter. Even if things had gone sour between them, she couldn't deny how he made her feel. 'I love him.'

Daisy looked pityingly at Nia. 'You know Scott and I had a thing?'

CHAPTER 23

Nia stared at Daisy and waited for her to deliver the punchline, but it didn't come.

'It was about a month before you two became official.' Daisy shook her head and smiled humourlessly. 'I was so stupid.'

When she opened her eyes again, they were filled with tears.

'But he had me, you know? He really convinced me that he was genuine.'

Nia felt sick. She didn't want to hear any more, but she was desperate to at the same time.

'At first I thought it was a joke when he spoke to me. I looked over his shoulder, expecting to see his mates lurking in the background, laughing at me.'

That was just how Nia had felt the first time Scott had spoken to *her*.

'But he was alone. We were in the art room and he asked me about my work. He seemed so interested in what I was doing, in *me*. And,' she laughed, 'those eyes. It was hard not to drown in them.'

Nia knew exactly what she meant.

'It was always just us, alone in the art room after school. We talked about everything. Well, at least that's what it felt like at the time. Now that I look back on it, I realise he just talked about himself. It was almost like a counselling session for him, I think. He poured out his heart to me, about how misunderstood he felt, and how much pressure was on him to be the perfect son. He told me about how his dad hit him once when he caught him playing dress-up in his sister's clothes.'

Nia's eyes widened. He'd never told *her* that story. She could imagine it being true, though, after meeting his dad once.

He'd pulled up next to the five of them as they'd walked home from school, leaning out of his work-van window and wolf-whistling. Nia jumped, eyeing him warily as the van slowed to match their pace. He was a big man, football tattoos covering his meaty, sunburnt shoulders.

'Who's the new bird, eh, Scott? Did you pay her to walk with you? There's no other way a girl like that would be seen dead with a scrawny little tosser like you!' A chorus of laughter erupted from the passengers in the van, and Nia's cheeks flamed as she felt their leering stares on her skin.

Nia looked up at Scott for an explanation. Who was this man? And why did Scott look ready to punch something, despite the water in his eyes threatening to brim over?

'Remember what we said,' Olivia murmured from the other side of Scott. Nia stared at her, shocked – her voice was gentle and soothing and everything Olivia was not. 'He may be your dad, but he's nothing. Remember?'

Scott's *dad*? Why wasn't she being introduced to him? Though, she realised as she averted her eyes from the lewd gesture he was currently making out of the window, maybe it was for the best.

Scott took a shaky breath and smiled down at Olivia. His arm was wrapped around Nia's shoulders but she'd never felt so distant from him. There was history between the four friends, especially Scott and Olivia. History that she wasn't a part of. Yet.

'Scott?' she asked gently. She could be there for him too.

'Shut up,' he snapped. His fingers dug sharply into Nia's shoulder, making her gasp.

The catcalls from the van got more obscene, but the men quickly grew bored and drove off when they realised they weren't going to get a rise from Scott. He'd kept his gaze unflinchingly ahead as he'd walked, seemingly drawing strength from Olivia's presence at his side. The pressure on Nia's shoulder didn't lessen, and she had to press her teeth together to stop herself crying out.

As soon as they'd left, Scott was back to his usual self – confident and relaxed. But he kissed Nia goodbye a little harder than usual that day, and his fingers had left a bruise on her shoulder.

But, somehow, what troubled her more were the secretive glances and whispers he and Olivia shared. At one point Olivia had stared deep into his eyes as she'd squeezed his upper arm, exchanging a silent message that only they could hear.

Nia never brought his father up after that. She told herself it was to spare Scott having to think about a relationship that was clearly painful for him, but in reality she didn't want him to direct that pain at her again.

Had he seen Daisy the same way he saw Olivia? And if so, why didn't he see Nia like that too? What was wrong with her?

'Bit by bit, we grew closer,' Daisy continued. 'I thought he was changing, that he wasn't the guy he pretended to be in front of everyone else. Whenever he visited the art studio after school, my day was brighter. We didn't do anything other than talk, or listen in my case, but I felt close to him, you know?'

Nia didn't know. Scott had never spoken to her like that, never confided in her.

'Then, one day, that all changed.' Daisy's foot jiggled on the floor as she stared down at her hands, which were busy picking a loose thread from the tattered cuff of her jumper. 'He was different from the Scott I thought I knew. He was more like the Scott he was before – loud, overconfident. He kissed me.'

Nia's jaw tightened in jealousy.

'I pushed him away. He was being weird – I didn't know, or even like, that Scott. But he *kept* kissing me.' She shuddered. 'It was horrible. So I bit him.'

Nia's eyes widened. 'That was *you*?'

She'd always wondered where Scott had gotten that scar from. It had been fresh when they'd first started dating. When it had healed, two little lines were left beneath his bottom lip. Nia must have spent hours gazing at them, along with every other detail on his perfect face. He'd joked that he'd had a fight with a small lion, and Nia had laughed it off, not wanting to push any further. Goose bumps prickled up her arms as she remembered his mouth on hers in the abandoned restaurant, and the overwhelming instinct to push him away.

Daisy nodded, as though she could see what Nia was reliving. 'He was pretty angry with me. He stormed off, and I assumed he'd just stop coming to see me.' She clenched her teeth. 'I hadn't been expecting him and his friends to ambush me on the way to school the next day.'

'What did they do?' Nia asked softly, though she was afraid she already knew. *Everyone* knew.

'Do I really have to say it?' Daisy asked coldly, staring deep into Nia's eyes.

Nia shook her head. It had been the talk of the school. Daisy had been pelted with eggs and rubbish. Bags of dog poo had been emptied over her head. Nia, Lucy and Anna had agreed it was horrible, but they still avoided Daisy, and so did everyone else. No one wanted a target on their own back.

No one had ever got into trouble for it, and eventually people stopped talking about the incident. The nicknames and the jokes aimed at Daisy stuck, though. Nia stared guiltily at the ground. No wonder Daisy had wanted to disappear.

'Did you know?' Daisy asked.

Nia looked up.

'Did you know what they were planning on doing?'

Nia shook her head. 'No, I promise. I wasn't even with Scott then.'

'You still *got* with Scott, though,' Daisy said sadly, 'knowing what he'd done.'

Nia opened her mouth to object, then closed it. Daisy was right. She'd known what Scott was capable of from the start, and it hadn't stopped her from falling for him.

Why hadn't she just *listened*? Not only to Lucy and Anna, warning her that he was bad news, but to her own head? Clearly her heart couldn't be trusted.

'Let's keep going,' Daisy suggested. Nia closed her eyes, sighing with relief.

She hadn't done that horrible thing to Daisy, she tried to convince herself as they carried on walking. She wouldn't have joined in, even if she'd been friends with the others at that point. But the gnawing feeling on the inside of her stomach told her that she would have. She would have thrown the first bag if they'd told her to.

Nia was so wrapped up in her own thoughts that she didn't notice Daisy had stopped until she bumped into her back. Irritated, she opened her mouth to snap at her, but instead 'Sorry' escaped from her lips.

Daisy looked at her in surprise. 'Don't worry about it.' Her pale eyes were fixed on Nia, barely blinking. Nia looked at the floor. When had it become strange for her to be nice to people? 'You OK?' Daisy asked gently.

Nia nodded. She was far from OK. Not only was she struggling with the guilt of losing Kayla again, she could now barely look Daisy in the eye without a wave of shame washing over her. Even if she hadn't been the one who'd tormented her, she hadn't tried to stop the others from making her life a misery. She'd averted her gaze, pretended she hadn't seen.

Nia, however indirectly, had been part of making sure Daisy was alone.

Was that why she'd disappeared?

'Why are you here?' she tried again. Daisy turned away

but Nia lightly touched her arm to stop her. 'No, I mean, did you disappear . . . did you run away because of . . . because of all tha—'

'Because of Scott?'

Nia nodded, her hand still paused on Daisy's arm.

But Daisy laughed and shook her head. 'No. It was horrible, but I didn't really have any friends at school before that happened anyway. It was better before, because I could just disappear. People didn't like me, but they weren't cruel either. So yeah, it made life at school worse, but school isn't everything, you know?'

Nia didn't know. To her, school *was* everything. Well, not what she was *supposed* to be doing at school. Not the lessons and the exams and the coursework. But the social life, what people thought of her. That was *everything* to Nia.

She wished she could be as carefree as Lucy and Anna. They had never worried about being 'cool'. Nia had pitied them for their naivety, their cringy selfies and childish ways. Didn't they know what they looked like? But now she realised that it was her who was the pitiful one. Olivia's dare wouldn't have lured *them* down here.

'So,' Nia said slowly, wanting to escape the regret swamping her chest, 'what about your family?'

'Come on,' Daisy said, as though Nia hadn't spoken. 'We're nearly back in the cell block.'

Nia hadn't been paying attention to where they were going. They were in the passageway that had given her the choices she wished she could go back and change: **COURTYARD B, CELL BLOCK B, HANGING ROOM.**

Nia froze, her breath trapped in her lungs as she stared at the sign. There was a dead pigeon hanging off it. Its wing was wedged beneath the plaque and its head lolled back against its dangling body.

She heard Daisy gasp as she spotted it too.

'Who did that?' Nia rasped, her voice threatening to tip over into a scream. 'Who *did* that!?'

Daisy's mouth opened and shut a few times before she shook her head and regained her composure. 'Wow.' She laughed that awful fake laugh and tried to flip her hair casually. 'He really jammed himself in there, huh? Stupid bird.'

Nia gawped at her. She couldn't seriously expect her to believe that the pigeon, the *same* pigeon from the cell block, had somehow got itself stuck beneath the Hanging Room sign?

'No,' Nia insisted. 'I *saw* that bird – it was stuck in the net when I climbed down. It—'

Nia paused, thrown by the way Daisy was looking at her. *Pity*.

'Nia, there are loads of pigeons in here. They get panicked because they can't get out. I'm always finding them in weird places.'

Nia swallowed. She could empathise with the pigeon. And she wanted to believe what Daisy was saying, because what was the alternative? Someone in here messing with her? Zombie birds? Or maybe she was simply losing her mind.

She caught Daisy watching her as she shuddered.

'You're lucky you didn't get really hurt in there, you know.'

Nia wrapped her arms around herself as her heart pounded

at the memory of the rope, the trapdoor, falling. 'How do you know I went in?'

Daisy's eyes darted around before answering. It gave Nia the impression that she was making up her answer on the spot. 'I heard the bang. Scared the life out of me, to be honest. I ran down the corridor to check on you, but you'd already disappeared by the time I got here.'

Nia frowned. If Daisy had been coming down the corridor from the cell block, then surely she'd have crossed Kayla.

'You must have seen her then! You must have seen my sister.'

Daisy tore her eyes away and shook her head. 'I didn't see anyone.'

Nia tried to ignore the hopelessness that made her want to sink to the floor again. Kayla was tiny; she must have sneaked past Daisy somehow. Maybe Nia had been in the Hanging Room longer than she thought, and Kayla had left as soon as she'd gone up the stairs, so Daisy wouldn't have even been in the corridor yet.

But the more she tried to convince herself it was true, the more the voices in her head told her she would never see Kayla again.

'Why did you go up there anyway?' Daisy asked. 'And why did you step on the trapdoor?'

Daisy was staring at her as though she were some kind of strange animal she wanted to understand better.

Nia shrugged.

'Morbid curiosity?' Daisy suggested. 'It's OK, I get it. Did you know it was still legal to hang people until 1998? That's why they kept some hanging rooms open, in case anyone ever got done for treason.' She chuckled, then looked embarrassed as she caught Nia staring at her. She really was as strange as everyone said.

'No,' Nia insisted. 'I wasn't curious – I hate this kind of thing.' She looked around them, trying to avoid the gaze of the lifeless pigeon.

'Hmm.' Daisy nodded. 'I didn't picture you as the kind of person who got their kicks from exploring dangerous, haunted buildings.'

Nia's eyes widened. Had Daisy seen something in here?

But Daisy laughed at her reaction. 'Don't worry, I'm just winding you up. There aren't any ghosts in here. It really is just an abandoned building. Though a creepy one, I'll give you that.'

Nia's eyes drew her back to the hanging-room door, her imagination in overdrive.

'I needed to get a picture,' she said, waving her dead phone lamely in the air.

'Why?'

'For them,' Nia whispered.

She turned away before she could see Daisy's reaction. She knew what expression would be on her face, and she didn't want to see it. She felt stupid enough on her own without someone else pitying her.

They weren't her friends, and she'd known that for longer than she wanted to admit. Even the last time they had all properly hung out, the night of the party, they hadn't exactly been pleasant to her.

CHAPTER 24

Nia could hear Olivia mocking the family photos on the kitchen wall as she ran upstairs.

'Here,' she snapped, thrusting the plate of food into Kayla's arms.

'Don't you want to read with me?' Kayla squeaked as Nia turned to leave. She was holding a book in front of her chest. Memories of snuggling under the covers as they took it in turn to read rushed back to Nia. They hadn't done that for years, so why was Kayla suggesting it now?

'No, Kayla,' Nia sighed. 'I don't.'

She closed her eyes, trying to ignore the creeping guilt from speaking to her little sister like this. But she couldn't get distracted. Not tonight.

'Just be quiet and stay put. Do not set foot out of this door, do you understand? If you do, I'll be so angry with you I'll never speak to you again.'

Kayla's chin wobbled, but she nodded.

Nia trotted down the stairs, jumping the last one and trying to regain her composure before entering the kitchen.

Scott, Olivia, Chloe and Max didn't acknowledge her return. They had opened the champagne and the bottle was empty. No one had poured a glass for her.

She tried to squeeze into the circle, but none of them moved to make space for her so she stood slightly on the outside, joining in with the laughter at a joke she hadn't understood.

How much was that champagne worth?

Maybe Mum and Mark would be in such a good mood when they got home that they wouldn't be too angry.

On that note, Nia thought, checking her watch, she should probably let her friends know that they'd have to leave by ten. How should she do it without sounding like a complete killjoy?

'Nia, why do you keep looking at your watch?' Olivia asked, her voice silky and innocent, disguising the bitchy comment that was sure to follow. 'Oh, gosh.' She brought her bejewelled acrylics to her mouth, which had formed a perfect circle. 'I'm so silly for forgetting; your bedtime is at eight, isn't it?'

The others smirked, and Nia tried to laugh along with them.

'Don't worry, sweetie. We'll be gone by then.' She looked around the kitchen, her lip curling into a sneer. 'I'm sure of it.'

Nia's face grew hot, and she wished she had a drink to hide behind.

'When do we have to be out by?' Scott asked, and Nia's blush deepened as he held her gaze.

'Oh, um.' She tried to toss her hair flippantly but was pretty sure it looked more like a startled twitch. 'Whenever.'

Oh god, why did she say that?

'Really?' Max asked in surprise.

'Mmmhmm.' Nia nodded.

'Awesome, no curfew!' Max high-fived Scott. 'Your parents must be pretty sound.'

Nia tried to picture Mum and Mark's reaction when they found four older kids in the house drinking their booze. Somehow she didn't think her friends would be describing them as 'sound' by the morning.

Olivia was grinning as though she could see straight through Nia's lies.

It wasn't long before the bubbles started going to their heads, and Nia wished she could have had some of the champagne too. She might have been able to enjoy herself if she was tipsy, instead of wincing every time one of them nearly broke something, and dreading the moment Mum and Mark returned.

'Oh-em-gee, guys,' Olivia said, holding her arms up so her perfectly flat stomach was exposed even more. 'Let's play truth or dare.'

'Yeah!' Chloe squeaked.

Max clapped his hands together. 'We'll need more drinks!'

Scott just smiled, as cool as ever, while Nia's stomach did backflips.

She tore her eyes off him when she realised Olivia was staring at her. 'Well, Nia?'

'Um, yeah, sure – let's play.'

Olivia rolled her eyes so dramatically that Nia wondered whether she would dislodge one of her false eyelashes. '*Drinks?*' she demanded.

'Oh, right.' Nia panicked, looking around the kitchen.

'Which room is your drinks cabinet in?' Olivia asked. 'The dining room or the sitting room?'

Nia stared at her as she peered through the doorway into the lounge. The dining table was right there, in the kitchen. Did she really think they had another room?

'Oh my god,' Olivia exclaimed. 'Does this house only have two rooms?'

Nia clenched her teeth together, wishing she could come up with something witty to snap back. But what could she say to bring someone like Olivia down?

'Ooh, vodka!' Chloe said, appearing from the cupboard in the corner. 'Someone in this house is a sneaky drinker!'

They filed into the lounge, Nia trying to ignore Olivia's mutterings about the vodka being supermarket own brand and cursing herself for not being brave enough to stand up to her.

Scott sat on the sofa, and Olivia immediately sat beside him, tucking her feet up so she had to lean unnecessarily close to him. Max dropped himself on to the armchair and Chloe curled up on his lap like a contented cat. There were no seats left for Nia.

'Chloe,' Olivia began as Nia sat on the floor. 'Truth or dare?'

'Truth.'

'Who is your best friend in the whole wide world?' Olivia smiled sweetly, batting her eyelashes.

Nia pulled a face. What kind of truth-or-dare question was that?

'Err, youuuu, of course!' Chloe simpered. Nia studied her. She'd probably jump in front of a bus if Olivia told her to. Maybe they all would.

'Aww, love you too, sweetie! Max, truth or dare?'

Nia frowned. Who had appointed Olivia as question master?

'DARE!' Max bellowed, throwing his hands in the air and making Chloe shriek. Nia hoped the neighbours hadn't heard.

'Hmm,' Olivia pondered, tapping a long nail on her glossed lip. 'Neck as much vodka as you can.'

Nia's eyes widened. She'd seen Max drunk. He was a mess. And he was a big guy – she wasn't sure she'd be able to control him if he got wasted.

'Drink, drink, drink, drink!' they chanted as he knocked back at least a quarter of the bottle, then passed it round for everyone to have a swig. Nia's stomach lurched just from the smell, and she couldn't bear to taste it, hoping her pretend sip had been convincing.

'Scott,' Olivia said, placing her hand on his thigh. 'Your turn.'

Nia tried to keep her face blank, but inside she was screaming, *Tell her to stop touching you!*

'Truth or dare?'

'Dare.'

Olivia thrust the bottle into Scott's chest. 'Drink, baby, drink!'

'Very original,' Nia mouthed into her lap. One day, she promised herself, she'd be brave enough to speak her thoughts so Olivia could actually hear her.

But not today.

She winced as Scott downed even more than Max had. She'd seen him drunk too.

'OK, my turn,' Olivia said as the cheers died down. 'I choose truth! Hmm, Olivia, who do you love more than anyone in the world?'

Wait, she got to ask herself a question too? And that had to be the worst question in the history of truth or dare.

Olivia looked around the room with misty eyes. 'You three are my favourite people. I just adore you all.' Her eyes lingered on Scott then flicked over Nia, making it clear she wasn't one of the three.

Nia hated Olivia more than ever at that moment, but that didn't mean she wanted Olivia to hate *her*. She dug her nails into her palms. What was Olivia's *problem*? Nia had never been anything but nice to her, and if she was so desperate to have Scott to herself then why hadn't she done anything about it before Nia had appeared on the scene?

Her almond eyes trapped Nia like a rabbit in headlights. 'Nia, truth or dare?'

Nia's brain scrambled. Which option could Olivia inflict the least damage with? She thought of the excruciating questions she could be forced to answer and decided she'd rather face the vodka.

'Dare.'

Olivia's eyes lit up in triumph, and Nia wondered if she'd made a terrible mistake.

'Kiss . . .' She paused, a Cheshire cat smile spreading over her face. 'Max.'

Nia waited for her to laugh, for someone to tell her not to be stupid, for Scott to speak up. But everyone was silent.

'Err . . .' Nia said, stalling.

Why was Scott just staring at his hands?

'Come on then, Nia,' Max slurred, standing up and lurching towards her. Chloe slid clumsily on to the armchair, her eyes wide with indignation.

Nia laughed again, but no one was laughing with her. They were just staring, waiting.

She held up a hand in front of her mouth as Max bent towards her. 'Er, obviously not!'

Olivia cocked her head to the side like a curious puppy. 'Why not?'

Chloe was looking at Nia as though she were about to rip her throat out.

Max was still hovering above her, so she kept her hand up. '*Because*,' she raised her eyebrows at Scott, who still seemed to be pretending that none of this was happening. 'Because I'm with—'

'Oh, come on already,' Scott interrupted, snapping his head up to glare at Nia. 'Just get on with it, will you?'

Nia's hand dropped slowly to her lap as she stared at Scott. Max saw his opportunity and sprang, his fleshy lips all over Nia's, his tongue poking against her teeth. Before she could shove him away it was over, and he was swaggering back to his seat.

The game continued, but Nia barely heard a word of it. She was fighting the desire to run to the bathroom and wash her mouth with soap. She couldn't forget the feeling of Max's wet lips. Scott didn't look at her once, but Chloe had resumed her position on Max's lap and hadn't taken her eyes off her.

Eventually they grew bored as Olivia's ridiculous questions and dares dried up. Scott rose to go to the toilet, and Nia waited for a minute before following him. She felt Olivia's cat-like eyes watching her leave.

He jumped as he opened the door of the downstairs loo to find Nia standing outside, biting her nails anxiously. 'Christ, what are you doing here?'

'Are you OK?'

Scott scowled and tried to brush past her, but Nia stood her ground.

'Yeah, whatever.' He still wouldn't meet her eye.

Nia was closer than she'd been to him since the night they'd broken into the restaurant, the night she'd pushed him away. She could see his pulse quivering in his throat, smell his aftershave. She hadn't told him that she'd bought herself a bottle and would spray it on her pillow at night.

'No, you're not, Scott.'

'Why did you ask me if you were just going to tell me what I'm thinking?' he grumbled.

'I didn't want to kiss him, you know that, right?'

'Didn't do a very good job of stopping him, did you?'

Nia's eyes burned at the injustice of it. She would have pushed him away, it just all happened so quickly. Couldn't Scott see that?

She reached for his hand and he let it hang limply between her fingers. 'It's *you* I want,' she promised.

'Yeah, well, you've got a funny way of showing it.' He took his hand back, and Nia wrapped hers around her stomach. 'You didn't want to be with me that night in the restaurant, and next thing I know you're sticking your tongue down my best mate's throat.'

She'd apologised so many times for that night, but he *still* hadn't forgiven her for not wanting to go any further with him.

'Some girlfriend you are.'

Nia flinched. She'd tried so hard to be the perfect girlfriend. She'd ditched her old friends and done all she could to impress Scott's. She'd suffered Olivia's insults in silence for *months*. What more could she do to show him how much she liked him?

'I'm sorry,' she whispered, wishing she could control the snot that was threatening to bubble out of her nose. 'I'll make it up to you, I promise.'

'Let's go upstairs.'

Nia froze. 'What, now?'

'Come on.' Scott grabbed her hand and tugged her after him.

Nia's mind went into overdrive. What was going to happen? What was he expecting of her? Shouldn't she be excited, instead of terrified?

She watched his back as they climbed the stairs, her heart pounding in her chest.

The front door opened.

The first thing Nia felt was relief. Then fear. Mum and Mark were home early.

Mum's smile was wiped off her face by the sight of her daughter being led upstairs by a boy. 'Nia?'

Scott laughed from behind her. 'Uh-oh.'

Mark appeared in the doorway, concern on his face. 'Nia, what's going on? Are you OK?'

'Her parents are home!' A shriek came from the lounge, followed by a scramble of feet and a crash.

Olivia, Chloe and Max flew through the hallway, their heads bowed, barging past Mum and Mark and nearly knocking over the pram. Scott dropped Nia's hand and squeezed past her, almost pushing her down the stairs as he legged it. Nia could hear their hysterical giggling as they ran down the street.

Mark softly closed the door behind them. He sighed and looked at Mum.

Nia knew that look. That look meant, 'It's not my place to give your daughter the telling-off of her life.'

Nia braced herself.

'Nia,' Mum began, and Nia grimaced. Mum wasn't angry, she was disappointed. But she hadn't seen the empty alcohol bottles yet, or the stuff Max had smashed as he lurched around the house.

'Why didn't you just ask if you could have a party?'

What?

'We could have got some decent snacks in, even asked their parents if they could have a couple of alcopops.'

Nia couldn't believe it. She could have had a party if she'd just *asked*?

'Obviously you couldn't have had it tonight, not when you're home alone with Kayla,' Mum explained as she hung her coat up. 'But we could have sorted something for tomorrow maybe.'

This was even worse than a telling-off. Nia was going to be ridiculed by the others now, for nothing.

Mum closed her eyes and took a breath. She looked beautiful in her dress, and guilt twisted Nia's guts. This was the first time she'd dressed up and done something for herself since Deon had been born. 'We'll need to talk about this, Nia,' she said seriously. 'But we've had such a lovely night; I really don't want to ruin it now.'

Nia could barely believe her luck. She wasn't going to get told off.

'I'm just going to put Deon down and check on Kayla, then we've got a bottle of champagne in the fridge that needs opening.' She squeezed past Nia on the stairs, carrying Deon, who continued to sleep peacefully in her arms. 'I'm only allowed a tiny bit, so I thought you might want to try it with us?'

Oh no!

'Um, Mum,' Nia said, as she followed her. How was she going to play this? Could she get away with blaming Olivia? But then Mum might forbid her from ever seeing them again.

'Shh,' Mum whispered as she lowered Deon into his crib, which was attached to her and Mark's bed. She closed the door softly behind her, her eyes full of love.

'About the champagne . . .' Nia tried again.

But Mum hushed her as she pushed Kayla's door open, frowning when she saw that the light was on. 'Kayla? Kayla darling, are you still up?'

Mum disappeared into the room and her words sent terror through Nia's heart.

'She's gone!'

CHAPTER 25

Nia gave herself a mental shake as she opened the door, exposing the red brick of the passageway that led back to the first cell block. Her feelings could wait until later. Right now all that mattered was finding her sister.

She pictured Kayla in her mind; the leggings and jumper she had been wearing, the book she took everywhere. She pictured exactly where she would find her, standing patiently next to the pool table, waiting for Nia to return. She imagined it so hard that she could almost feel the tiny weight of her as she ran into her arms.

She set off, not waiting to see if Daisy followed her. She walked quickly, but soon her legs forced her into a jog. Her ankle throbbed as she ran, but it felt good. Every step was taking her closer to Kayla.

She was panting by the time she arrived at the door, but she didn't stop to catch her breath. The door groaned as she heaved it open.

'KAYLA!'

Nia pictured Kayla running, her arms outstretched, her head colliding with her stomach as she clung to her.

'Kayla!'

If she wished it hard enough, imagined every little detail, could she make her sister appear?

The cell block was empty.

'Kayla?' Her voice was smaller now, the all-too-familiar sense of despair engulfing her.

She turned back to the door. Daisy stood there looking scared, as though she was waiting for Nia to attack her again.

'Don't just stand there!' Nia shrieked. 'Help me look for her!'

Daisy opened her mouth to respond, but seemed to think better of it, and nodded. Nia checked one side of the cell block and Daisy the other. She made sure to go properly into each cell so she could look into all four corners and behind the door.

'Make sure you check beneath the hedges, in case she's crawled underneath,' Nia called, then paused, confused. *Hedges?* She was thinking about when Kayla had gone missing before, she realised, and the places they'd searched for her on that dark, freezing night. The stress of this whole situation must be getting to her. 'I mean, just check everywhere, OK?'

When she'd finished on her side, she checked Daisy's too, just in case.

But she finally had to accept that Kayla wasn't there.

Daisy was standing outside the isolation cell, watching Nia as she swept through the cell block yet again, praying she'd missed something and Kayla would somehow appear in the spot she had just checked.

As despair threatened to overwhelm Nia, she heard something. A bang – distant, but loud. Nia's head turned towards the sound, her body locked in position and her breath paused. But everything was silent.

'Did you hear that?' she whispered, turning to Daisy.

Daisy was also frozen, and Nia couldn't read her expression.

'You heard that, right? There *is* someone else here!'

Daisy cleared her throat and twitched, snapping herself out of her trance. 'No, it's just the prison.'

'What do you mean?' Nia asked.

'The prison, it makes noises sometimes,' Daisy said, as if it was the most obvious thing in the world. 'It's like any old building, you know? There's a door that bangs in the wind sometimes, in a different cell block – that's probably what you just heard.'

Nia narrowed her eyes, not trusting Daisy but not knowing what to do about it. She couldn't exactly go charging off towards the source of the sound, getting lost yet again. How would that help Kayla?

No, she'd stay put, stick to Daisy and watch her like a hawk. She'd slip up soon, she *had* to. And then Nia could finally find Kayla.

But in the meantime, Nia would keep searching.

She barged past Daisy and into the isolation cell. Nia ignored her winces as she threw the pile of clothes against the wall, shaking each garment as though Kayla would fall out of a pair of leggings.

She flipped the mattress, and a wave of déjà vu made her

pause. She'd done this in Kayla's room, the night she'd disappeared.

She shook her head – she couldn't get distracted. That was then; this was now. Ignoring her repulsion, she lunged towards the rat-nest pile, determined not to leave a single inch of the cell block unsearched.

But Daisy's hand darted out, seizing Nia's wrist.

'Don't!'

'Let me go. I need to look for Kayla!' Nia screeched, her voice choked. 'I need to look *everywhere*!'

'OK,' Daisy said, her calmness a stark contrast to Nia's hysteria. 'OK, let's look everywhere.'

She kept her hand gently on Nia's wrist. The touch, and Daisy's steady gaze, felt reassuring, and Nia wondered if she really could trust the strange girl who lived in a prison.

'Just let *me* search here, OK?'

Nia nodded. Daisy let go of her arm and crouched down over the pile of clothes. Nia could see that the material was moving – the repulsive creatures had probably been disturbed by her shouting. How could Daisy bear to get so close?

Daisy moved slowly, and carefully peeled back a layer of material to expose the nest. The mother rat looked up at her, but this time her gaze didn't seem hostile. She looked relaxed and almost like she was pleased to see Daisy. Her babies wriggled beneath her, sniffing blindly. Nia found herself worrying that they would be cold without the material covering them.

'Hey, Hades,' Daisy whispered. She took a packet out of her pocket, broke off a piece of biscuit and handed it to the rat. 'Sorry to disturb you.'

She carefully covered the family again, and stood, speaking gently. 'Sorry, Nia. Kayla isn't here.'

Nia closed her eyes. Of course Kayla wasn't curled up under a few T-shirts with a family of rats. She thought Daisy was the crazy one, living down here and giving weird names to rodents, but now Nia worried that it was actually her who was losing the plot.

'Where *is* she?' Nia asked, but her tone wasn't accusatory this time, just desperate.

'Nia . . .' Daisy said softly, but Nia didn't want to hear anything that wasn't going to help them find Kayla.

'She has to be here, she *has* to be!' Nia was pacing, the tiny cell only taking two strides to cross. 'Where else could she have gone? You're *sure* you didn't see her when you were following me?'

'I promise. I didn't see her,' Daisy said, her eyes filling with tears.

'Could she have climbed back out the way I came in?' Nia asked, striding out of the cell. She grimaced as her ankle throbbed. God knew how much damage she'd done by running about on it.

She craned her neck upwards to look at the dangling walkway.

No, impossible. It was so high off the ground that Nia couldn't even reach it, so Kayla didn't have a chance. Looking at the twisted metal and the sharp drop to the ground, Nia was amazed they had made it down in the first place.

She turned to confront Daisy. 'How did *you* get in here?'

'I just—'

'There's no way you could climb up and down that platform.' Nia approached her and Daisy backed off, the same fear in her eyes as when Nia had first confronted her. She was on to something, she was sure of it. And this time she was going to get the truth out of Daisy.

'There's another way in, isn't there? And that's where Kayla will be.'

Nia found herself growing hopeful. Daisy was lying to her – she had to be – but that meant that she knew where Kayla was. All Nia had to do was get Daisy to tell her. 'What about that door, the one you said blows in the wind – is that the other way in?'

'Nia, I can't . . . I mean, there isn't—'

'Stop *lying*!' Nia screamed. To think she'd felt sorry for Daisy. She was a sneaky little liar and she was keeping her from Kayla. 'Tell me how to get out of here or you'll regret it.'

Daisy stopped backing away, hesitated for a moment, then sprinted to the side. Nia was after her, running as hard as she could and yelling through the pain in her ankle, determined not to let her get away. But Daisy was fast, freakishly fast. The space between them was widening, and then Daisy jumped.

Nia gasped as Daisy launched herself into the air, seeming to defy gravity. Daisy windmilled her arms, then gripped the bottom of the floating walkway like a lemur on a tree. She scrambled upwards, her hands gripping lightly and her feet flat against the metal grid as though she were walking across the ground instead of a vertical strip of bouncing metal. She made it up to the platform in seconds then stretched across the wall, clinging to the brick and balancing her toes on the metal rods.

Nia's mouth hung open as she watched her monkey-like acrobatics. If she could do it, did that mean Kayla could too?

'Do you believe me now?' Daisy called down, her voice nearly lost in the huge room.

'Go and check the corridor!' Nia called. 'Check if Kayla's there!'

Daisy hesitated, and Nia fought the urge to shout at her. Why wasn't she moving? Couldn't she see how urgent this was? A seven-year-old was lost; she should be *running*.

She saw Daisy sigh before turning to step into the corridor, the door still hanging wide open above the huge drop. Nia crossed her fingers on both hands. Wait, was it bad luck to cross two sets of fingers? She'd believe in anything if it meant Kayla would be safe, so she uncrossed one, just in case.

'Please, please, please,' she muttered, wanting to hear good news so badly that she could almost *see* Kayla standing next to Daisy in the doorway.

A movement in the dark made her heart leap. Was it . . . ?

No. Just Daisy, shaking her head.

'No!' Nia shouted, her knees folding. She stared upwards, the image of Daisy swimming in her tears. 'Daisy, are you *sure*?'

'Yes, I'm sure,' Daisy called, her voice echoing around the room.

Nia's legs felt weak beneath her and she sat heavily on the floor. The overwhelming feeling of familiarity swept over her again, as though she'd been here before, in this exact same situation, feeling this exact same despair. The same shame.

How could she have let this happen? Again?

Her mind whirred through the various points in time she

would return to if she had the chance – a time before she burned bridges with anyone who truly cared about her. The night of the party? The unanswered messages from Lucy and Anna? The day Scott had kissed her for the first time?

Tentative hands wrapped around her shoulders, snapping her out of her thoughts and pulling her closer.

'I'm sorry, Nia,' Daisy whispered.

Nia sniffed, wishing she could control the tears that just kept coming and coming as though they'd been building up for months and had finally been released.

'I'm scared I'll never see her again,' Nia said when she could finally get her breath. She felt Daisy's hands tense on her arms.

Nia wiped her nose on her sleeve. Her heart wanted her to give up, to curl up on the dusty floor and accept that her sister was gone. But her head told her that it was time to get out of here, that Kayla needed her, that she could never stop searching.

She wasn't sure she'd be able to climb back out like Daisy had. But Daisy could go and get Mum, and then the search for Kayla could begin properly. They'd find her in a corner Nia had missed, or wandering a different corridor, not hurt or trapped in one of the ways Nia's mind insisted on imagining. She managed to let go of the idea that there was someone else in here with them, someone much more sinister than Daisy Evans.

'I can't believe how easily you did that,' Nia mumbled, nodding at the walkway.

'It wasn't easy the first time,' Daisy admitted. 'It was me who made it collapse – the bolts were barely hanging in the wall because the brick had gotten so damp. I thought I was going to die when the grate gave way beneath my feet. But since then I've had practice at climbing down. Lots of practice.'

Nia thought of the screwdriver that had been jammed into the wall above. Daisy must have put it there. '*Why*, though?' she asked once again. 'Why do you keep coming down here?'

Daisy squirmed and looked sideways at Nia. 'Because of him,' she said finally, nodding towards the isolation cell.

CHAPTER 26

Cold fear gripped Nia's heart. She'd just accepted that they were alone down here, but was Daisy now suggesting they weren't?

'Him?' she asked faintly.

Daisy stood and held out her hand to Nia. 'Come and see.'

What could Nia do? The second she thought she could trust Daisy, she realised she knew nothing about her at all. But she took Daisy's hand and let her pull her into the cell. Maybe she was finally going to find out who had her sister.

Daisy pointed at the drawings on the wall and repeated, 'Because of him.'

Daisy wasn't talking about the Ratman, Nia realised with a jolt. She was talking about Andrew Warren. 'You *knew* him?'

'He was my dad.'

Nia tried to hide her astonishment as Daisy continued to gaze at the artwork on the walls. A tear trickled out of her eye, and she let it roll down her cheek.

Nia had no idea what to say. How did you comfort

someone who had lost a family member, especially in such horrible circumstances?

Luckily, Daisy spared her, and continued to explain. 'He was the only person who ever got me, you know?'

Nia nodded, though she didn't know, not really. She didn't even get herself, so doubted anyone else did.

'I lived with him when I was a kid. It was just the two of us. We didn't have much money, but we were happy. He taught me how to draw, and we'd spend the weekends collecting materials to turn into art at home. You should have seen our house – the council would have had a heart attack when they got it back off us.'

She laughed, but a second tear joined the first. Nia tried to fight the sympathy Daisy's story was making her feel. She needed to stay angry, so she could find Kayla.

'I had to go and live with my mum when Dad got locked up. I didn't know her, even though we lived close by. Dad told me she had a drug problem, but she must have convinced social services that she was clean.'

Nia felt a prickle of guilt as she thought about her own family. She had so many bad things to say about Mum, so much resentment. But she knew she was lucky really.

'I don't know why my mum took me in,' Daisy continued. 'She made an effort at first, but the cracks started to show pretty quickly. She took me shopping for a treat but she got caught shoplifting, so we had to leg it out of the shopping centre with security guards chasing us. And she couldn't stop slating Dad, making fun of his art and his mental health. I couldn't be close to someone like that.

'She was using drugs again too, and I was pretty much left to fend for myself. There was never any food in the house, and the electricity got cut off because she didn't pay the bills.'

'Dirty Daisy' had been one of her many nicknames at school. Nia dropped her gaze to her trainers.

'Then Mum got a new boyfriend and I couldn't stay with her any more, not with him in the house. I missed Dad, so I came to the last place he'd been alive.' Daisy's eyes brightened. 'I wasn't expecting to find something this amazing – I knew straight away this had been his room when I saw the walls. I guess he was in a special cell because of his mental health.'

She looked around the room, as though deciding to live in an abandoned prison was the most normal thing in the world. 'I'm so glad I came here. I'd never have seen all this if I hadn't.'

Nia frowned and wondered if it was possible that Daisy didn't know why her dad had been kept in the isolation cell. She found herself looking at the drawings with fresh eyes, seeing a troubled artist instead of a scary criminal. 'Which ones did you do?'

Daisy became suddenly animated as she pointed at the walls, talking Nia through her creations. She was trembling with passion, and Nia wondered if this was what Scott had seen when he had visited her all those times in the art studio. She tried not to think about why he had chosen them both. Did he think they'd be easy to manipulate?

'This one,' Daisy said, forcing Nia's thoughts away from Scott. She pointed at the girl on the wall, created from a mixture of rubbish and food wrappers. 'This one is my favourite.

It's supposed to be me, but as my dad saw me.' She looked cautiously at Nia.

'It's beautiful.'

Daisy could barely contain her smile, and Nia thought about how easy it was to make people feel good, and how rarely she did it.

'But what about this one?' Nia nodded towards the poster of Daisy's face. The holes where her eyes should have been stared blankly back.

Daisy blushed, the redness creeping up her white neck and all the way up to her hairline. 'I guess my art has always been a bit . . . dark.'

'And some of these,' Nia said slowly, pointing at the blackened drawings on the other side of the cell that she still didn't want to look at. 'They're pretty . . .'

'Terrifying?'

Nia nodded and chewed her lip, hoping she hadn't offended Daisy. A strange feeling was taking over her body, a weird dizziness. She couldn't stop looking at the vandalised poster of Daisy, the scratched-out eyes. *Missing girl, missing girl, missing girl.*

'He wasn't well,' Daisy said faintly, her voice wobbling and snapping Nia out of her trance. 'When he was with me, he was . . . better. Most of the time. But they locked him up anyway.'

Nia swilled the words around her mouth, knowing she should swallow them but unable to hold them back. 'What did he do?'

CHAPTER 27

'He shouldn't have been in here,' Daisy said, her voice darkening. 'He needed *help*, not prison. The charge they got him on was so stupid – "anti-social behaviour" or some rubbish, when really he was just trying to escape the noise in his own head.' The anger in her face faded, replaced by something exhausted, defeated. 'He never hurt anyone,' she whispered.

Daisy lowered herself to the ground as though she was suddenly too tired to remain standing. She sat among the blankets that had been strewn around the cell when Nia had ransacked the place in her search for Kayla. Nia guiltily wondered whether she should offer to help remake what must've been her bed.

Daisy's fingers curled around a tattered cloth, and she clutched it to her chest. Nia realised it was a T-shirt and didn't need to ask who it belonged to.

She sat beside Daisy, not close enough to touch her but close enough to just *be* there, she hoped. She sneaked a look at the poster again and her mouth opened in horror. The picture had changed – it wasn't Daisy, lost with scratched-out eyes, it was Kayla. Nia's breath caught in her throat. She blinked and the poster flicked back to a picture of Daisy.

'I miss him. I never found out what happened to him,' Daisy continued, as Nia pressed her trembling hands between her knees. 'They just told my mum that there had been an "altercation", whatever that means.'

Nia felt the blood drain from her face. Daisy didn't know. She hadn't seen the incident book.

'But Dad wasn't the kind of guy who got into altercations. He would do whatever he could to avoid them.'

How was it possible Daisy hadn't seen the incident book? Should she tell her? Would it help? Nia's brain swung back and forth between her options. The drawings on the walls seemed to press closer towards her.

Show Daisy the incident book, and she'd find out how her dad died. Keep it from her, and she wouldn't have to find out how her dad died.

'I begged my mum to find out more. Surely there has to be an investigation or something, if someone dies in prison?'

Nia realised with shock that Daisy was looking at her, waiting for an answer. 'Um,' she rasped, her mouth dry. 'I guess.'

'They wouldn't give her any more details. That's what she told me anyway.' Daisy pulled the T-shirt closer, stroking it across her chin. 'I just wish I knew more, so I could have some kind of closure, you know?'

Daisy sighed and at the same time as she said, 'Actually, it's probably for the best that I don't know,' Nia said, 'I know what happened to him.'

'What?'

Nia's eyes widened. Had Daisy heard her? Could she take it back?

'You know what happened to my dad?'

No, she couldn't.

'I, um, I . . .'

Daisy was right. It *was* better that she didn't know. What good could it possibly do her to see the long list of incidents blamed on her dad? Nia remembered the impression she had been given of Andrew Warren when she'd first come across his name. He seemed like a violent thug. Daisy shouldn't have to read that.

'Hello?' Daisy laughed, but her eyes gave away how frantic she was. 'Earth to Nia?'

Think, Nia. How could she get out of this and spare Daisy the pain she was sure to feel if she read the logbook? Her eyes darted around the room, but her mind remained blank under Daisy's scrutinising stare.

'Nia?'

'I, um . . . I just read about it in the paper,' she said lamely, knowing there was no way Daisy would accept that answer.

'There was only one paragraph about it in the local paper,' Daisy said, her voice hardening.

'Yeah,' Nia agreed, forcing her voice to sound light and airy. 'I just meant I know that he died, that's all.' She knew she was doing a terrible job of lying – she couldn't even look Daisy in the eye.

'No, that's not what you meant,' Daisy insisted, her eyes narrowing. 'Nia, tell me what you were going to say.'

Nia's mouth froze open as she finally met Daisy's gaze. 'Daisy.' She shook her head, willing Daisy to tell her to leave it, that they should talk about something else.

'Nia, it's my *dad*,' she begged. 'Tell me what you know!'

Nia closed her eyes. 'OK,' she whispered. She opened them to see Daisy standing, every muscle in her body tense. '*OK.*'

She stood, wishing they could get on with searching for Kayla. But there was no way Daisy would just let this drop, not now. And Nia needed Daisy on her side, so she could climb out of the cell block and get Mum.

'I found something,' Nia said, and left the cell.

Daisy scurried after her, her light footsteps barely making a sound on the cell-block floor.

'There's nothing in there,' Daisy said from behind her as Nia approached the guard box. 'They took everything when they cleared this place out.'

Nia opened the door, wishing she could protect Daisy from what she was about to show her.

But something in the guard box made her stop dead.

Lying on the table next to the red logbook was Kayla's precious book – the one she took everywhere.

Nia stared at it, trying to understand what it meant.

'Kayla?' she breathed.

Kayla had been here.

'No,' Daisy said from beside her, making Nia jump. 'No, that wasn't here before. I would have seen it.'

It took Nia a moment to realise that Daisy was talking about the logbook, not the sure sign that Kayla had been here, in this room. As Daisy reached towards the red book Nia snatched

Kayla's paperback, pressing it to her chest. *Black Beauty*.

'Daisy,' she spluttered, 'this is Kayla's. Kayla has been here, she—' Nia was almost sobbing with relief. Her sister was close.

But Daisy's attention was on the logbook, her thoughts focused on her own family. Nia stayed silent, leaning on the desk for support and studying her face as she read. Her ankle was hurting more than ever now, and she wondered if she'd done some serious damage running around on it.

She would let Daisy read, let her understand what had happened to her dad. Then they would find Kayla and get the hell out of here.

A range of emotions passed over Daisy's face, from astonishment, to disbelief, to anguish. Nia felt as though she were experiencing all of those feelings along with her. She prepared herself for Daisy's tears to fall. She wouldn't hesitate to reach out to her this time. She'd hold her close, even let her wipe her tears on her shoulder if that was what she needed. It was the least she could do.

But Daisy's face was contorted with anger, not sadness, when she finally reached the end of the book. 'Where did you get this?' she growled.

'I told you, I found it when I came down here,' Nia stuttered. 'It's—'

'No,' Daisy spat. 'I know this place. I know everything *in* this place. That book wasn't there. I would have seen it.'

'It was hidden underneath the desk.' Nia pointed to the space with her toe. 'I was poking around, looking for something cool to send a picture of to my friends, and I saw it.'

Daisy was breathing so heavily that Nia wondered if she

were having some kind of asthma attack. 'And did you?'

'Did I wha—'

'Did you send a picture of it to your pathetic friends?' Daisy waved the book in the air and Nia took a step backwards. The desk dug into the backs of her thighs.

Daisy's expression – her entire demeanour – had changed. She was vibrating with fury and glaring at Nia in a way that scared her.

'I—'

'I thought you might be different, but you're just like them,' Daisy snarled. 'You deserve everything you get, Nia.'

CHAPTER 28

Nia gasped as though Daisy had shoved her. She deserved everything she got? What did *that* mean?

Daisy was small and looked like a strong breeze could knock her over, but she was ferocious. 'Did you all have a good laugh about him?' Her face twisted with hatred as she did a scarily accurate impression of Olivia. 'Oh-em-gee, this guy is such a *freak*. He totes deserved what happened to him.'

There was a long pause as Nia stared at her, unable to speak.

'And I bet *you* were just loving it, weren't you?' Daisy hissed, her eyes bulging alarmingly. Nia's eyes darted to the doorway behind Daisy. Could she get past her? 'I bet you thought this was it – your chance for fame and glory. Your chance to finally be Little Miss *Popular*, just as you've always dreamed of.'

Nia winced at the venom in Daisy's voice. Was that really what she thought of her? She hugged Kayla's book closer. She couldn't deal with this, not now. She needed to get out of the guard box, out of this godawful prison.

She needed Kayla.

'Well, congratulations, princess!' Daisy shouted, and Nia jumped. 'You did it. Now Olivia thinks you're the coolest person she knows, and Scott has declared his undying love for you. Who cares who gets trampled in the process, right?'

Nia swallowed, her lip quivering. The worst thing about what Daisy was saying was that she knew it was true. She didn't care who she had to hurt to gain her friends' approval, even if that person was herself.

'*Is* that what happened, though, Nia?' Daisy asked, snapping her back to the present. 'Are you popular yet? Was breaking into this place enough? Will *anything* ever be enough?'

Nia remembered Kayla's face the night she had threatened her, slamming her bedroom door and closing her inside so she could party with her friends. She had been cruel to her sweet, kind little sister. She had *lost* her. Nia dropped her gaze and an image flashed into her mind of Kayla curled up cold and lonely in the dark.

Daisy shook her head in disgust. 'When I first realised you were coming down here, I thought . . .' She laughed and raised her eyes to the low ceiling in the guard box. 'I thought that you might be like me, not them. I thought you might be coming down here to escape from everything that's out there.' She pointed at the open door on the upper level. 'I was at the end of the passage – the one that leads from the visitor room. I thought I hadn't hidden in time and you'd seen me, but I guess it was too dark.'

So there *had* been something at the end of the tunnel, something moving in the gloom. If only Daisy had revealed herself then – things might be different.

'When I realised you were desperate enough to climb down into the cell block, I hid and waited to see what you would do.' Daisy gestured at the door Nia had heard opening when she thought the Ratman was after her and Kayla. 'I couldn't see you, but I could hear you snooping around and I hated the idea of you going through my stuff. But I told myself that you must be hurting to have come down here, and that we could help each other. That we could be . . . friends.'

Nia couldn't look at Daisy. She hadn't done anything to deserve her concern, but Daisy had wanted to help her from the second she saw her.

'But now I see that you're just like the others. All you care about is being *cool*. Well, you have no idea where that could lead you, Nia, none at all.'

Nia shivered at Daisy's sinister words. Was she still reading too much into things, or was Daisy always on the verge of revealing something else, some terrible secret about this place?

'It might have been better if you'd fallen when you climbed down here,' Daisy said quietly.

'Better?' Nia croaked, her throat sore and dry.

Daisy closed her eyes, and her fury seemed to ebb away as quickly as it had arrived. 'I'm sorry, I didn't mean . . . This is so messed up.'

Nia nodded. It was becoming more messed up by the second.

'I'm sorry too. I didn't mean to make fun of your dad. I would have never done it if I had known who he was . . .' Nia trailed off weakly, not bothering to finish the lie.

Daisy didn't acknowledge that Nia had spoken. 'It's not true, you know, any of this.' She shook the folder in front of

Nia's face. 'All this stuff they said about him, it's lies.'

Nia nodded, but Daisy didn't see.

'I don't know why, but someone obviously had it in for him. *More* than one person, by the looks of all these incidents. Something was going on and the guards were too thick to notice. It's obvious, though, isn't it?'

Nia blinked, wondering how she should reply, but glad that Daisy's anger had been drawn away from her.

'Even you must be able to see how obvious it is, what he was doing?'

Nia nodded slowly, hoping she'd given the right answer.

'They thought they were punishing him by putting him in isolation,' Daisy continued, 'but that's exactly what he wanted.'

Daisy looked out of the guard-box window and across the cell block. Her voice was quiet now, barely louder than a whisper. 'Someone out there wanted him dead, and the isolation cell was the only place he was safe.'

It made sense, especially after everything Daisy had said about her dad. He wasn't a fighter. He wasn't the man the incident log made him out to be. He was scared.

'I wonder where he died,' Daisy breathed. Her eyes were unfocused, her thoughts surely straying to the same morbid places that Nia's had when she'd first read the entries.

Nia watched Daisy and wished she could say or do something to take her pain away. Even though Daisy was an outcast, someone who had spent the last ten minutes screaming about how rubbish Nia was, she liked her.

Maybe Daisy was right. Maybe they did have something in common. Nia wasn't sure what, but she felt it – something that connected them. Maybe Nia was as big a weirdo as Daisy.

The difference, she realised, was that Daisy was a *nice* weirdo. Nia wasn't sure if she could say the same for herself.

'I'm sorry,' she whispered. 'I'm so sorry for showing you the incident book. And for ignoring you at school. And for calling you Disappearing Daisy.' Nia bit her lip, scared by the tide of apologies that had started to tumble out of her mouth.

Daisy stared at her for so long that Nia considered waving her hand in front of her face. She didn't like being scrutinised like this. What did Daisy see when she looked at her? A wannabe Olivia, or a girl not dissimilar to herself? Maybe Nia was a bit of both.

'It would be easier if you were just a straight-up bitch,' Daisy said softly.

Nia swallowed. 'Easier?'

Daisy sighed, finally releasing Nia from her gaze. 'I just . . . I don't know if I can trust you.'

A snort of disbelief escaped Nia's nose before she could catch it. Daisy looked up sharply.

'Sorry,' Nia said quickly, not wanting angry Daisy to make a reappearance. 'It's just, that's a bit rich.'

'You're just as twisted as I am, Nia.'

The flare of venom was back in Daisy's voice, but this time Nia didn't cower from it.

'You're not serious?' she screeched, unable to keep the disbelief out of her voice. 'I'm no angel, I know that, and trust me, I feel horrible about it. I've promised myself I'm going to change the second I find Kayla and get out of this shithole.' Nia swallowed, the mention of Kayla's name immediately bringing tears to her eyes. 'But you're the one who has been living in a prison and blatantly lying to me since the second we met! And don't think I haven't picked up on those weird little hints you keep dropping – "*It might have been better if you'd fallen*". What the hell did that mean? Better than *what*, Daisy?'

Nia prepared herself for Daisy's retort, hoping she could keep the tears at bay long enough to respond. Nia wasn't expecting the sudden look of fear that passed over Daisy's face.

'What?' she asked. 'What is it?'

Daisy blinked rapidly and shook her head as though clearing her thoughts. 'Maybe I was wrong.'

'Wrong about *what*, Daisy?'

'About you. About what you deserve.'

If Nia had felt dread at Daisy's words earlier, it was nothing compared to what she felt now.

'You have to understand—'

But whatever Daisy was planning on saying was interrupted by the sound of laughter, rising and falling like a hysterical hyena. It was coming from behind the door they'd taken to get into the cell block.

CHAPTER 29

Nia's heart stalled, then began pounding so quickly she could feel it in her throat. Her eyes were fixed on the cell-block door, her lips parted in horror as the manic laughter got louder, closer.

She prised her gaze away to look at Daisy, who was watching Nia with a tortured expression.

'Who?' Nia whispered, sounding as small and scared as she felt.

Daisy opened her mouth, but only air came out. She shook her head helplessly.

Nia turned back to the sound. Another feeling was coming over her, a feeling that she shouldn't be scared, she should be furious. Whoever, or *whatever*, was coming had to know where Kayla was. Her hand found the lifeless phone in her pocket. She could use it in the same way she had when she'd thought Daisy was the Ratman. She could wait next to the door, and when the moment was right she wouldn't hesitate to bring the phone smashing down into their skull.

But another chorus of laughter made her jump. It didn't sound human. Could she even inflict any damage on it, whatever it was?

Daisy made a strange croaking noise. Her gaze flitted between Nia and the door as though she were making the most difficult decision of her life. Finally she settled on Nia, her eyes bulging and wild.

'RUN!' she hissed.

Nia didn't need to be told twice.

But her ankle couldn't take any more abuse, and she half crumpled to the ground as she tried to stand, Kayla's book slipping from her fingers. Daisy clutched her under the armpits, groaning as she yanked her up. Nia screamed silently as pain reverberated up her leg. But adrenaline, and Daisy wrenching her mercilessly forward, urged her on.

What was Daisy so scared of?

They hobbled away from the sound, which was growing increasingly more frenzied. Daisy panted beneath Nia's arm, and Nia wished she didn't have to rely on her. How was she supposed to trust her? She knew more, *much* more, than she'd been letting on. She'd been lying to Nia this entire time.

But what choice did Nia have? It was either trust Daisy or stay put and take her chances with the Ratman.

'Where are we going?' Nia whimpered, not knowing how much more she could take. 'I thought that door was the only way into the cell block?'

'It isn't,' Daisy grunted, not slowing down for a second. 'I lied to you.'

'No shit,' Nia growled.

There was another door, opposite the one Nia and Kayla had fled down. 'I heard something,' Nia remembered. 'Coming from behind this door – that's why me and Kayla ran away in the first place.'

'It was me,' Daisy said, pulling them ever closer.

'But it's locked!' Nia insisted. She'd tried it when she had searched every last inch of the cell block looking for Kayla. She'd rattled the handle, kicked the door, pounded her fists against it while she shouted her sister's name. It was a hundred per cent locked.

Daisy led Nia to the wall next to the door and unwrapped her arm from around her shoulders. She fumbled in her pocket, and produced . . .

'A *key*?' Nia hissed. The feeling that she shouldn't be following Daisy anywhere grew stronger.

'I'll explain later,' Daisy gasped, her face flushed from the strain of supporting Nia.

She pulled Nia through and locked the door behind them. Nia's heart slowed a little. Did this mean she was safe now?

Maybe, but Kayla wasn't. Kayla was still out there.

The thought physically tugged Nia back towards the door. She put her hand out towards Daisy, praying she would understand. 'Kayla,' she whispered.

But Daisy shook her head. 'I can't . . . I just need to *think*, OK?'

Nia nodded and wished she knew what kind of dilemma Daisy was wrestling with. She was obviously torn between helping Nia and . . . *what*? Nia had no clue.

Daisy seemed to melt to the floor. She curled up with her

head resting on her knees and wrapped her arms around her legs, as though she were trying to disappear. Nia watched her, trying not to make a sound, scared that whatever Daisy was figuring out would not go in her favour if she distracted her.

But the minutes ticked by and Nia wondered just how long she was supposed to wait for Daisy to decide if she would help reunite her with Kayla.

She shuffled to the locked door and tentatively pressed her ear against it. The laughter had stopped. It was so quiet that Nia wondered if she had imagined the whole thing, if the terrifying sound had been in her head. But Daisy's reaction proved that it hadn't been. They were running from something very real.

At least they were safe here, for now.

She glanced at Daisy again. She hadn't moved. Nia resisted the urge to poke her with her toe.

She looked around, noticing that this corridor was slightly roomier than the one on the opposite side of the cell block. Lighter too, thanks to the small window high up on one of the walls. Through it, Nia could only see more red brick and the constant pattering of rain.

She thought of Mum and wondered what she would be doing at that moment. Would she ever speak to Nia again?

There was another door on the left, just before the corridor bent around a corner. Nia leaned on the wall and dragged herself towards it. It couldn't hurt to learn as much about this place as she could so that she'd be ready for . . . whatever came next.

The door was open, and she pushed it away from her

carefully. She glanced at Daisy to see if she stirred. But she must have been lost deep in thought, because she didn't react at all.

A sharp, strangely sweet smell hit her nostrils and she gagged. As her eyes adjusted to the gloom, she realised she'd found a storeroom. Much like the visitor room, it seemed to have been left in the same state it would have been in if prisoners were still here. A mop balanced in a bucket in the corner. It was full of filthy water – that must be the source of the smell. A workbench was littered with notebooks. Nia moved closer, scanning the titles that were written in black sharpie – MAINTENANCE LOG, WORK ROTA.

There was a glass-fronted box nailed to the wall above the desk. It was filled with tools – hammers, files, chisels, even a saw. The remains of a padlock lay on the workbench and the wood of the cabinet was splintered where it had been smashed open.

Nia stepped towards the box, her hand reaching out for a hammer. It would make a better weapon than her phone. But there was something in her way, an old tarpaulin on the floor. Her toe touched something solid as she leaned over it.

'No! Don't go in there!'

Daisy's voice made her leap in surprise. She was lunging towards Nia, her arms outstretched to pull her back. But it was too late. Nia had already seen it. Poking out from beneath the tarpaulin was something contorted and grey. It was a human foot.

CHAPTER 30

Nia recoiled from the tarp, crashing into Daisy and sending them both to the floor. She shuffled backwards, her limbs tangling with Daisy's, her eyes never leaving the foot.

She willed her view to change and reveal that the limb was in fact something else, something innocent that belonged in a storeroom. But the longer she stared, the more certain she grew that this couldn't be blamed on her imagination, or stress, or anything other than the fact there was at least *part* of a dead body in there with them.

She clamped her mouth shut, not wanting to breathe the same air that the rotting flesh existed in. As she took in the details – the puckered grey skin, the overgrown toenails and the sickly smell – a single maggot wriggled from under the tarp and slid off the end of the foot on to the floor.

Nia scrambled out of the room and vomited against the wall in the corridor.

She was vaguely aware of a hand tentatively patting her shoulder as she bent double, her breathing ragged and painful.

There was a body in there. *A dead body.*

Her thoughts turned to Daisy. Daisy, who had tried to stop her finding it. Daisy, who hadn't freaked out when she had. *Daisy.*

'What,' Nia breathed from her bent-over position. 'The. *Fuck*, Daisy?'

The hand on her shoulder withdrew.

Nia stood slowly, grimacing at the disgusting puddle at her feet and praying her head rush wouldn't send her down to the floor. Daisy stood with her back against the opposite wall, her head turned to the side to avoid Nia's furious stare.

'You need to start talking,' Nia hissed. She wiped her mouth on her sleeve and wished she had a bottle of water. 'Right. Now.'

'I . . .' Daisy started, her face twisting as she went through a bombardment of emotions. 'I'm sorry you had to see that.'

'*Sorry I had to see it?*' Nia whispered. 'There's a body, a dead body, and you knew it was there! I think there are bigger issues here than the fact I happened to stumble upon it!'

Daisy withdrew even further into her baggy clothes. Nia wondered if a slap would convince her to start talking.

'What—' Nia swallowed, unsure what questions she should be asking. What did she actually want to know about the corpse that lay less than three metres away from her? She licked her lips, pulling a face at the taste of bile, and settled on, 'Who is it?'

Daisy inhaled sharply. Nia was suddenly reminded of the presence lurking on the other side of the door to the cell block and spun round. The door was still locked. When she returned her focus to Daisy, the girl's face was contorted with misery.

Nia could make no sense of the strangled sounds that escaped Daisy's lips as she tried to speak through the sobbing.

And then the thought hit Nia so hard that she staggered backwards from the force of it . . . Kayla.

Kayla was missing. Nia had been sure that the only place she could be was back in the cell block. Daisy couldn't look Nia in the eye.

Kayla.

Nia leapt back into the storeroom and flung the tarp away to reveal the body beneath.

She turned to vomit for the second time.

Oh god. Oh god. Oh god.

Why had she looked? *Stupid, stupid Nia.* She would do anything to un-see the gruesome sight of dead flesh and empty eye-sockets. It wasn't Kayla, of course it wasn't. The foot was *grey*, for god's sake. It had obviously been there for . . . Nia had no idea how long it took for a body to decompose, but it clearly couldn't be Kayla.

Her eyes were pulled back towards the body, despite her head screaming at her to get out of the room and never look back.

It was a man. An old man, by the looks of the grizzled beard that clung to his bony jaw. His mouth hung open, revealing a few lone brown teeth. His eyes weren't gone, as Nia had first thought, but they were completely translucent – a kind of milky grey-blue colour.

Nia had seen enough. She wobbled out of the room, her hand gripping the doorframe as the floor tilted beneath her feet.

Daisy was still crying, a high-pitched keening that would

have made Nia want to reach out to her, if she hadn't felt so completely numb. She slid down the wall opposite Daisy and watched her, unable to fathom what could have happened or how Daisy was connected.

Did she *know* the dead man?

Nia looked into the storeroom from where she sat. She could still see the foot.

Who was he? A fresh thought came to her and she dismissed it quickly. It couldn't be Daisy's dad, though the level of distress Daisy was currently in did make Nia wonder for a moment. But Andrew Warren had died in prison. They'd left a lot of crap behind when they'd left this place, but a body would have been a whole new level of negligence. There was no way.

Then *who?*

And – Nia forced down the acid rising in her throat and prayed the thought wouldn't make her sick again – how had he died?

Looking at the whiteness of his facial hair, and the state of his teeth, it wouldn't be that unreasonable to assume he'd died from natural causes. At least, it wouldn't have been, if it wasn't for the laughter they'd heard in the cell block. Laughter that quite clearly belonged to someone Daisy was afraid of.

Kayla.

It was time to get Daisy talking. Nia took a breath. The floor felt more solid beneath her now that her focus was back. But as she watched Daisy cry, trying to decide whether to coax or scare the truth out of her, there was a sound in the cell block.

'Nia!'

The voice stopped Nia's heart. Daisy snatched her head up, her eyes wide with shock.

'NIA!'

It was Kayla. There was no mistaking it. Her little sister was out there, screaming for her.

CHAPTER 31

'Kayla's gone!' Mum said.

'What?' replied Nia, squeezing into Kayla's box of a room. 'No, she isn't.'

But Mum was right. Her bed was empty.

Nia threw back the covers, despite the sheets still being smooth and undisturbed. She tossed the pillows over as though Kayla could somehow be underneath them, all the time repeating her name. Mum was doing the same behind her in an urgent whisper, so as not to wake Deon.

The under-bed drawers next – maybe Kayla was hiding? No, empty. Kayla wasn't the kind of kid to play tricks.

The curtains were yanked open, revealing a locked window. Nia jiggled the handle, just to make sure. Mum was checking the wardrobe, looking between every single item of clothing as though Kayla might have made herself 2D.

Mark was flying through the other two bedrooms, flinging doors open, calling Kayla's name so frequently that he wouldn't have been able to hear even if she had replied.

'Where has she gone?' Mum shrieked, grabbing Nia by the arms. 'Nia, where has she gone?!'

'I don't know. I don't know!'

'You must know! She was here when we left. What happened?'

Nia shook her head helplessly, desperately trying to think. She had told Kayla to stay in her room – that was the last time she saw her. She'd brought her dinner, but the bread and ham looked like they hadn't been touched. Then she realised.

'Cream cheese,' she whispered.

'What?'

'Cream cheese. I forgot the cream cheese!' She pointed helplessly to the untouched food on the bedside table.

'She won't eat sandwiches without cream cheese,' Mum whispered, and Nia nodded, their eyes locked in horror.

'She'll be downstairs then!' Mark cried, overhearing from the landing. 'She'll be getting it from the fridge!'

But Nia and Mum shook their heads at the same time as he thundered down the stairs. 'We ran out this afternoon,' Mum said softly.

They knew what it meant, but they didn't want to say it out loud. The reality was too impossible, too horrible to speak of.

'Well, what then?' Mark shouted when he found the kitchen empty. 'Where is she?'

Mum closed her eyes. 'The shop.'

Nia was the first out of the door. The cold hit her like a sledgehammer to the chest, but she didn't turn back for her coat. She was running, flying past lampposts, leaping off kerbs and across roads without checking for traffic.

She could hear a strange groaning sound as she ran, and it took her a while to realise it was her saying, 'Please, please, please,' over and over as though the word would make Kayla appear, safe.

The shop was closed. Nia leaned on the door, sucking air into her burning lungs. Would Kayla have got there when it was still open?

No, she realised. If Kayla had arrived before closing time Mrs Singh would be looking after her right now – she knew the whole family from how often they visited the shop. She'd have brought Kayla home the second she'd arrived.

Nia looked around, the cold making it hard for her to catch her breath, her lips already chattering uncontrollably.

Think, Nia, think.

Where would Kayla have gone?

She heard footsteps and spun round, daring to believe. But it was Mark, sprinting towards her, her coat clutched in his hands.

'She's not here, she's not here!' Nia shrieked.

'Put this on,' Mark ordered, his voice calm despite the panic in his eyes.

Nia tried to push it away – she didn't deserve to be warm. But Mark insisted, wrapping it around her shoulders. 'It's freezing out here. You need your coat.'

Nia couldn't bear to look at him. This was all her fault, so how was he acting so caring towards her? If she were Mark and someone had lost *her* daughter, she wouldn't be worried about them getting cold.

Terror gripped her heart.

'Was Kayla's coat gone?' she whispered, though she feared she already knew the answer.

Mark swallowed. 'No.'

Nia wailed and covered her mouth with her hand. There was barely anything to Kayla and she felt the cold terribly, but she couldn't reach the coat rack. Nia tried to remember what she'd been wearing, but couldn't. She hadn't even helped her into her pyjamas. She was the worst sister in the world.

An icy wind howled through the alleyway beside the shop, singing a haunting song.

Nia continued to search, but every second that passed made her feel more hopeless. 'Make sure you check beneath the hedges, in case she's crawled underneath,' she called to Mark. But it was too dark, too cold, too impossible to find a tiny seven-year-old out here. Her thoughts wandered to Mum and the baby, and she caught up with Mark again.

'Mark, where's Mum?'

'At the house,' Mark answered, not pausing his search. 'She called the police and she's waiting there for them, in case Kayla comes home.'

At least she and baby Deon weren't out here because of her, scrabbling around in the dark, freezing.

Kayla must be so *cold*.

They needed to speed up. They needed more people, more ground covered. Surely she wouldn't have just stayed here, by the shop, once she'd realised it was closed? She'd have tried to go home, wouldn't she?

So why hadn't she made it?

Nia shook her head. Thoughts like that weren't helping. She

ran to the nearest front door and hammered on it with both fists, needing whoever was inside to hear how urgent this was. Mark looked up in surprise, then nodded when he realised what she was doing.

A light came on and a reedy voice called through the letterbox, 'Who is it?'

'Hello?' Nia had to shout over the worsening gale. 'My little sister is missing, have you seen anything?'

The door opened immediately, revealing an old woman in her nightgown. She shuddered as the wind swept into her hallway but kept her worried eyes focused on Nia. 'A little girl? Wait, I know you – I've seen you in the shop with your little sister. Oh my, it's not her, is it, the girl who's gone missing?'

Nia nodded, nervous energy making her bounce on the spot. 'Yes, it's her – Kayla. We think she came here earlier tonight, but we're not sure how long ago. Have you seen anything, heard anything?'

The old woman was shaking her head, and Nia didn't waste time hanging around to hear her apologies. She jogged to the next door and repeated the process, with the same results.

Before long, the street was filled with concerned neighbours. They wrapped their winter coats around themselves. Some brought torches, some brought dogs, some brought useless words of sympathy that Nia didn't want to hear.

The same questions kept being asked, 'Who's missing?' 'How long has she been out here for?' 'Why was she on her own?' In the confusion, new people who arrived didn't realise that Nia and Mark were the family and failed to conceal their predictions, 'A child won't last long out here, not in this weather.'

Too many people; no one *doing* anything. Nia began to worry she'd made a mistake – would it be harder to find Kayla with all these bodies around, making noise? What if they were trampling on evidence or something?

The shopfront was illuminated and the crowd squinted and shielded their eyes. Nia almost cried with relief when she saw the police car pull in, its headlights blindingly bright in the dark night. They'd find Kayla.

The police gave instructions. 'Spread out and don't leave a single stone unturned,' and the crowd dispersed. Nia and Mark stuck together, retracing their steps to the house. The sound of Kayla's name could be heard all around. A few times Nia thought she heard someone shouting, 'I've found her!' but it was just wishful thinking.

Nia had no idea how much time had passed. It felt like hours. The volume of police officers increased, their dogs straining at their leads, desperate to get on with the job. Nia wanted to tell them that Kayla was scared of dogs, but Mark told her that wasn't important right now. She noticed that there were fewer people on the streets, and her fear mixed with anger – had they given up?

Nia swore that she would never stop searching, but the cold crept into her veins and made her dizzy. She stumbled over a kerb, her numb foot responding sluggishly. Her phone slipped out of her pocket, the back-camera and torch shattering as it hit the pavement. Mark gripped her elbow, stopping her from crashing to the ground after her phone. She couldn't focus on him; everything felt woozy.

'I'm taking you home,' he told her.

She could hear her feeble protests as though they were coming from someone else far away, but she didn't have the strength to argue as he guided her. The heat of the house hit her as they opened the front door, and Mum appeared, staring intensely, wordlessly demanding an update.

'No sign of her,' Mum and Mark said at the same time, their faces crumpling in unison.

Nia was taken through to the living room, where a young police officer wrapped a foil blanket round her.

She began to shake.

She could hear Mum and Mark filling each other in, but it was clear there was nothing new to be shared. A two-mile radius had been thoroughly searched, with not a single hint of Kayla's presence being revealed.

'I'm heading back out there,' Mark said after a few minutes of warming up. 'I can't stay here; I have to do something.'

'I'll come with you,' Mum replied, reaching for her coat.

Mark shook his head. 'You can't, love, you need to stay in case Deon wakes up. And for Kayla . . . when she comes home.'

Mark pulled Mum into his chest as she cried.

'Are you warming up?' the officer asked Nia.

She glanced up at him. He didn't look much older than her. She nodded, though the trembling seemed to be getting worse as the sensation flooded back to her fingertips, making her flesh burn and itch.

The front door clicked and Nia snatched her head up, but it was just Mark leaving. Mum came back into the living room, her eyes puffy.

'You must be freezing,' she said to Nia. 'I'll make you a hot chocolate.' She turned to the officer. 'Another cup of tea, Dan?'

'Yes, please.'

Nia rose to her feet, shooting a scathing look at Officer Dan. 'No, Mum, you shouldn't be making people drinks!'

But Mum raised her hand and insisted, 'It helps. Keeping busy, doing something, *helps*.'

Nia nodded and let her go, not really understanding, but knowing not to argue. They sat and drank their drinks, Nia refreshing the post that she had put up, asking people to keep an eye out for Kayla. Shame overwhelmed her whenever she read a comment blaming the parents for not keeping a better eye on her.

Every time the officer's walkie-talkie made a sound, Nia and Mum jumped, staring hopefully at the device. But it was always a short update, confirming yet another section of the town had been searched with no sign of Kayla.

Minutes merged into hours.

And Kayla didn't come home.

CHAPTER 32

Kayla had finally been found at two a.m., shivering in someone's shed. Another hour outside in the freezing cold and she'd have died. But she was safe.

That time.

And now, because of Nia, her life was in danger again.

Nia rose to her feet, unable to keep the tremor out of her knees. She rushed towards the door, wishing she had a plan.

'NIA!'

She flinched. There was no mistaking it. It was Kayla, and she sounded terrified.

As her hand gripped the cool, rusting metal of the door handle, she turned to see how Daisy was reacting to the screams. She was frozen, her mouth open in a horrified grimace, her eyes as unblinking as the corpse in the store cupboard. However Daisy was involved in this mess, it was clear she wasn't going to be any use to Nia right now.

Nia would just have to hope that she wouldn't be a hindrance either.

She turned the key in the lock and opened the door.

Kayla stood in the middle of the cell block looking impossibly tiny. Nia lopsidedly sprinted towards her, gritting her teeth through the pain in her ankle. It could be a trap, it probably *was* a trap, but Nia didn't care. She needed to get to Kayla, to pull her close and hug her like she should have done every day since she was born.

Kayla burst into noisy tears as Nia skidded down on her knees so she could wrap her little sister's entire body around hers. She rocked her back and forth, cradling her like she had when she was a baby and Nia had insisted on carrying her everywhere like a doll. Nia's sobbing joined Kayla's, and she squeezed tighter.

Nia opened her eyes to see the cell block swimming in tears. Droplets flicked off her cheeks as she looked back and forth, searching for the owner of the demonic laugh. There was no one. But with fifty-odd cells on this floor alone, Nia knew that not being able to see them didn't mean they weren't there.

She reluctantly pulled Kayla away from her chest and held her at arm's length with trembling hands. 'Are you OK?' she asked, checking her over. She looked scared, and her eyes were swollen from crying. But Nia couldn't see any signs of injury. 'Are you hurt?'

Kayla nodded her head and Nia gasped. 'Where? Where are you hurt?'

But Kayla frowned and hiccupped. 'No, I mean I am OK. I'm not hurt.'

Nia hugged her again, breathing a sigh of relief. Only Kayla could claim to be OK in this situation. She should be screaming at Nia, calling her a terrible sister for leaving her. But Kayla was the purest, most kind-hearted person. Nia knew now that she would stop at nothing to protect her. She just wished it hadn't taken her so long to figure that out.

'I'm sorry,' she whispered, stroking the back of Kayla's plaits. 'I'm sorry for losing you again.'

Kayla's tears returned. Nia wished they were being reunited back in the soft-play centre, somewhere she could focus on making things right between them and the rest of her family. Somewhere safe.

'Kayla,' she said, stroking a tear off her face. Where to start? She wanted to know everything that had happened since she'd lost her outside the hanging room, but they couldn't spend time on the detail. Nia needed to know what they were up against. 'Who took you?'

Kayla's eyes widened with terror and Nia's heart clenched. What had happened to her?

'I don't know,' Kayla finally whispered.

Worry swept over Nia. They couldn't afford to have a repeat of Kayla shutting down like earlier.

'Please, sweetie, try to think. I know it's scary, but I need to know what's going on so I can keep us safe.'

Kayla nibbled her lip and frowned as though she were trying her hardest. 'I couldn't see their face.'

Nia's imagination fired the possibilities around her head. Had Kayla been blindfolded? Was there something wrong with the face of the person who had her? Did they even *have* a face?

It wasn't important, not now, Nia realised. They just had to get out of there, then they could dwell on the details later. She looked over her shoulder at the door that led to the storeroom. It *had* to lead to another way out. Or, at the very least, somewhere they could hide until the police arrived.

Nia shuddered as she thought of the storeroom. Had the old man been doing the same – looking for somewhere safe to stay hidden?

Stop it, Nia. This kind of thinking wasn't helpful. She had to stay strong.

'Let's get out of here,' she said, and rose gingerly to her feet. She tried not to focus on the hope shining out of Kayla's face. Her sister really thought Nia had a plan. Nia didn't want to admit that all she had was fear.

Nia grimaced as her bad foot touched the floor. The previous adrenaline had disappeared and left nothing but pain behind. 'I've hurt my ankle,' she told Kayla, trying to keep her voice steady. 'It's not bad, but I might need to lean on you a little, OK?'

Kayla nodded seriously but staggered under Nia's weight as they took their first steps.

It was going to take an excruciatingly long time for them to reach the door.

Please let it be unlocked.

Daisy wouldn't leave them in here, would she? Nia had no idea. One minute Daisy was someone she could empathise with – someone strange and confusing, but also talented and kind. But the second Nia thought she understood her, she became dark and secretive.

Nia just hoped she'd done enough to convince Daisy that

she didn't in fact deserve everything she was going to get.

Almost there.

A metallic clang echoed around the cell block. The demented laughter joined it, bouncing around the room as though the sisters were surrounded. Kayla screamed, but Nia was too terrified to make a sound.

She turned slowly, tugging Kayla behind her back to shield her. Standing on the other side of the cell block, lovingly stroking the gleaming blade of a long knife, stood a figure.

CHAPTER 33

Nia understood what Kayla had meant when she'd said she couldn't see his face. There was a pillowcase over his head. Rough eyeholes had been cut in the fabric, but they didn't quite line up, so all Nia could see were two black holes. He wore a plain tracksuit, but the baggy clothing didn't hide the size of the man. He was large and muscular, and would be much, much stronger than Nia.

In the hand that didn't hold the knife, he grasped the dead pigeon. Nia watched as he squeezed so hard that the bird's head came off. Its limp body fell to the ground.

He slowly raised his bloody hand and waggled his fingers at Nia, waving like a young girl would. He let the mangled pigeon head drop to the floor. Nia shivered as he brought the knife to where his mouth would be, running it across the pillowcase as though he was licking the blade.

Nia kept her fingers gripped around Kayla's shoulder, terrified she'd disappear again if she let go. The thought that this . . . *freak* had kept Kayla captive all this time made Nia want to scream.

How would Kayla ever recover from this nightmare?

But Nia was getting ahead of herself. They had to get out of here first.

She took a slow step backwards, gently pushing Kayla towards their escape route. The masked man took a step forward.

She stepped again. This time his step was bigger. It was clear he wasn't going to allow them to maintain the distance between them.

Shit.

How would this sick game of cat and mouse end? What did he *want*? Why hadn't he already hurt Kayla, if he'd had her all this time? Was he just messing with them?

What the hell was she supposed to do?

She took another step back, trying not to wobble on her bad leg. The last thing she needed was for him to know that she was injured.

He stepped with them.

Nia tried to speak, but only a strangled croak escaped her mouth. She cleared her throat and tried again. 'What do you want?'

She wished she could keep the fear out of her voice.

The man cocked his head to one side. He made another creepy gesture by twirling his finger around the knife. And then he laughed.

It was the most horrible thing Nia had ever heard. How did such a big man have such a high-pitched childlike giggle?

The laughter stopped so suddenly that the silence made Nia jump. The man's shoulders were still, as though he were deadly serious.

Kayla's shoulders trembled beneath Nia's fingers.

She sneaked a glance at the door. They were close. But would they be able to get to it, open it, get through it and close it behind them before he reached them? And that's if it was even unlocked. Nia sucked air into her lungs as she imagined the blade of the knife slicing into her flesh.

How was she going to get them out of this?

Daisy.

Her grip tightened around Kayla, and she took another step backwards that was quickly copied by pillow-face.

Daisy must know something. Daisy was the key. Daisy had been living down here for weeks with this psychopath and was still alive.

They needed to get through that door.

And, Nia realised with startling certainty, even if she had to push Kayla through and slam the door after her so that she could face the killer alone, she would do it. She would have to trust that Daisy would do the right thing when presented with a tiny, wonderful seven-year-old.

Nia swallowed and stood a little straighter. She felt better, now that she had a plan. Even if that plan likely ended with her lying dead in a pool of her own blood.

They must be nearly at the door now, and there was still a good distance between them and the masked man. Nia turned to check how far they had to go. Standing just a metre away, between them and the door, was another man. But this one didn't wear a mask.

It was Scott.

CHAPTER 34

Nia nearly sobbed with relief. Scott was here. He was *here*. He must have been so worried about her that he'd come to find her, and now they were safe, because Scott wouldn't let the masked man hurt them.

But something about Scott's expression was off. He was . . . grinning.

Nia felt the smile slide off her own face and she stopped herself from running towards him. His expression hadn't changed, and for a horrible moment Nia wondered if he was actually dead, propped up against the door somehow.

But then he blinked, and his easy smile grew even wider, revealing the dimples that had enchanted Nia since the day she first set eyes on him.

'Scott?' she whispered. She drew Kayla closer towards her.

She stood sideways so she could see both the masked man and Scott. She didn't know which one of them to shield Kayla from.

'Hi, babe,' Scott said lightly, as though they'd bumped into each other in town. Nia waited for him to explain, but he seemed to think that his greeting was adequate.

What the hell was he doing down here?

Nia's head swivelled between them. She desperately wanted to believe that there was somehow an innocent explanation, that Scott wasn't involved in . . . whatever *this* was.

'What are you *doing* here?' Nia breathed, praying his explanation would mean an end to this nightmare. Maybe it would even be something they could laugh about together in future.

Scott shrugged, effortlessly cool as always. 'Just fancied a look around.'

A look around.

That's what he always said when they found somewhere worth exploring, like the abandoned restaurant. *'Let's have a look around.'*

OK, Nia told herself. *Coming inside the prison isn't so strange, for Scott. But he wouldn't come alone . . .*

Nia turned towards the masked man and her fear was replaced by cold fury as the reality clicked.

The man started giggling again. His high-pitched shrieks made him bend double at the waist. When he stood, the pillowcase was in his hand. Max.

'Sike!' he shrieked, pointing his finger at Nia before dissolving into another fit of laughter.

Of course.

Scott soundlessly joined in the laughter, his eyes still on Nia. Max was struggling to breathe, as though Nia's appalled face was the funniest thing he'd ever seen.

'Oh my god, Nia,' Max spluttered. 'Your face. That was priceless.'

But Nia was watching Scott. He was still grinning, not even the slightest bit concerned by the fact that Nia wasn't remotely amused.

'Scott?' she said sharply. She'd never spoken to him like this before, but she was struggling to contain her rage as much as Max struggled with his laughter. 'Have you . . . have you been in here this whole time?'

Scott nodded. 'We got here as soon as you told us where you were. I couldn't believe you were finally going to see our special place.'

Special place?

'But the messages,' Nia spluttered. 'The photo of you all in town . . .'

'It was taken in Cell Block D,' Scott smiled. 'And we've been together the whole time. Well, apart from when we split up for certain tasks.'

His eyes glittered as he grinned over her shoulder at Max.

'What *tasks*?' Nia whispered.

Max's booming voice made Nia jump. 'Leaving birdy for you to find, making sure you were in the right place at the right time, looking after your sis,' he said, counting the cruel tricks they had played on her on his fingers. 'Oh, and messing with the trapdoor in the hanging room so you'd have a little shock.'

Nia stared at Scott in horror as Max dissolved into more fits of laughter.

Scott shrugged again, a smirk twitching the corner of his lips. He gently tipped his head to one side, reached out and stroked a frazzled lock of hair away from Nia's forehead. 'Chill out, babe. It's just a laugh.'

'I'm still waiting for the punchline,' Nia snapped.

Max let out a low whistle. 'Ooooh, time for a domestic!' He leaned towards Nia and she recoiled, remembering his mouth pressing against hers that night at her house. 'If you guys want to make up afterwards, there's plenty of cosy rooms here.' He made a filthy gesture with his fingers and Nia resisted the urge to slap them away.

She turned back to Scott. 'I don't understand. This was all . . . a joke?'

'Prank of the century, baby!' Max crowed. Nia felt Kayla flinch behind her, cowering away from him. Another wave of anger flooded her body.

She rounded on Max, who was a good foot taller than her. 'You *kidnapped* my baby sister, for a prank?'

The smile dropped from Max's face. 'God, Nia, you've always been such a boring bitch.'

Nia's chin wobbled. How was it possible that even now those words hurt her? Why was part of her still desperate to prove that she wasn't boring, that she belonged with them?

'I hardly *kidnapped* her,' Max continued, gesturing in the air with his knife. 'We just hung out for a bit, right, kid?'

Kayla whimpered and hid her face in Nia's hoody. Nia pushed her need to please away, replacing it with a deep hatred. She would never, *ever* care about impressing Scott and his friends again. What they'd done to Kayla was unforgiveable.

'It's not funny,' she hissed at both of them. 'None of this is *fucking funny*.'

Scott pulled a face at Max and muttered, 'Time of the month,' which prompted another round of laughter from Max.

Nia was done.

'I'm getting out of here,' she said, curling her lip in disgust, but realising she still had no clue *how* to get her and Kayla out.

Scott stood a little straighter, making it clear he wasn't about to step aside and let them through the door behind him. Maddeningly, Nia found she still couldn't look him in his stupid, pretty eyes without blushing.

'Scott,' she sighed. God, she was tired. What did he *want* from her? Was she just a plaything to him?

He stepped towards her, so close she could feel his breath on her face. His fingers traced a line down her cheek, pausing to gently pluck her bottom lip. 'I thought you might want to stay for a bit.' He paralysed her with his eyes, the multitude of colours taking her breath away even now. 'We could hang out. I've missed you.'

Nia's heart was fluttering like a panicked bird. This is what she'd wanted. This is why she'd come down here in the first place. Was she going to throw that away, all because she couldn't take a joke?

She raised her chin and returned his gaze. She hadn't decided what her response would be until the words left her lips. 'Fuck you, Scott.'

Pride swelled within her chest. She had done it. She had broken the spell. But her elation was cut short by the sudden crack of Scott's hand against her cheek. She gasped, staggering against Kayla. Tears came before she could stop them, and she raised her fingers to the hot mark he had left on her face.

He'd hit her. Scott had *hit* her.

His playful smile had gone, as had the bright specks of colour in his eyes. They looked dark and furious.

'Ouch, that was a stinger!' Max winced, though he didn't seem at all surprised by what Scott had just done.

Scott leaned towards Nia and she trembled. 'That was a mistake,' he told her softly.

Nia tugged Kayla behind her so that she was sandwiched between her and the wall. Scott was many things, most of them not very nice, she saw that now. But *this*? This was something different. This wasn't cruel pranks or peer pressure. Nia felt it with every fibre of her being – things had just gotten serious, and she was in danger.

'Aw, man,' Max said, his obnoxious voice echoing around the cell block. 'I thought for a second you might be up for being part of the gang, Nia.'

A dainty giggle joined the sound of Max's booming voice. Nia looked around frantically for the source of the sound. She should have known the boys wouldn't be alone.

CHAPTER 35

Olivia and Chloe emerged from one of the cells. Olivia sashayed towards them like a model on a catwalk.

'Hi, Kayla!' Chloe said brightly as she tried to copy Olivia's signature walk.

Nia felt Kayla shift her weight to peer out from behind her. 'Hi, Chloe,' she said softly.

A jolt of nausea hit Nia. She turned to Kayla, terrified that somehow she was also involved in this whole set-up. 'Kayla, how do you know Chloe?'

Kayla swallowed. 'She brought me down here, from up there.' Kayla pointed up at the hole in the wall two storeys above them.

Nia thought back to when Kayla had appeared in the isolation cell, confused and unable to explain how she'd got down there. 'Why didn't you tell me how you'd got into the cell block?' Nia whispered, wishing the others weren't listening to every word she said.

Kayla's lip trembled as fresh tears fell. 'She said that if I told anyone, a ghost with a dead face would kill us all,' she squeaked. Nia wrapped her arm around Kayla, hushing and comforting her.

She turned to glare at Chloe. 'What the hell is wrong with you?' she hissed. 'What kind of thing is that to tell a little kid?'

Chloe giggled and hid her mouth behind her hand. 'I know, it was a bit extreme. But I panicked! I didn't want her to tell you everything the second she saw you, did I?' she asked, as though Nia would somehow *understand*. 'That would totally ruin the plan. Actually, it was kind of genius, if you think about it.'

'Too right, babe,' Max said proudly. 'We were dead impressed that you thought on the spot like that!'

Nia shook her head in disbelief. They were talking as though they'd pulled off some kind of master plan, as though nothing about this situation was twisted and wrong.

Olivia watched the conversation with an amused smirk.

'Don't worry, Nia,' Chloe huffed, as though irritated that Nia wasn't impressed. 'I just played with her for a bit in the visitation room, then we came down through the stairway by the soft-play. I don't know why you didn't go that way too instead of climbing down there like a lunatic.' Nia flushed with embarrassment as she looked at the dangling deathtrap above them. There were *stairs*? 'And then I just delivered her to you. No biggie.'

Nia looked at Kayla, who was clutching the back of her hoodie and trembling. She still couldn't look at Max.

No biggie?

But as Nia opened her mouth to tell Chloe exactly what she

thought of her, Olivia decided to make her presence known. She didn't have to do much; she never had. All it took was a slight shift, a minute movement that sent a ripple of light through her cascading hair, and she had the rapt attention of the whole room.

'Can we *please* get on with this,' she sighed. 'I'm bored.' She studied her immaculate manicure, somehow revealing her toned stomach as she stretched her hand out in front of her body.

God, Nia hated her. But, just like Scott, Olivia invoked feelings in her that she couldn't suppress, no matter how much she wanted to. She was just so damn *perfect*. So cool, so cold. It was as though she simply allowed the world to continue existing around her, perfectly at ease with being at the centre of its axis. And still, after all this time, all this pain and cruelty, Nia wished Olivia would like her.

She clenched her jaw, knowing she would need to fight her urges to impress Olivia if she was going to get her and Kayla safely out of there.

'You've had your fun,' Nia agreed, glad that Olivia was as over this as she was. 'Now I need to get Kayla home.'

Olivia jutted her hip out to one side and pouted at Nia like a sad puppy. 'Aw, Nia. Even you're not stupid enough to think you'll be seeing your home ever again.'

She's just trying to scare you.

As though controlled by puppet strings, Scott and Max took a menacing step towards them. Nia made herself wider to block them from Kayla, eyeing the knife in Max's hand.

They're just trying to scare you.

'We can't exactly have you running to Mummy and telling her about our little friend, can we?'

Nia screwed her face up. 'What, Daisy?'

'Ugh.' Olivia grunted in disgust at the mere mention of Daisy. 'No, not Daisy Evans, *obviously*.'

Nia shook her head, not understanding.

'For god's sake, Nia,' Olivia snapped. 'I'm sick to death of always having to explain things to you. You're so embarrassingly slow.'

Nia cursed the deep blush that rose up her neck to her cheeks. *I don't care what Olivia thinks of me. I don't care what Olivia thinks of me.*

'Obviously,' she repeated slowly, as though the word itself might be too much for Nia to understand, 'we can't let you go because you'll blab about the guy we killed.'

CHAPTER 36

Nia swallowed. She'd been so shocked to discover who was behind her and Kayla's torment that she hadn't even thought about the body in the storage cupboard.

They'd *killed* him?

No. They can't have. Olivia, Scott, Chloe and Max were many things. But sixteen-year-old murderers? That was too extreme, even for them.

Though, Nia shivered as she glanced around the cell block, this whole day had been pretty extreme.

She made what she hoped sounded like a dismissive snort. 'Right, sure.'

'I know you met old Sam,' Olivia said sweetly. 'We listened to you hurling your guts out.'

His name was Sam.

The boys chuckled.

'How does he smell now, by the way? I haven't seen him since, you know.' She drew a line across her throat. 'I imagine he's a tad ripe by now?'

Nia shuddered, remembering his long toenails and white eyeballs. They had to be lying. This was all part of their game. They were just trying to freak her out.

It was working.

'OK, Olivia,' Nia nodded. 'You killed a guy, you're dead scary.'

That was the wrong thing to say. The mocking twinkle in Olivia's eyes vanished and was replaced with hateful fury. Nia tensed, sure Olivia would launch herself at her in a whirlwind of sharp nails and teeth.

But Olivia wasn't the kind of girl who got her hands dirty.

'Scott,' she said sharply. For the second time Scott's hand flew out, cracking against Nia's cheekbone. Nia screamed as she felt the skin split beneath his knuckles. She heard Chloe gasp in the background, but couldn't be sure if her reaction was from horror or excitement.

The tears came fast and washed Nia's bravado away. This wasn't a joke. Nia now believed that they were deadly serious about killing the man in the cupboard. *Sam*.

'Talk back to me again and he'll break your nose.'

Nia wasn't about to question anything Olivia said, not again. And the sneer on Scott's face told her that he wouldn't hesitate to do Olivia's bidding. He wasn't just a puppet . . . he was actually enjoying this.

'Old Sam made the mistake of getting too big for his boots,' Olivia explained, her tone back to light and innocent. 'We kept him around for a while when we first broke into this place. He was useful at first, getting us booze and providing entertainment.'

The other three sniggered, and Nia's skin crawled. Max had slung his arm round Chloe's shoulders, who looked like she could barely support his weight.

'He'd been living in here ever since the prison closed,' Olivia continued airily. 'Not a bad find for a crusty old homeless guy, really.'

Nia fought to keep her face neutral, not wanting to provoke a reaction from Scott or Olivia, who looked ready to pounce. She squeezed Kayla's shoulder, wishing she had told her to put her hands over her ears.

Olivia's demeanour switched suddenly from relaxed and commanding to irritated. Nia held her breath and looked at Scott, who had also picked up on the signal and was flexing his arm. The bond that she'd sensed between them clearly ran deeper than she'd ever imagined.

'Are you remotely interested in any of this, Nia?' Olivia snapped. 'Honestly, it's like talking to a lamppost or something. I mean, you always were dull, but right now it's like you're fully brain-dead.'

Nia gawped. Olivia was annoyed with her for not being a rapt enough audience. This was a show, and Olivia was the leading actress. Nia needed to do a better job of being an adoring fan if she was to avoid being hit again.

'Sorry.' She cleared her throat. 'Um, what happened?'

Olivia sighed before resuming her story. 'We had a party.'

She smiled at her friends, who grinned back. They reminded Nia of a pack of hyenas.

Nia really didn't want to know what had happened at the party. 'What happened?' she whispered.

Olivia stalked towards Nia, her hips swaying elegantly like a cat's, her almond-shaped eyes locked on to Nia's. She paused a few centimetres away, and breathed into her ear, 'Would you like the graphic version?'

Nia tensed and shifted her weight, hiding Kayla behind her. What was she supposed to say? She knew whatever answer she gave would not work out in her favour.

'Not really,' she whispered.

The others laughed. Though Nia noticed that Chloe's smile faltered as she chewed the inside of her lip. Maybe she wasn't getting as much of a kick out of this as the others.

Olivia smiled pityingly at Nia. 'Poor baby.' She ran her bejewelled nails down her cheek as she spoke. 'We had some drinks, had a dance and made a fire. Just a normal Saturday night, you know?'

Nia felt sick, remembering the remnants of a fire she'd seen in the other cell block while searching for Kayla. She could see Max shifting his weight from one foot to the other, as though the story was making him excited.

'But Old Sam decided to totally ruin the vibe.' Olivia shook her head and rolled her eyes. 'We only wanted to give him a tattoo. I decided we would brand my name on to his chest; make him part of the group for good.'

Olivia had her hand on her heart, as though she genuinely believed that she was doing a kind thing.

'He was a bit scared, of course, so we had to hold him down. But *then*,' she widened her eyes in astonishment, 'he started shouting about calling the police on us. Can you believe it, after all we'd done for him?'

Nia closed her eyes and felt herself sway. When she opened them, Olivia was even closer. It was almost . . . intimate. Nia wanted to scream.

'So we made sure he didn't tell,' Olivia smiled. The light shone on her sticky pink lip gloss. She leaned forward and wrapped her arms around Nia, stroking her hair as she whispered, 'And we'll make sure you don't tell either.'

Olivia stepped backwards suddenly and slashed at Nia's face with her talons. Nia shrieked, bringing her hand to her cheek. *Blood.*

Olivia looked impossibly beautiful when she smiled. 'I've always wanted to do that.'

Max nodded. '*Cool*.'

Nia was distracted by the searing pain in her cheek and didn't see Olivia's hand dart forward again until she triumphantly stood back with a handful of Nia's hair in her fist. 'And that!' she giggled.

Nia sobbed. They were going to kill her.

CHAPTER 37

All four of them pressed closer to Nia. She shrank down, using her arms to protect Kayla instead of herself. Surely they wouldn't hurt Kayla?

Would they?

'Wait,' Olivia said suddenly.

A flicker of hope bubbled in Nia's chest.

But it quickly burst.

'We should let Daisy do the honours.'

After all that had happened today, Nia had thought she couldn't be surprised by anything else. She was wrong.

'Daisy,' Olivia called towards the door. 'Time to come out!'

The door opened without a moment of hesitation and Daisy appeared. Nia's heart felt like it was going to explode. She *couldn't* be part of this.

But her hopes were killed when Scott put his arm round Daisy's shoulders and pulled her into his chest. He planted a kiss on her cheek.

'You *bitch*,' Nia hissed. A bead of blood dropped off her jaw and splashed on to the concrete.

At least Daisy had the grace not to look at Nia. She looked ashamed – her eyes were fixed on the floor as she stood rigidly against Scott. Though that could be fake, just like everything else had been. Nia hated her even more than the others. At least they had been fairly transparent about what they were like since the day Nia had met them, even if she had pretended not to see it.

But Daisy... Daisy had made Nia believe they had some kind of *connection*.

Max rubbed his hands together, squeezing Chloe's neck in the crook of his arm. 'Ooh, this is gonna be good!'

'How could you?' Nia whispered, trying not to look at Scott and his horrible smile. 'Was that stuff about your dad all a lie? Some crap to make me feel sorry for you so I'd let my guard down?'

Daisy looked like she was about to speak, but Olivia cut her off. 'Daisy's been part of this since the second you stepped foot down here. She's the mastermind behind this whole thing, really.'

Nia kept her eyes on Daisy, desperate for a sign that Olivia was lying. Daisy wouldn't look at her.

'She kept track of you while we persuaded you to keep exploring,' Olivia explained, waggling her phone at Nia. 'We wouldn't have been able to do any of this without her, or you, for that matter. Honestly, Nia, you almost made it *too* easy.'

As desperate as Nia had been to understand what had happened, she wanted nothing more than for Olivia to shut the hell up.

'We were all ready to reveal ourselves when you got to the hanging room. We were thinking about sending you for a little dangle.' She giggled, and the others joined in. 'But then you gave us an even better opportunity.' Nia was flooded with shame when she realised what Olivia meant. 'I can't believe you left her, again. Good god, Nia, are you *trying* to get your little sister killed?'

Nia pressed Kayla closer into her back. She wished she could turn and give her a proper hug. This was all her fault.

'Anyway, Max picked her up that time while you were off exploring. And then we had great fun watching you running around screaming like you'd completely lost your marbles.'

Nia jumped as Max did an impression of her, making his voice way too high-pitched and screaming, 'Kayla, oh my god, Kayla. Where arrrrreee youuuu?!'

More laughter, and Nia struggled to contain her tears.

Olivia had a hand to her mouth, somehow looking cute as she giggled. 'Honestly, it was so tragic. The courtyard next to the hanging room was how we got into the prison the first time. We were hiding just the other side of the wall while you ran in circles crying!'

Scott was shaking with silent amusement, and Nia forced herself to focus on Olivia. She didn't want to cry, not now, not in front of them.

'We sent Daisy in eventually, just to mess with your head a bit more. It was quite touching actually, especially when she found the incident book we left out for her.'

Nia noticed Daisy stiffen.

'We found it in the governor's office, Daisy,' Olivia said

sweetly. 'Thought you might be interested to read up on your pops.'

Daisy was just as powerless against the four friends, maybe even as desperate to please them as Nia had once been. Could them planting the incident book be enough to make her realise she'd picked the wrong side?

'Anyway,' Olivia continued, snapping her fingers at Nia to get the attention focused back on her. 'We eventually got bored so told Kayla to call for you. We weren't sure if you'd even come, though – you're not exactly the model sister.'

Olivia was right, but Nia had noticed something – Daisy hadn't shut the door behind her. It was open, just a crack. Nia needed to get herself and Kayla through that door, but how could she distract the others enough to make a run for it?

Make them put on a show.

'Is this the first time you've done something like this?' Nia asked, turning her attention back to Olivia, making it clear she was still the star of this show.

The way Olivia's eyes sparkled told Nia she'd asked the right question.

'Funny you should ask,' she said keenly. 'This all started because of you, actually.'

Nia couldn't let the way Olivia's words made her stomach lurch distract her. *Keep her talking.*

'The first time was after that lame-arse party you threw.' The others all groaned at the memory, but Nia was amazed to find that she no longer gave a crap about what they thought.

'We left your tiny little hovel and were, like, practically dying of boredom. We couldn't believe our luck when we stumbled upon your little sister wandering about in the dark.'

Olivia had Nia's full attention now.

'One little shove and she was stuck in a shed.'

The friends laughed. Nia felt like she might be sick again. Kayla had said something about being pushed, but they'd all dismissed her. There was a pile of patio furniture leant up against the shed door, so the police suggested it'd fallen on Kayla, forcing her into the shed and trapping her inside.

'It's a miracle you ever found her,' Olivia continued once she had her giggles under control. 'Imagine – she could be more rotten than Old Sam by now!'

The laughter started again, and Nia swallowed bile. They were sick, sick, *sick*.

She wouldn't let them hurt Kayla again.

'Anyway,' Olivia said breezily. 'It made us realise how easy it was to mess with people, so we went for a walk around town.'

Ever so slowly, Nia shifted her weight, so she was no longer leaning against the wall. She felt Kayla move with her and prayed she would react when the time was right.

'We came across some woman.' Olivia shook her head. 'She was quite tragic. Mutton dressed as lamb, you know? Anyway, she was totally wasted, staggering about by the river path.'

'*Embarrassing*,' Chloe chipped in.

'We thought she might want to sober up,' Olivia said sweetly.

'If she hadn't been such a pisshead, it would have been a nice three a.m. dip in the river,' Max interrupted before dissolving into a fit of high-pitched laughter. Nia noticed Olivia shoot him a scathing look. She really did hate being upstaged.

'As I was *saying*,' she snarled, and Max quickly shut up, 'her death was ruled an accident. A tragic end for a tragic woman.'

Nia tried not to let Olivia's words register. She couldn't let the horror of them affect her. She was inching towards the door, so slowly no one had noticed her move . . . she hoped.

'The second time was a little more gory,' Olivia continued. 'We—'

But Nia didn't let her finish. With a scream partly caused by the pain shooting through her ankle, she launched herself forward, pulling Kayla with her. She kept Kayla pinned to her side and cushioned her with her own body as they both tumbled on top of Olivia.

Olivia screamed, her eyes wide with fury, her lips peeled back over her teeth. She wasn't quite so beautiful any more.

Nia had planned what she was going to do, but the thought of it still made her feel sick. She raised her head, before swinging it down sharply on to Olivia's face.

Olivia's gargling screams made Nia's head hurt even more than the impact. But there was no time to study the splintered pulp that was now Olivia's nose. The others had leapt into action.

Chloe's screams joined Olivia's, and Nia was pleased to see that she was as useless as she'd hoped in this situation. 'Your nose!' she shrieked, over and over. 'Oh my god, Olivia, your perfect nose!'

But Scott and Max were on her, just as she knew they would be, hands roughly grabbing her around the middle. With the hand that wasn't holding Kayla, Nia clutched a fistful of Olivia's silky hair and pulled.

She hadn't thought it possible for Olivia to scream any louder, but it was.

The hands around her waist let go as the boys realised what Nia was doing.

'If you hurt me, I'm taking a chunk of her with me!' Nia shouted, giving the hair a tug to show that she meant it.

The boys backed away. Nia could see the knife in Max's hand and didn't doubt that he'd use it on her when the time came.

Nia swivelled on to her bum, cradling Kayla beneath her arm and keeping a tight hold of Olivia's hair. She brought her lips to Kayla's ear and whispered, 'When I say, you need to get through the door and pull it shut behind you, OK?'

Kayla whimpered, but nodded.

A drop of blood trickled on to Nia's eyebrow. That headbutt must have hurt her more than she realised.

She shuffled backwards, dragging Olivia with her, who was screeching unintelligibly and gargling snot and blood. Scott and Max followed closely. They looked ready to rip her to shreds, but paralysed by fear of what might happen to their beloved leader. Daisy and Chloe stood in the background, their mouths open in horror.

They reached the door.

'You're not getting out of here,' Scott snarled, his eyes wide and frenzied. 'You know that, don't you?'

Nia returned his gaze, feeling nothing but disgust. 'I know.'

Then she wrenched the door open and pushed Kayla into the corridor. She saw Kayla stagger to the floor and look back over her shoulder, before Nia pushed the door shut behind her.

The action had meant letting go of Olivia's hair. The boys didn't waste a second before attacking, landing agonising blows over Nia's body. Nia pressed herself against the door, protecting her head with her arms and praying Kayla was running away from this horror. Praying that she would find a way out. Praying that her own end would come quickly.

She felt someone try to pull the door open, ramming it again and again into her ribs. Nia braced herself. The last thing she would do would be to stop them going after Kayla, at least for as long as she could maintain consciousness.

But the edges of her vision were blackening. She didn't have much longer. She foggily wondered if Max had already used the knife, or if he'd save that honour for Olivia.

A heavy object crashed down beside her and the assault stopped as suddenly as it had started. Nia peeked out from behind her arms to see Max lying next to her. A thick stream of blood flowed down from his temple and turned the whites of his eyes red.

CHAPTER 38

Hands gripped Nia's armpits and heaved her away from the door. A foggy voice in the back of her head told her that she should be resisting. Kayla might not have had the time she needed to get away. But her body wouldn't respond.

Beneath the sound of Olivia's continuing screams, Nia could hear shouting. What was going on? And... she groggily squinted at the form on the floor with her... what had happened to Max?

She forced herself to concentrate. The room swam reluctantly into focus. The knife wasn't in Max's hand any more – it had somehow ended up a few metres away.

Nia sucked air painfully into her lungs, her senses clearing. Scott stood in front of her. She cringed, preparing herself for him to land another blow on her battered body. But he wasn't looking at her. His eyes were focused above her.

Nia winced as she craned her neck upwards. It was Daisy who had pulled her out of the way of the door. Was she claiming Nia for herself, determined to be the one who got to kill her? Whatever strength she had left, she would use it to inflict damage on Daisy Evans. She knew it didn't make any sense, but Daisy's betrayal hurt worse than that of her own boyfriend.

But the raised voices were starting to piece together in Nia's head now, though the words still didn't make sense to her. Olivia's screeching was almost outdone by Chloe's sobbing over Max. *Olivia wouldn't like being upstaged in her climactic scene*, Nia thought darkly, and almost laughed before the pain in her ribs stopped her.

Nia frowned, trying to follow the conversation between Daisy and Scott. Scott's mouth was flapping open and shut, but only half his words reached her ears.

'. . . stupid . . . regret . . .'

'. . . try me.'

Concentrate, Nia.

The grip around her wrist never wavered, and Nia began to worry that she wouldn't get a chance to give Daisy what she deserved. What were she and Scott talking about? Were they arguing about how to kill her?

Nia craned her head up again and saw something she'd previously missed. There was a hammer in Daisy's hand. But it wasn't pointed towards her . . . it was aimed at Olivia.

The words started to make more sense.

'One step closer,' Daisy growled, 'and she'll need more than a nose job to fix her face.'

'You wouldn't dare.' Scott looked possessed, and Nia suddenly found herself feeling frightened for Daisy. Daisy, who wasn't dragging her away from the door to hurt her, but to *save* her.

Daisy responded to Scott's words by swiftly kicking Olivia in her side. Nia flinched as Olivia's bloody face turned towards her, grimacing in agony. Her nose was a mush of unidentifiable pulp.

Nia had done that.

Was she any better than them, if she was capable of hurting someone that badly?

Daisy and Scott were still arguing, and Nia tried to pull her attention back to them.

'I should have done this a long time ago,' Daisy spat, and Nia realised she was crying. 'I should have done this the second you hurt Sam. You're monsters!'

Daisy tugged Nia's arm, pointing her towards the door. Nia concentrated on what little energy she had left, sensing she was going to need it very soon.

She flexed her feet. The pain in her ankle now felt like nothing compared to the screaming fire in her ribs. Were they broken? It hurt to breathe.

As she continued to subtly check herself over, she noticed Scott change. The anger melted out of his body and the soft sparkle returned to his eyes. 'Shit, I'm sorry, Daisy. You're right. This has gotten really out of hand. Let's just move past this, yeah? We can—'

'PISS OFF, SCOTT!' Daisy screamed, and Nia jumped. 'You're not going to fool me again. I've seen what you're like, what you're *really* like. You can't pretend it's the others any more – it's *you*!'

Nia let out a painful breath. For a second she'd been scared that Daisy would fall for Scott's charm offensive. She hoped she would have been as strong if he was aiming it at her instead of Daisy.

Daisy tugged Nia's arm, and Nia gave a tiny nod. She shifted her weight on to her feet.

Scott was trying again, and Nia understood why – this approach had never failed him in the past. 'Babe, please. I just wan—'

But Daisy screamed and let go of Nia, darting towards Olivia. Scott's face contorted into genuine terror, and Nia wondered if this was the first time she'd seen him reveal a true emotion. The power she had always imagined Olivia had over them all was real. The look in Scott's eyes told Nia that he would die for the girl.

As Scott dived to protect Olivia, Daisy twisted in mid-air, changing direction and launching herself at the cell-block door. She tore it open and Nia seized her chance, scrambling through the gap on all fours and into the corridor on the other side.

'Run!' Daisy screamed.

She started to heave the door shut behind Nia.

But Nia's hand darted out, grabbing Daisy's wrist. 'You're coming with me!' she wheezed, crying out in pain as her lungs pushed against her battered ribs.

'Let me go!' Daisy insisted through the gap in the door.

But Nia held fast. She didn't yet understand how Daisy was involved in all of this, but if she left her behind with Scott she didn't stand a chance.

Giving in to Nia's insistent pulling, Daisy flew around the door to join her. Together they heaved it shut, barely getting it closed before Scott landed on it, hammering his fists and screaming. Nia grabbed the handle and leaned against it, sobbing as she fought Scott pulling it from the other side. Daisy grappled with the key, her hands shaking violently as she tried to get it into the keyhole.

Finally she turned it, and locked the door.

Nia went to sink to the floor, the relief sapping the last dregs of her energy. But Daisy was tugging her arm again. 'He has a key,' she gasped. 'He has a key!'

CHAPTER 39

Nia groaned. She couldn't do this any more.

But she had to.

She set off at a low run behind Daisy, one arm wrapped around her ribs while the other hunted for support along the wall.

Please let this be over soon.

Daisy was going too fast, darting round corners so quickly that Nia called out for her to slow down. The sound of Scott's frenzied pounding suddenly stopped, and dread almost made Nia stop running. He must have come to his senses and remembered his key.

'*Kayla*,' Nia grunted, hoping Daisy would understand, because Nia wasn't sure she could get any more words out.

Daisy draped Nia's arm around her shoulders for the second time that day. Nia screamed through her teeth as she was forced to stand straight.

'We'll find her,' Daisy insisted.

But Nia didn't share her confidence. She'd already lost Kayla in here once. This place was a maze – how were they supposed to guess which way a traumatised seven-year-old had gone?

Daisy seemed to read her thoughts and started calling Kayla's name. She kept her voice muted so she wouldn't lead Scott directly to them. 'Kayla!'

Nothing.

'You need to call her,' Daisy puffed from beneath Nia's arm. 'She still thinks I'm one of them.'

Aren't you? But Nia couldn't afford to be suspicious. Daisy was her only hope.

'Kayla,' she wheezed.

God, it hurt to talk.

She pushed her energy into her throat and shouted, 'Kayla!'

Daisy hushed her, glancing over her shoulder. But surely Scott couldn't know which way they'd gone? It felt like they'd taken a hundred turns down this winding corridor. Nia glanced at the signs as they staggered along – more storerooms, routes to other cell blocks, the canteen, more exercise yards.

Would any of these signs have whispered promises of safety to Kayla?

'Where are you taking me?' Nia croaked. She didn't know how much further she could keep going like this.

Nia almost didn't hear the sound above the noise of her own laboured breathing, but Kayla's tiny voice resonated in her heart.

'Nia.'

She spun round. A strangled shout of relief and agony escaped her lips as she saw Kayla in the corridor behind them. She opened her arms to hold her, but Daisy wouldn't let them stop, and pulled her onwards.

'If she found us,' Daisy whispered, 'so can Scott.'

Nia couldn't stop the whimper of terror that escaped her mouth.

'Kayla,' Daisy called over the top of Nia's head. 'We need to keep moving. Come on!'

Nia could see Kayla hesitating as they continued through yet another door. 'It's OK, Daisy's helping us,' Nia called to her, then murmured for Daisy's benefit, '*I think.*'

'I'm getting you out of here,' Daisy insisted, before adding, 'I'm so sorry.'

Nia didn't have time to unpack Daisy's guilt. She wanted to know everything – how she was involved, what she had done. But all that mattered now was getting away from Scott.

The patter of Kayla's feet behind her told Nia she was following close behind, thank god.

'Scott doesn't know about this route,' Daisy explained, not easing the pace for a second. 'But it's not . . .' Daisy grimaced. 'It's not very nice.'

Not very nice?

Nia would crawl through a nest of man-size tarantulas at this point, if it meant getting to safety. Did Daisy really think she would care about *nice*?

'The door is just up here,' she panted. Nia found a fresh surge of energy at the thought of it being close. 'Well, it's not really a door, exactly. More of a grate, really.'

Oh god, sewers.

Nia discovered she could still object to their escape route after all.

'Here,' Daisy announced.

She ducked out from under Nia's arm, staggering slightly and rubbing her neck. Nia was amazed by how far she'd managed to drag her. She reached her arm out to Kayla, pulling her close and stroking her hair. Kayla was still shaking, and Nia was scared she would never be able to stop.

They had arrived at a crumbling door, set strangely low in the wall – it was shorter than Nia. Its hinges were rusted and a sign on the wall said: **STRICTLY NO ACCESS**.

Nia raised her eyebrows at Daisy.

'It's the only way.'

Daisy had to use two hands to prise the door open. It screamed in protest, the sound echoing down the corridor. Nia turned, praying it hadn't alerted Scott to their location. A blast of icy air greeted them, and Nia recoiled. If the main part of the prison smelled damp and old, whatever was behind the door was ancient.

A flight of steps appeared, leading down.

Nia's eyes widened as she looked at Daisy. 'We're on the ground floor.'

Daisy nodded. 'There's a basement.'

Nia did not want to go down there. It felt wrong, like travelling deep into the ground was taking her even further away from freedom.

'Are you *sure* this leads to a way out?'

Daisy nodded. 'I promise. You just need to follow the tunnel until you get to a—'

'Wait,' Nia interrupted. 'You're not coming?'

'I—' Daisy hesitated. 'I can't.'

Nia shook her head in disbelief. 'Daisy, he'll *kill* you.'

'I know,' Daisy whispered, fresh tears gathering in her eyes. 'But they said they'd blame Sam's death on me if I ever told anyone what happened down here. They said the police would believe them over some weirdo like me who was living in a prison on her own. So I kept quiet.' She sobbed, her chest heaving as she cried. Nia blinked, trying to keep up with the confession tumbling out of her mouth. 'They said they'd kill me too and I knew they meant it. They were keeping me around to toy with me, I knew that, but I was so scared I just didn't know what to do! And then when they told me to play along with their prank on you, I did what they told me to. I thought they were doing some kind of messed-up initiation thing. I thought you were one of them.'

Daisy covered her face and cried freely into her hands while Nia gawped at her. How long had she been keeping all of this in, fearing for her life?

'But when I realised you were different, I knew I couldn't let them get away with it any more.' She kept her face hidden. 'I'm just sorry I didn't stop them before they hurt you.'

Nia closed her eyes, the weight of Daisy's revelation heavy on her shoulders. Daisy wasn't one of them, she never had been. She was the weird kid, the artistic loner who'd rejected Scott. He must have been delighted to reclaim some sick power over her when they'd found her living down here.

'Daisy,' Nia whispered. 'It's over now. Let's go.'

But Daisy shook her head, her eyes still shielded by her hands. 'I can't – they'll tell everyone I killed Sam! But I didn't, I tried to stop them, I promise I did. He was just a kind old man who stayed down here when the weather was really bad outside, he didn't deserve—'

Nia hated to interrupt Daisy when she evidently needed to offload, but they couldn't wait in this corridor any longer. They weren't out of danger yet.

'Daisy!' she said. 'You don't need to worry about getting blamed for anything – that ship has sailed, don't you think?!' Nia understood that Daisy's fear was ingrained, but it was time to snap out of it.

Daisy slowly lowered her hands, and Nia gestured to herself, the fact she couldn't stand up straight, the bloody injuries on her face. Evidence that it hadn't been Daisy Evans who had killed poor old Sam.

Daisy let out a short bark of laughter and said, 'Oh yeah.'

Nia couldn't help but return her grin.

'OK, let's go.' Daisy rubbed the wetness off her cheeks before leading the way. She seemed lighter after her deluge of information and emotion. She started down the stairs, using her torch to light the way.

Nia made Kayla go next. Daisy may have been confident that Scott didn't know about this route, but she wasn't. She turned to tug the door shut behind them, but it screamed in protest and she quickly withdrew her fingers. She paused, listening for signs that the noise had brought Scott running, but all was quiet.

Her feet wobbled on the uneven steps. There was no handrail, so she held the wall for support. The sandy stone was cold beneath her fingers. She had to duck her head to avoid smashing it against the ceiling, which was curved and rough, unlike the straight brick edges of the passageways in the older part of the prison.

She turned to check over her shoulder every few steps. The stairway was clear.

For now.

'So you know how the main prison is Victorian,' Daisy said as they travelled ever lower, 'and they added some new bits on in this century, like the visitation wing and the gym?'

'Hmm,' Nia replied, disturbed by Daisy's abrupt transformation from hysterical victim to prison tour guide. She really must think they were safe from Scott now. That was some comfort.

'Well, this bit,' she continued, unable to hide the excitement in her voice. 'This bit is even older.'

They arrived at the bottom of the steps. The tunnel was low. The floor was made of the same rough, uneven rock that continued upwards to form the walls and ceiling, like some ancient cave. Along the corridor there were holes cut into the wall, almost like . . . doorways. Nia peered into the closest one and saw that it opened into a tiny room, even smaller than the cells in the Victorian cell block.

'Welcome,' Daisy said, her voice muted by the dense walls surrounding them, 'to the Georgian section of the prison.'

CHAPTER 40

Whatever Nia had been expecting, it wasn't this.

She had thought Daisy would lead them to, at best, some kind of hidden escape route, like a way the guards could get out if there was trouble. Or, at worst, they were going to have to wade through the sewers. She never for a second thought there would be another level to the prison, a place where prisoners were kept in holes under the ground.

'What the . . .'

'I know, grim, isn't it?' Daisy whispered.

She and Kayla didn't have to crouch to avoid hitting the low ceiling, but Nia's thighs were aching.

'Did they seriously keep people down here?' Nia had been creeped out by the Victorian section of the prison, but at least up there they had space above their heads, room to walk around and stand up. Down here it was more like a tomb.

'Yeah,' Daisy said as she continued walking, the light from her torch flicking left to right. 'Men and women, just shoved down here together.'

Nia noticed that Daisy's voice had a tremor. Maybe she was talking so she wouldn't dissolve into tears again. Nia wasn't sure which she would have preferred.

'How do you *know* all this?' Nia asked, flinching as a chunk of crumbling stone fell from the ceiling and bounced off her shoulder.

'I googled it,' she said simply. 'I wanted to know everything about this place – there's so many secrets here.'

Nia shuddered.

'The tunnel leads to a train track,' Daisy continued. 'There's a platform at the station that used to be solely for the prisoners. Years and years ago, the train would take them straight from the prison to Ellesmere Port, where they'd be shipped off to Australia. Mad, isn't it?'

Nia was starting to wish Daisy would stop talking. She didn't want to know any more. This whole thing was just too much. All she could think of were bodies crushed up against each other in this horrible cold tunnel. It made her want to scream.

'How much longer, Daisy?'

Daisy turned to look at Nia, her expression concerned. 'Not too far now. There's a tricky bit in a minute, though.'

Nia groaned. Wasn't this tricky enough? Her entire body hurt, and she longed to stand up straight. But she smiled encouragingly at Kayla, repeating, 'Not far now.'

'Nia,' Daisy said softly as they walked. 'I didn't know they had Kayla. I promise. If I'd have known, I—'

'It's OK,' Nia interrupted. 'I know.'

And Nia found that, as peculiar as she was, she finally trusted Daisy.

They arrived at the 'tricky' bit Daisy had described.

'Daisy, the tunnel's caved in!'

'It's not as bad as it looks,' Daisy insisted. 'I managed to get through last time.'

This was crazy. Nia was following the kind of person who squeezed through piles of rubble in ancient tunnels just because she was curious about what lay beyond. Surely this wasn't the way?

But Daisy was already wriggling through a gap, angling her shoulders and somehow managing to fit through the impossibly small hole. Nia and Kayla were plunged into darkness as Daisy took the light from her torch with her.

Nia squeezed Kayla's hand.

'I'm through,' she called, though Nia could barely hear her. She shone her puny torch back through the hole for them.

Nia sucked air through her teeth, already feeling how much squeezing through that hole was going to hurt her sore ribs.

She turned to Kayla, stroking the top of her head. Crouched down like this, they were almost nose to nose. 'This is it, sweetie, one last difficult bit, then we'll be back with Mum.'

She felt tears gather in her eyes as she watched them appear in Kayla's. They were both going to need a lot of therapy once this day was over.

Nia felt a lurch of fear as Kayla disappeared into the hole, but Daisy's shout quickly came. 'She's through, I've got her. Your turn, Nia!'

Nia looked at the hole, then looked down at her body. There was no way she would fit through there. *No way*. This place was made for Daisy Evans – it was like it had been designed for the slight girl who could jump impossibly high, climb like a gibbon and apparently burrow through rubble.

She sighed. She had to at least try. Then, when she couldn't get through, Daisy and Kayla could carry on without her and get help.

While Nia waited alone in an ancient underground prison.

In the dark.

With Scott up there somewhere, furiously searching for the girl who had broken Olivia's face.

Wishing her mind would stop insisting on imagining the worst possible outcomes, Nia slid her arms into the gap. It made her think of a documentary she had watched with Kayla, where they'd seen a foal being born, its legs coming out at an angle so that its shoulders weren't quite as wide. Nia had screamed and covered her face, cringing away from the blood and gore. Kayla hadn't been disgusted by the birth of the horse. She had been fascinated, her eyes never leaving the screen as she repeated words like 'dystocia' and 'placenta', committing them to memory along with all the other information she stored in that humungous brain of hers.

Nia shouted in pain as her ribs touched the cool stone. There was no way she could get through – she'd black out from the agony. She turned on to her back instead. It was a little better. She shimmied further into the hole, already feeling the squeeze around her hips.

She was jammed, just as she'd predicted. She craned her head to see Daisy's feet on the other side, the tatty material of her trainers highlighted by the beam of the torch. There was no way Nia was getting through the hole, and she heaved her body back, defeated.

She couldn't move.

She tried again, wriggling different parts of her body to try and shift herself back out of the gap. But she had somehow wedged herself so tightly that she couldn't rotate her hips at all.

'Daisy! I'm stuck!' she shouted at the shoes in front of her.

But Nia couldn't hear Daisy's reply over the sound of her own sharp scream as a hand grabbed her foot.

CHAPTER 41

NO!

He'd found them. Scott had found them, and he would kill them all.

Nia knew she would be scaring Kayla but couldn't stop the petrified screams as he pulled her backwards, away from their escape route.

'DAISY!' she shrieked.

But it was useless, and Nia felt herself sliding towards Scott, her ribs bumping against the rough stone of the collapsed tunnel.

A final tug brought her back through the hole. She landed on her tail bone with a thud that winded her. She wrapped her arms around herself and gasped for air as she stared at Scott's knees.

The tunnel was illuminated by the torch on his phone. He crouched down, pressing his face up to hers. Nia didn't understand how she had ever thought him beautiful. He was the most hideous thing she had ever seen.

'You bitch,' he snarled. 'You'll pay for what you've done.'

Nia's breathing was returning to normal, not that it would help her now. She'd managed to figure Olivia out, which had been her undoing. But Scott? Nia had no idea how to fight him. What were his motivations? Olivia? Well, Nia had broken Olivia's nose and now Scott was hell-bent on revenge, so she couldn't exactly use that to her advantage.

Maybe Scott was simply a straight-up psycho and there was absolutely nothing Nia could do to stop him.

'Where is she?' he asked, his face barely centimetres from hers.

It was Daisy he wanted? Of course. Daisy had hurt Max, maybe even *killed* him. For a wild moment Nia considered begging him to let her go in exchange for Daisy.

No. This whole situation was because Nia had risked everything for Scott's attention.

Well, she had it now.

But Scott shouted through the hole, 'Kayla! Come back here or I'll bash your sister's brains in!'

Nia's eyes widened in horror. He wasn't after Daisy – he wanted *Kayla*.

'What are you doing?!' Nia whispered.

Scott grinned down at her and ran his hand down her bruised face. Even now, he touched her as though he owned her. 'You're going to pay,' he said simply. 'And you suddenly seem to give a shit about your little sister, so I want you to see her in pain.'

The floor tipped beneath Nia as though she were going to faint, despite the fact she was sitting down. He was evil.

Pure evil. To think she had kissed him, pined after him, almost let him . . .

'KAYLA, RUN!'

She felt a twist of satisfaction at the look of anger on Scott's face. But his hand gripping her throat wiped her smugness away. Kayla would be safe, and that was all that mattered. But Nia was still scared of dying.

She just hoped it would be quick.

'I'm going to make you regret that,' Scott said, his grip tightening and snatching her air away. 'I'm going to make you wish you'd never been born, Nia.'

She couldn't breathe.

Her hands desperately searched for something that could help her. An object protruded from her pocket and she wrapped her fingers around its smooth shape, frantically working it loose.

Scott hadn't noticed. He was staring into her eyes, smiling as the life seeped out of her. He pressed his lips to hers and kissed her as he strangled her.

Nia brought the lip gloss up and jabbed the wand deep into Scott's eyeball.

There was a moment of shocked silence, and then Scott started screaming.

His hold around her throat loosened and he rolled to the floor. His hands hovered near his eye, afraid to touch the lip-gloss handle.

Nia watched him, paralysed. Had she done enough? His screams seemed to be getting quieter, as though he were pushing past the pain. He turned his face towards her, his lips peeled back to reveal his teeth.

Olivia's favourite shade jutted out of his eye, blood and slime mixing with bubblegum pink.

She'd only made him angrier.

There was a clattering sound behind her. An object had been posted through the hole in the rubble. Daisy's hammer.

Scott lunged for it, but Nia got there first. She swung the hammer into the lip-gloss wand, driving it deeper into Scott's face.

He stared at her, the malevolence gone. All that was left was a bewildered teenage boy, who didn't understand how things suddenly weren't going his way.

He blinked, and Nia hit him again. His eye disintegrated into a bloody pulp.

He folded slowly to the floor, a low groan coming from deep in his chest.

Nia couldn't move.

Scott lay face down. She should check if he was breathing, she knew she should. In fact, if this was a film, she would be screaming at the main character to carry on hitting him until there was no chance he would ever be able to hurt her, or anyone, again.

But she wasn't in a film, and she *wasn't* like the others. The idea of bringing the hammer down on his prone body made Nia feel so repulsed that she clenched her teeth to stop her stomach from emptying yet again. She couldn't do it.

A sound snapped her out of her stupor. Daisy, screaming her name.

Nia gasped, and a wave of emotion finally hit her. She

covered her mouth, her eyes still stuck on Scott. She could feel Daisy, who must have come back for her, plucking at her clothes, insisting she get up, that he might not be dead, that they had to go, *now*.

The blood was rushing to Nia's head, her lungs noisily sucking in the stale air. Her mind stayed trapped with Scott, but somehow her body responded to Daisy's demands. She crawled through the hole in the rubble on her stomach, screaming, sobbing, the pain unbearable.

There was part of her that just wanted to give up, that told her that she should rot down here, that she deserved this.

I deserve this.

Daisy's hands gripped her wrists hard, as though she could sense what Nia had been thinking.

'Nia, breathe,' she said, loud and clear, no agitation in her voice.

Nia tried to speak, but all that came out was a strangled groan.

'We're going to get you out of here, Nia,' Daisy told her. 'I'm going to pull your arms, and it's going to hurt like hell, but then we'll be out.'

Nia moaned in anguish. She couldn't do it.

A tiny voice backed Daisy's up. 'You can do it, Nia!' Kayla squeaked.

'I can't,' she whispered, tears dripping on to the ground below.

'What feels stuck?' Daisy replied. Her voice was calm and Nia clung to her lack of fear.

'My hips – I can't move them at all.'

'You can,' Daisy said firmly. 'If you got your shoulders

through, your hips can follow. Your shoulders are the widest part.'

Nia found this hard to believe, but remembered the foal, and the way it had slipped out easily once its shoulders were finally free. She remembered Kayla nodding wisely, as though she had known exactly how it would happen.

She twisted her hips in the same direction that she'd twisted her shoulders, screaming as her ribs wrenched around. Her left hipbone found a gap, a pocket of space just big enough to allow her to squeeze through, dragged the rest of the way by Daisy.

She lay panting on the floor, staring at the tunnel ceiling. She'd done it.

'You two stay here,' Daisy said. 'I'll run out and get help.'

But a wall of fear hit Nia, and she clutched Daisy's sleeve. 'No!' She knew it was stupid, that there was no way Scott could fit through that hole. But the idea of being left down here, with him just metres away from her . . .

'We all go. Together,' Nia insisted.

Daisy looked like she wanted to argue but, much to Nia's relief, she nodded. With grunts of effort from Daisy and shouts of agony from Nia, they got her up to standing. Nia didn't understand how they made it – she felt as though she might shatter into a thousand pieces. But finally they reached the steps leading upwards.

Daisy leaned Nia against the wall and scurried up the stairs, pushing the door open and flooding the tunnel with light. Nia let out a huge breath of relief.

She made Kayla go in front of her, still unable to shake the feeling that Scott was pursuing them. The only way she could manage the steps was on all fours, whimpering every time she moved.

One more step to go.

She shielded her eyes with her arm, blinking in the daylight. Daisy had been right – there were train tracks, rusted and overgrown with weeds.

'Oi!'

The shout made Nia jump and she nearly lost her footing, tumbling back down the steps into the tunnel below. She looked around properly and saw that they had come out of some kind of outbuilding. The train track was surrounded by a sheer brick wall on both sides. Nia could hear train announcements in the distance, something about not riding skateboards in the station.

'It must be a security guard,' Daisy whispered, as a furious-looking man marched towards them. 'The proper station is on the other side of that wall.'

'You can't be in here!' the guard shouted as he puffed, stepping over loose bricks and rubble on the platform. 'This platform is strictly off limits – it's bloody dangerous!'

He paused when he got closer and saw the state of Nia. Then, when his eyes drifted over to Daisy, they widened in shock. 'Wait, you're . . .'

Daisy dropped her gaze. Her fingers plucked at her sleeve.

'Please,' Nia said, allowing the tears to run down her grimy cheeks, 'can you get my mum?'

EPILOGUE

Nia's eyes sprang open.

Her mind was foggy, struggling to process her surroundings. Memories returned to her in fragmented chunks. The desire to run and hide was overwhelming.

Her head ached and her throat was dry and scratchy. Scott's furious, bulging eyes flashed into her brain and she inhaled sharply. Had he caught up with her and knocked her unconscious?

Where was Kayla?

Nia sat up, blinking.

She wasn't alone.

The images around her registered quickly – walls, desk, curtains, wardrobe, a shadowy figure watching her from the corner of the room.

Nia gasped, a rush of understanding hitting her. She held her arms open and Kayla ran towards her, curling up against her chest like a baby monkey.

'We're safe,' Nia whispered, stroking her hair and rocking

her in her lap. 'We're safe.'

Kayla's sparrow-like body trembled against hers and Nia's tears dripped on to the top of her soft head.

They were safe.

But would they ever *feel* safe?

She was fully awake now, the familiarity of her bedroom enveloping her like a comfort blanket. The hallway light was on, as it had been every night since they'd escaped the prison, three weeks ago.

And every night Nia woke in the small hours, sure she was back inside the prison, certain she had lost Kayla again. The fear would linger until Kayla crept into Nia's room, needing Nia's comfort as much as Nia needed to reassure herself that her little sister wasn't still lost.

It was over. They were home, and they would never have to go back to that place. The prison had been closed for good the very next day – it took a couple of murders for the owners to realise it might not be the ideal location for a children's play centre.

She felt Kayla's heartbeat slow and regulate with her own. They practised breathing in through their noses and out through their mouths, just as their counsellor had taught them. It helped, in moments like this.

But no amount of breathing would ever soothe the burning guilt Nia felt for putting Kayla in this position in the first place.

Part of her felt pleased, privileged, that Kayla sought comfort in *her* arms every night instead of those of their parents. But another part wanted to push her away. She didn't deserve the love of this sweet, trusting little girl.

I am not to blame. This is not my fault. It was not my crime.

The mantra came into her head unbidden, and she let it repeat until it almost felt true. The therapist would be pleased.

Nia scooted over, pulling Kayla into bed with her and carefully tucking the covers around them both. She would stay here until morning, and Nia was glad of it. She wasn't sure she'd ever be able to sleep alone again.

Her digital alarm clock told her it was only ten thirty. The whole family had been crashing into bed early each evening, exhausted by the raw emotion that radiated from them all. Baby Deon's teething didn't help matters, and Nia wished she could do more to take the dark circles away from under Mum's eyes. She couldn't imagine how stressful it would have been for her when she'd realised both her daughters really were trapped inside the prison.

Nia had been over the events of the day more times than she could count, repeating the detail to the police, her parents and their therapist. Mum's version of events was almost more upsetting, and Nia felt horrible when she remembered how sure she'd been that Mum wasn't coming to rescue her.

In reality, the second Nia's phone had died, Mum had called the police. But they'd been delayed by the property owners struggling to find a key into the building. Nia had laughed bitterly when she'd heard this, thinking of the sets Daisy and Olivia had found.

When the security guard at the train station had raised the alarm, Mum practically sprinted out of the prison and down towards the station, squeezing Nia and Kayla so tight that they had to ask her to let go. Daisy tried to fade into the background, but Nia refused to let go of her hand.

Nia closed her eyes, nuzzling into Kayla's hair, hoping sleep would claim her quickly. The therapist told them that sleep was good, that they were healing.

Max had been killed. Daisy's hammer had hit him in precisely the right spot, felling him like a skilled lumberjack taking down a giant redwood tree. The idea that he was there one moment, huge and aggressive, kicking Nia in the stomach over and over again and then . . . gone. It still made her shudder.

But even more disturbing was that Scott *hadn't* died. One of the things that woke Nia night after night was the sensation of her fist plunging the lip-gloss wand deep into his eye socket, the firmness before it gave way and sank even further. She would stare at her own hand, repulsed by what it had done, terrified of what she was capable of.

He'd lost the eye and was still in hospital now. Did he think about her? She thought about him, as much as she wished she could wipe him from her memory. She thought about the possessed expression on his perfect face when she'd broken Olivia's nose. She thought about how close he'd been to killing her. She hoped she would feel better once he was finally transferred to a young offender institution, but knew she was kidding herself.

Because Olivia was still out there.

Nia suspected the police found it hard to believe that Olivia and Chloe had even been there at all – there was no evidence of their presence by the time a team had entered the prison, and Scott would never give Olivia up, or even Chloe, if it meant risking Olivia's safety.

Nia turned her head away from Kayla, scared her little sister would catch her fear.

Olivia and Chloe were missing. Hopefully they'd fled and were far, far away. But Nia knew they could be *anywhere*.

They could be—

Nia's phone pinged.

She stopped breathing, praying it was in her head, that she was reliving the trauma. She slowly swivelled her eyes to the bedside table. The screen was lit up.

Kayla's breathing was slow and snuffly – she was already asleep. Nia wished she was too, instead of staring wide-eyed at her phone.

She had to know.

She saw long, silky hair and glossed cupid-bow lips as she stretched her hand over Kayla, careful not to jostle her as her hand clasped her phone. She tugged the charger out and reluctantly unlocked the screen.

Daisy

Wakey, wakey.

Nia's heart lurched before her head could intervene with common sense. It wasn't Olivia, of course it wasn't.

Nia

Am now.

Daisy

Thought you would be. Wonder if we'll ever be able to sleep normally again?

Nia let the tension melt out of her muscles and adjusted herself so she could use her phone more comfortably. She was going to have to beg Mum for a double bed if their sleeping arrangements continued.

Nia

That'd be nice.

Daisy

Kayla in with you?

Nia

Always.

Nia sighed gratefully as she looked down at Kayla's sleeping form. They were safe.

Daisy

Pam made brownies today. Shall I bring some over in the morning?

Nia smiled. Pam was Daisy's new foster carer, and she'd

really hit the jackpot. Pam was both chilled and caring, giving Daisy her freedom but also being there when she needed her. The never-ending selection of baked goods was a bonus.

Nia

God, yes.

A Sunday morning lazing around eating brownies sounded good to Nia. She'd have to get up early to wash her hair, ready for when Daisy arrived—

No, Nia realised. *I don't.*

She didn't even have to get out of her pyjamas. She could appear downstairs looking like she'd slept in the garden and it wouldn't matter, not to Daisy.

Maybe she could invite Lucy and Anna over too. They'd turned up at her house when they'd found out about her ordeal, armed with a care-box full of face masks and chocolate. Nia hadn't been ready to see them – she was immobile in bed, her broken ribs aching and with stitches threading the gash in her forehead together.

Their presence had made Nia sob with gratitude. Just like Mum and Mark, they'd forgiven her.

Now she just needed to forgive herself.

But it was difficult to move forward when every time she closed her eyes, she saw red bricks and heard the echoes of evil laughter.

She still felt a flutter of panic every time her phone went off.

But it was all over. Nia just wished she could be as sure of it as Daisy was. She told herself that Scott would soon be in prison, and Olivia and Chloe would be following as soon as they were found.

And they *had* to be found soon. Surely two sixteen-year-olds couldn't evade the police for ever.

Could they?

Nia tried to ignore the creeping doubt that reminded her Olivia was far from being a normal teenager.

'We're safe,' she whispered. Kayla wriggled as her breath tickled her ear.

Weariness crept over her, and Nia was amazed she could still feel tired after sleeping so much. Her eyes started to droop as another message came in. She blinked in confusion at the new notification. It was the group chat, the one she'd shared with Scott, Olivia, Max and Chloe.

Olivia

You're going to pay.

ACKNOWLEDGEMENTS

This story has been on such a journey since my original sleep-deprived scribbles as I watched my daughter play in the soft-play centre set in an abandoned prison (yes, it's real!). So many people have been involved along the way, from the initial spark of an idea through to publication.

First, thank you to my agent, Stephanie Thwaites, whose constant reassurance and boosting of my writing stopped imposter syndrome from taking hold. And Isobel Gahan, whose support during the publishing process was invaluable.

To my editors, Rachel Boden and Nazima Abdillahi – your endless cheerleading and excellent editorial insight made me genuinely excited to receive each round of edits. And thank you to everyone else at Hachette working behind the scenes to bring this book to life – Laura Pritchard, Jennifer Alliston, Carla Brown, Beth McWilliams, Jasmin Kauldhar, Nic Goode, Annabel El-Kerim, Senait Mekonnen and Binita Naik. Thank you Paul Blow for the striking and unique cover – you perfectly captured the essence of the story.

The WriteMentor community has been thanked in many acknowledgements, and rightly so. Stuart White leads a team of incredible, selfless mentors, who I have had the privilege of working with three times. Thank you, Carolyn Ward, for your terrifying inspiration and beta reads, Gerardo Delgadillo for your insight and support, and Cynthia Murphy, for encouraging me to let my imagination fully explore the depths of the prison.

To my local writer friends, whose friendship and no-nonsense advice has kept me going through all the times I was tempted to quit. Sandra Dingwall, Amy Beashel and Liz Pike – thanks for the laughter.

A special thank you to the wonderful woman who encouraged me to write in the first place, when I was sure I had no business doing so. Lynn Huggins-Cooper – you knew exactly how to coax words out of a tentative new writer.

To my critique partner, who is also my debut sister, my shoulder to cry on, my writing guru and my terrible-TV partner. Ravena Guron, you're a brilliant writer and a brilliant friend.

Ree, you were one of the first people I shared my terrible early attempts with, and you gave such kind, supportive feedback that I decided to keep going. Thank you.

And finally, my family. Mum and Dad – without your support, I would never have found the headspace nor had the self-belief to try. Tom – thank you for being so enthusiastic about every step of the process and being cool with me occasionally disappearing into the wilderness to write. And Robyn – hopefully one day you'll be able to enjoy Mummy's stories without getting nightmares.

RESOURCES

Childline is a free, private and confidential service for anyone under the age of 19 in the UK. Trained counsellors are available to talk about anything, big or small.
childline.org.uk

Runaway Helpline is run by the UK charity Missing People and has been supporting young people for many years. Staff and volunteers are trained professionals who want to help young people through anything they are finding tough.
runawayhelpline.org.uk

Anti-Bullying Alliance (ABA) is a unique coalition of organisations and individuals, working together to achieve a vision to stop bullying and create safer environments in which children and young people can live, grow, play and learn.
anti-bullyingalliance.org.uk

National Bullying Helpline is a helpline providing assistance to individuals struggling with bullying issues, whatever the nature of the abuse.
nationalbullyinghelpline.org.uk

Young Minds is the UK's leading charity fighting for children and young people's mental health.
youngminds.org.uk

The Mix has information and support for anyone between the age of 13–25. Connect with experts and peers who provide support and tools for everything from homelessness to finding a job, from money to mental health, from break-ups to drugs.
themix.org.uk

Our Time provides information and workshops for children and young people whose parents or carers experience mental health problems.
ourtime.org.uk

© Florence Fox

After growing up in rural Shropshire, Tess James-Mackey set out to explore the world and find her place in it. She quickly rushed straight back to Shrewsbury when she realised she'd been where she belonged from the start. She now lives in a quiet suburb with a noisy partner and daughter, two extremely noisy cats and a less noisy tortoise.

When Tess isn't analysing insurance risk, she's busy writing teens into spine-chilling situations inspired by her own lived experiences – from soft-play in an abandoned prison to camping in the wilds of the Black Mountains, and raising a child with a terrifying imaginary friend.

You can find Tess on Twitter @Tess_JMack